I0788577

FIELDS *of* CLOVER

Better to Have Loved and Lost…

by

Gregory Hugh Brown

Fields of Clover

Copyright © 2021 by Gregory Hugh Brown

ISBN
978-1-954932-30-2 (Hardcover)
978-1-954932-29-6 (Paperback)
978-1-954932-28-9 (eBook)

Forward

The characters that I write about within the pages of this book were from a time period vastly different from our own. The beginning of my story takes place in the early 20th century which had not changed markedly for the lives of my characters as compared to the lives of the 19th century pioneers that came before. In the early 20th century and late 19th century people in the rural areas of northwest Alabama, where my ancestors lived, had not yet entered the modern age. They still built their own homes, as my grandfather did, plowed their own fields with oxen or mules, grew their own food for themselves and their animals, hunted for deer and other game, fished in the abundant streams and lakes of northwest Alabama, made their own clothes from threads made from fibers spun on spinning wheels which were then woven into fabric on hand made looms that they or their ancestors made for them. They were largely self-sufficient relying on their large families of children to farm the lands that they lived on. The societal and cultural mores of these times were different by necessity as these pioneers struggled to survive in the wilderness they traveled hundreds of miles by ox cart to claim and settle as their own. Therefore we cannot look at them through the same rose colored lenses as we often view our modern societies and cultures.

Although the early pioneers were a rugged bunch, their life spans were often short and diseases of all kinds plagued the land resulting in a high mortality rate. Often the women died in childbirth and the men would take second wives to care for their children and to produce more children in order to work the fields of their large farms. Having a large family was as much of a practical manner as it was one of mutual commitment and love. In fact some men would have additional second or third wives who they did not marry in order to produce large families of children. This was an accepted practice and the children by the unmarried wives bore the last name of their father just as the married wife's children did. Most times they all lived under the same roof or at least in close proximity to each other. The married women accepted this practice by their men, as in those days, they had very little to say about it.

This marital practice or lack of it came largely from the customs of the

Indians that the pioneers lived amongst or close to. The pioneers adopted the Indian's farming methods, hunting practices, and medical practices including the uses of medicinal herbs for treating and healing wounds and their techniques for setting broken bones. There were many customs and beliefs that the pioneers learned from the Indians whose lands they would eventually claim as a result of the Indian Removal Act of General Andrew Jackson which forced the Indians westward to reservations in Oklahoma Territory and other locations. The pioneer men would in many cases marry Indian women because pioneer women were scarce in those times. It was a Godsend for the Indian women because it gave them the chance to become part of white society and it prevented them from being removed by Andrew Jackson's removal policy. My 4th great grandfather, William Mansell, married Morning Dove White, a full blooded Cherokee Indian and they eventually moved to what is now Hamilton, Alabama, which is where my story begins.

Clover McKinley Palmer was the product of these ancestors and of their hard fought pioneer lives, societal structures, cultural and religious beliefs and, most importantly, their DNA. He is the central figure for which "*Fields of Clover*" is titled. His life and his pioneer ancestors' lives were vastly different from ours because of the limitations of their technology, transportation, news media, and all the innovations of our modern society that they had not yet been introduced to. So we must consider all these factors and place these people within the context of their times. To do otherwise would confuse our notions of who they were and why they lived and worked and loved and learned as they did.

Fields *of* Clover

Fields of Clover is based in large part on my brother James Roger Brown's *"Autobiography in the Shape of Alabama II"*, a family genealogy that he finished in 1997, the year that he passed away of HIV complications. He had completed a painting similarly titled *"Autobiography in the Shape of Alabama (Mammy's Door)"* in 1974 which is now in the collection of The Museum of Contemporary Art of Chicago. The painting was homage to "Mammy", our great grandmother, and her son Clover. With this book, I hope to continue the homage to them and meld their history of facts together with the fascinating stories that they and their ancestors told about their lives and the times that they lived in. There were many facts found within the ancestral research used as sources for the writing of this book but there were also many colorful tales from the ancestors discovered in that research that have been drawn from as inspiration for the writing of this book as well. All truth is relative to what we have proven to be factual from research but is also limited to what we as readers are willing to accept and, like most stories, is more a legend than it is totally fact.

My writing of these facts and legendary tales begins on this Friday the thirteenth of January 2017, my lucky day. This story is my own legend about my grandfather, Clover McKinley Palmer and his ancestors and, like all legends, is a convoluted layering of facts and fables; facts from ancestral research and fables from the colorful tales of colorful ancestors that go back many generations in time. The roads to be traveled may be tried and true, withstanding the tests of time, or they may have diversions onto side roads that have many unexpected twists and turns. The detours contained within them have been placed there by family necessity as generations pass by.

The roads traveled in my book are best traveled by navigation of the separate routes necessary to reach our final destination. The book is comprised of four parts which segment the more factual ancestral background to be found in Part I – Ancestral Fields, the tall tales, ancestral letters, and family memories to be found in Part II – Legendary Fields, the ancestral twilight of the spiritual realm to be found in Part III – Spiritual Fields, and the resilience of the human spirit to be found in Part IV – Triumphant Fields.

Part I
Ancestral Fields

Chapter One

Roads Chosen

My story begins, as many stories do, beside a road that our characters have chosen to travel. For them the road they have chosen will lead to destinations that only destiny could have charted. Little did the travelers know that this spot would mark the beginning of their journey and they knew even less about how life's fickle twists and turns had brought them here. Life is that way and the kaleidoscope within which it is contained may twist and turn in infinite directions which will offer the participants a cacophony of confusing colors and patterns to choose from. Often it will be the most tempting and beguiling of patterns that will confuse us and lead us astray. Often destiny does not offer us much of a choice and leaves us with the luck of the draw.

So, the story begins on the side of the road not far from where Clover McKinley Palmer and Cora Lee Goodson lived outside the town of Hamilton in northwestern Marion County, Alabama. Cora Lee lived in her father's house up on the little hill above Harlon Boyette's place, not far from Taylor Road. Clover lived in and was born at his grandfather's place, the old Doctor Russell Porter Palmer homestead further out in the country. Clover was 21 and Cora Lee was 19 and love had brought together their hearts as one. It was a slightly sunny and windy Saturday on March 29 of 1919 that they met with Clover's uncle, preacher Bud Palmer, along with two witnesses on the side of the road next to a little pine tree where they would marry and begin their journey through life together.

Clover and Cora Lee had similar ancestral histories as did many people in this part of Alabama. From the 1700's and before their families had arrived in Virginia from England, Ireland and Scotland. They then moved westward over the centuries through North Carolina, South Carolina, Georgia and finally into Alabama. Their ancestors may even have crossed paths in Isle of Wight, Virginia where many early settlers arrived in America on ships from England, Ireland, Scotland, France, Germany and other countries in Europe. Later, during the westward expansion of our country, it was common for early settlers to obtain federal grand grants, made possible by seizure of Indian lands, and move their families to new locations in North Carolina, South Carolina, Georgia, and Alabama. This was the case with both Clover and Cora Lee's ancestors as they moved west by covered wagon or ox cart toward Alabama over the centuries. These early pioneers were skilled at clearing the lands and building their own log homes and barns from which they could begin establishing an agrarian lifestyle that would make them self sufficient and able to support and raise their families. Clover's family had lived in northern Alabama since the early 1800's and lived in the log houses that their ancestors had built. Cora Lee's family moved from North Carolina to Georgia in the early 1800's and into Alabama in the late 1800's and eventually moved to Hamilton, Alabama in the early 1900's, where Cora Lee was born.

Cora Lee's father, John Thomas Goodson, left Georgia and moved to Anniston, Alabama to find work at local factories there. His main vocation was farming, however, and he was considered by most to be exceptional at it. While Anniston provided John with income to help support his growing family, it did not provide good farming land as it was very rocky. So John left Anniston for Hamilton, Alabama which provided him with very good farming land. Cora Lee's father John and her brother Oscar went back to Anniston in winter to work and took Cora Lee with them. Cora Lee's half sister, Rowena, lived there and was able to get a job for Cora Lee at Woolworth's during World War I. Cora Lee's father worked on day shift at a local factory and her brother worked on night shift while Cora Lee took the outside job at Woolworth's so that they could both sleep. Their relative, Uncle Bill Driver lived outside of Anniston and owned an apartment that they could live in while working in Anniston, but they went back to Hamilton in spring to farm.

In Hamilton, Cora Lee's brother Tom had married preacher Watt's daughter, Mary Ethel Watts. Tom Goodson's mother in law, the preacher Watt's wife, had kept Cora Lee until she was school age. Cora Lee would visit Tom Goodson and Mary Ethel many times later and that is where she first met Clover. She met Clover during one of her visits as Clover was there repairing one of Tom Goodson's clocks. Clover was very good with his hands and was much in demand as a carpenter, furniture and clock repairman and was very ingenious at just about any vocation. Clover was a good son and often did odd jobs to help his mother, Mary Dizenia Palmer, or "Mammy" as she was later called by her grandchildren and great grandchildren. Mary Dizenia had to raise Clover with the help of her grandfather, Russell Porter Palmer and her grandmother, Morning Dizenia Palmer, who provided their home for them to live in. Russell Porter Palmer lived to be 89 years old and passed away on July 27, 1908 when Clover was 9. Morning Dizenia passed away a little over three years later at age 85 on October 1, 1911.

Clover could not help but notice the pretty young girl who had come to visit Tom as he worked on the scattered pieces of the clock spread out on the kitchen table and he would steal a glance at her whenever he thought she wasn't looking. As Cora Lee visited with Mary Ethel in the kitchen, she thought to herself: "Who was this handsome young man who seems so clever and so intent on watching me as he fixes Tom's clock". For both Clover and Cora Lee it was one of those magical moments in life as they continued to exchange glances with one another. Tom and Mary Ethel could not help but notice that Clover was not nearly so interested in repairing the clock as he was at sizing up his chances with Cora Lee. After catching up with all the local gossip with Mary Ethel, Cora Lee decided that it might be best to head back up the road to her father's house and she bid her goodbyes to all as she shot an admiring glance toward Clover and departed. Clover at once darted his eyes over at Tom and gathered all the pieces of his clock and put them into a box that he placed on the kitchen counter top. He looked at Tom and told him "I believe I am going to need a few parts for that clock of yours, so I am going down to the general store to place an order". Tom and Mary Ethel just smiled and agreed with him as they knew what Clover really had up his sleeve and they didn't want to hold him up.

Cora Lee did not live far away and, as her father's place was just a short walk up the road, she always walked there when she visited Tom and Mary Ethel. As Clover left Tom's place he looked and saw Cora Lee walking up the road and he hurriedly followed behind her. Clover sped up his pace and caught up with Cora Lee and began walking by her side. Cora Lee was a little surprised when Clover overtook her but as she later recounted: "I had to walk with him as there wasn't anything else that I could do." As they were walking Clover told her that: "There was a beautiful girl somewhere for him and he thought he had found her." Cora Lee really didn't know then that he was talking about her.

So, Cora Lee first met Clover at her half brother Tom Goodson's and his wife Mary Ethel (Watts) Goodson's place which was next to her father's house on Taylor Road. The next day, after their first meeting and walk on the road, Clover sent the most beautiful letter to Cora Lee and they continued writing to each other and meeting whenever and wherever they could. Clover was as good with words as he was long on good looks and his letters and their romance flourished fast and furious as the days raced forward. Soon Cora Lee forgot all about her boyfriend, Walter Purser, that she had been dating before Clover, with his dashing good looks and debonair manner, entered her life. Clover would come to court Cora Lee at her father's house up on the little hill above Harlon Boyette's place. Cora Lee liked her father's place because it had a stacked chimney with a double fireplace with hearths that faced both rooms, which with plenty of homemade quilts piled up over you, kept you warm and cozy in the winter. There was one room they called the "Big Red Room" and the other room was the parlor or what we call a living room today. The house also had a long side room with beds that had feather mattresses and pillows for all the family to sleep on and there was also a long kitchen on the other side with a big wood burning stove to cook on and a long wooden table with 12 ladder back chairs with woven rope seats that the family and workers would sit down in front of and have their meals.

The parlor was where Clover and Cora Lee dated on Sunday afternoons and it had a nice Victorian love seat where they could sit close to one another. There was also an old pedal pump organ there against the wall that Clover would play hymns that he had written for the church or he would play tunes that he knew by ear. They would go on Sunday morning to the Sacred Harp Singings at the church in Barnesville or to the White House Church of Christ out in the country alongside the highway to Tupelo. Some Sundays they would have picnics or what they called food on the grounds after the service where neighbors would bring all kinds of country cooking dishes to eat on the tables outside the church. Clover enjoyed going to these singings as he had a very good singing voice and he was also a very talented song writer and musician. On Sunday after lunch Clover would come to Cora Lee's and sit politely with her in the parlor and visit discreetly as decorum demanded in those days. It was nice to snuggle up with Cora Lee on that love seat, but they had to keep a watchful eye out for John Thomas Goodson, Cora Lee's father. Clover would leave around 4:00 p.m. which was milking time for the cows at

Thomas Goodson's place and people had to get about doing their chores around the farm.

After not so long a time of getting to know each other better and romancing one another as much as those times permitted, they both realized that they were head over hills in love with each other. Many romantic outings took place in Clover's car, a used "T" Model Ford, and they would normally drive out on Sundays to the Sacred Harp Singings together in it. The roads in those days were dirt and pretty rough with potholes and rocks so it was not unusual for the car to have a flat tire. On more than one occasion, Clover had to get out of the car in his nice Sunday clothes and repair the flat. Everybody carried repair kits and patches in their cars then and it was fairly common practice to repair flats if you drove on those roads. Needless to say, fixing a flat provided a little extra time to whisper sweet nothings and cuddle with your sweet heart on the way to church – after all, you needn't be in a great hurry to fix the flat and you had a built in excuse for being late to church. Clover arrived more than once to the Sacred Harp Singings with dirt on his white shirt and his thick head of black hair all mussed due, of course, to having to repair a flat tire. Usually no one said anything about Cora Lee's hair being mussed up as well. Love's call beckoned and they could wait no longer. Clover and Cora Lee decided to get married and they planned to run away and get married on the next Sunday. Clover would get the marriage license and they would find a preacher.

This plan would've worked out well hadn't Clover's mother, Mary Dizenia, found the marriage license in Clover's pocket as she was about to wash his clothes. She found out about their plans and had decided on telling Cora Lee's Father. Mary Dizenia was very possessive of Clover and did not want him running off and getting married to anyone. So Clover and Cora Lee had to get married secretly and before Mary Dizenia got the chance to meet with Thomas Goodson, Clover made plans to meet Cora Lee and her brother Tom's wife, Mary Ethel, at a little country store on Saturday, the day before they were to have run away. So Clover went to the courthouse and got another marriage license, and went and got his uncle, preacher Bud Palmer, and Willie Calvin his best friend to be a witness. They all met at the country store and walked a little ways down the road where Cora Lee saw a little pine tree on the side that had just started to grow and she picked that spot for them to marry. Bud Palmer married Clover and Cora Lee on the side of the road next to the little pine tree just before you turned down to Harlon Boyette's house next to Cora Lee's father's place. The only ones that knew Clover and Cora Lee had married were Clover, Cora Lee, Bud Palmer, the preacher, Willie Calvin, the witness, and Mary Ethel, Tom Goodson's wife. In spite of the objections of Mary Dizenia, they were married and their marriage would grow like the little pine tree on the side of the road into timber both tried and true. Why Mary Dizenia was so opposed to the marriage has always been a complete mystery and the union provoked a grudge of silence from her toward Cora Lee which never ended even when the two of them had to work hard together to raise the kids during the depression. Nonetheless, Clover and Cora Lee were to begin a colorful and challenging life together and as the kaleidoscope twisted and turned over the next decade, they would have six children together; four sons and two daughters, one of which became my mother, Mary Elizabeth Palmer (Brown). And so, this is how Clover met Cora Lee and how they came to be married on that Saturday of March 29, 1919.

Chapter Two

Clover Conceived

"Fields of Clover" is an apt title because I believe that Clover was named for the fields of clover that he was conceived in. I believe this because of the associations one can make with the flower and also because Clover is a very uncommon name that I have never heard used by anyone. In fact the name Clover is usually a feminine name and not one that is used but just rarely (there were only about 150 girls named Clover in 2015 in this country and few if any boys). I have heard Grover used many times but not Clover. My grandfather is the only Clover I know of and it just could be that he was named for the place in the field of clovers in which he was conceived. Even if my grandmother meant to name him Grover and just misspelled, that is highly unlikely. Grover would have been the name of a Democratic president, Grover Cleveland. Mammy was a staunch Republican like all of her ancestors before her and there is no way that she would have named her son after a Democratic president. Clover's middle name was McKinley though, most likely named for the Republican president of their time period, William McKinley. Keep in mind that this is what I believe and not what I know in fact to be.

Since I will never know with certainty what happened, I would like to believe that Clover was a love child conceived of two lovers who on one fateful day in April of 1898 cast all their cares and caution to the wind. As that cool, brisk wind wafted amongst the freshly bloomed purplish clover heads, they longingly watched the fields of flowers wave rhythmically against the pristine blue sky. The effect of this moving natural panorama projected around them was hypnotic and dreamily entrancing. Their senses, already ripened and bursting with juices were stimulated and totally exhilarated in such a manner they had never experienced before. They were aroused and soon became locked in each other's embrace as their passion warmed with each repeated caress. Taking an innocent stroll along a pastoral country path, they fully expected to find a suitable picnic spot offered to them. They found instead a fragrant and captivating field of clovers that opened up destiny's kaleidoscope and offered a powerful temptation that entrapped them. And so they became lost, as many lovers have done, with the desire to possess each other completely. Soon, their soft handmade quilt seemed to float over the flowing sea of clovers and they fell gently from grace upon it as if pillowed from harm by billowy, comforting clouds artfully patterned in an angelic azure sky. It certainly could have been this way for this loving couple, and not even the fact they were first cousins would've stopped them from consummating their forbidden act. As they sunk feverishly amongst the upright flowery heads with which nature surrounded them, all sense of right or wrong left them. How could any of this be wrong as only their love ruled them now? Only love mattered now and love would fully pursue its course to its destined end. That destiny had joined them together in their act of love and formed a perfect unison within their souls which had only now to be consummated. Perhaps then, it is not so far-fetched that Mary Dizenia would name her son Clover after the fields that love sprang forth from that fateful April day of 1898.

That scenario could well have happened and certainly similar scenarios have happened with so many lovers. We have only to remember our own youths and the temptations that we have succumbed to. There are other possible scenarios that can be imagined if we begin to connect some of the facts that we have about the parties concerned. In this way, the facts may be connected like the dots in a "connect the dot drawing" and we may be able to see the picture more clearly. I will start by referring to a letter that my Aunt Iva wrote to my brother in which she gives some specific details about Blue John and his family. William Russell Palmer was John Russell (Blue John) Palmer's father. William Russell was one of the sons of our great, great, great grandfather, Doctor Russell Porter Palmer of Hamilton, Alabama. William Russell Palmer moved to Arkansas as a young man and established a successful jewelry and watch repair business (watch and clock repair must have run in the Palmer family). Aunt Iva writes that he became quite well off and had a very good life there but little else is known of who his wife and children were except, of course, that "Blue John" was his son. From a letter of Destie Parrish, a niece of Mary Dizenia, we learned that William Russell divorced his wife and moved away. Some years later he was said to have been killed in an automobile accident. From these sources we do get at least some specific information about William Russell and his son John Russell (Blue John).

What we also know about "Blue John" from other relatives' accounts is that he vacationed in Hamilton, Alabama in summer at various times and stayed with Doctor Russell Porter Palmer at his homestead. Russell Porter Palmer was both his and Mary Dizenia's grandfather. There was a six year difference in their ages and at first Blue John was probably just the "Arkansas Glamour" as my Aunt Iva put it. Mary Dizenia would've been 14 to Blue John's 20 years of age and probably an early crush for him was manifest upon this impressionable young girl. "Blue John" and Mary Dizenia must have been attracted to each other early on as they were on common ground, not only as first cousins, but as sons and daughters having difficult relationships with their fathers. In Mary Dizenia's case, her real father, Zacharias Gaines Palmer, had died when she was just nine months old and her mother soon remarried a man named George Weaver. Her mother's new husband was, according to Mary Dizenia, "a bad step father". What Mary Dizenia meant by him being a "bad stepfather" was never elaborated on other than to say that he was mean to his wife and children but one can surmise that it could've amounted to harassment or worse and most likely caused psychological problems for Mary Dizenia. Her mother, Nellie Armstrong Palmer, died eleven years later when Mary Dizenia was 12 years old and she spent most of her youth with her stepparents or being passed from one family to the next. It would've been normal for Mary Dizenia and "Blue John" to be close as they were first cousins. First cousins usually are close and sometimes the male and female cousins will have "crushes" on each other. I can remember having crushes on my female cousins and them having crushes on me when we were children and we still remain very close today. Blue John came each summer from Arkansas over the next four years, so there would've been a considerable amount of time for the couple to become more acquainted before their relationship turned more serious.

If we could go back and ask more questions, how would the story go? Since going back is not an option, the only way to approach this is to read between the lines and ask what we would've done in "Blue John's "and Mary Dizenia's shoes. In my case, I would examine my own personality traits as well as those traits of my living relatives that I know well enough to draw some comparisons. The study of one's ancestors helps one to better understand one's self and to assess how the persons in question may have reacted in certain situations. Another thing to take into consideration is that the name of a person can sometimes be suggestive of certain personality traits. For example, "Blue John" suggests someone that is sad or moody and therefore someone that may be difficult to deal with in family and social situations. His name was John Russell Palmer so why did they call him "Blue John"? There had to be a reason for it. The most common explanation for it from family sources was that he was called "Blue John" because he liked to drink sour milk as a child. The old timers often used the term "Blue John" to indicate "bad cheese" or "sour milk". So that is certainly a possibility as well. Another question to ask is why did "Blue John" get sent to Hamilton, Alabama or why did he himself choose to go there (after all he was an adult of 20 years of age or more) to visit his relatives so often and for such long periods of time? I don't know of many young people then or today that like to visit their relatives for several days, let alone several months as "Blue John" did. So, let us just assume that "Blue John" was a problem and that he needed some time away from his parents. He likely needed some good loving care and some good discipline provided by his grandfather who practiced the old Palmer ways. I don't know if this is true and I don't know, even if it is true, what kind of problems if any "Blue John" had. I do know that he got his first cousin Mary Dizenia pregnant. That fact is indisputable and none of Mary Dizenia's descendants would have been born, including me, if it were not true.

We don't know about "Blue John's" physical appearance, but I know enough about my Palmer relatives to tell you that they are handsome. My Aunt Iva says that she thinks she saw a photograph of Blue John that Mammy kept and he was a very "cute" young man. I think then that we can trust my aunt's appraisal and that we can deduce that "Blue John" was a good looking young man that was destined to break a lot of young girl's hearts, my great grandmother's included. How was it was then that Mary Dizenia chanced upon this heart breaker and fell so completely stricken with him that she bore his child? Most likely, she visited her grandfather often over that four year period that she knew Blue John. She didn't get along with her step father who was mean or she was forced into staying with relatives that really didn't care for her as a loving family should. She needed the time away. Having a handsome first cousin there on vacation that was daring, devil-may-care and rebellious probably suited her mood at this point in her life. "Blue John" was probably very appealing to Mary

Dizenia on many levels and she was young, vulnerable and susceptible to his persuasive powers. Most importantly, I think Mary Dizenia fell in love with Blue John and he with her.

I know from talking to my Palmer uncles that the northwestern Alabama hills were full of moonshine stills. Likewise, I know that my Palmer relatives were all partial to the spirits provided by those stills and that they kept plenty of jugs around to sample the elixir when the occasion or compulsion would arise. It would have been so easy for a couple of rebellious cousins to sneak off with one or two of these jugs and drink from them in the woods next to Doctor Russell Porter Palmer's house. No one would miss the jugs or the cousins for the amount of time that it would've taken "Blue John" to seduce Mary Dizenia in that field of clovers that I speculated about before. By the time old Russell Porter Palmer came running out of the barn trying to find out where his missing jugs of whisky went, it would've been too late. "Blue John" would've done what "Blue John" did best – break young girl's hearts. This time it was very different though because this young girl was Doctor Russell's granddaughter who would soon become pregnant by her first cousin, Russell's grandson, and in a few months would give birth to his great grandson, Clover McKinley Palmer.

This could be a possible scenario as well but whatever way it happened, Doctor Russell had quite a predicament to deal with and at the time he didn't realize just how much of one he had. Indeed, his predicament would've placed the entire Palmer family upon the "horns of a dilemma" they'd never experienced before. After finding out that Dizenia was pregnant with "Blue John's" child, what could Doctor Russell Porter Palmer do? He was a doctor and had sworn by his oath to save lives, so he couldn't very well get his shotgun and shoot his unabashedly brazen grandchild, but he would've been sorely tempted to and would've had to be restrained by Morning Dizenia and his family. After all, you don't just go and shoot your son's child even if he did get your granddaughter pregnant. That's what he would've had there, "the horns of a dilemma", and the Devil was in the details of those horns. Irrespective of what actually happened and knowing exactly what the details were, I don't know just when Doctor Russell found out that his granddaughter was pregnant and when he found out who did it. There are many unanswered questions that will remain unanswered, and in many ways, I believe Russell Porter and Mary

Dizenia would have preferred it to stay that way.

On January 8, 1899, nine months (this is curious also because Blue John would have had to be at Russell Porter's house in April of 1898 to have gotten Mary Dizenia pregnant, not sometime in summer when relatives said he always visited) after Mary Dizenia Palmer's and Blue John Palmer's rendezvous with destiny, Clover McKinley Palmer was born at Doctor Russell Porter Palmer's home. Mary Dizenia had just turned 17, 4 days earlier on January 4, 1899. Her stepparents would have no more to do with her as an unwed mother and they sent her to live with her grandfather. So this old pioneer of 80 years of age took in my great grandmother and cared for her until Clover's birth and provided a place for them to live afterward until he passed away at age 89. There Mary Dizenia was, so young and so abandoned by her first cousin Blue John who had made love's sweet promises just nine months before. Blue John moved back or was forcefully taken back to his father William Russell Palmer's home in Arkansas from whence he had come on his fateful vacation just months ago.

Blue John was said to have moved to Osceola, Arkansas sometime soon afterward, which was the same place that Mary Dizenia's niece, Destie Parish, lived. Of special note here is that Mary Dizenia later made annual visits to Osceola, Arkansas every summer without fail to visit Destie who we know she was not all that close to. These visits could have been made to see Blue John. There were accounts of him turning up again to visit later but nothing of any consequence was ever related about him to solve the mysteries about just who he was and why he behaved as he did. John Russell Palmer or "Blue John" as they called him had forever changed the course of his first cousin's life and by so doing had launched many new destinies and many new lives that would plant the seeds of proud generations to come, mine being one of them. William Russell Palmer's son, John Russell or "Blue John" Palmer and his brother, Zachariah Gaines Palmer's daughter, Mary Dizenia Palmer, had continued the family lineage in a way that no one had anticipated and in a way that future generations would be ashamed and fearful to admit. So not a whole lot of inquiries by family members were ever made into what actually happened in that "field of clovers" so long ago.

Mary Dizenia or "Mammy", as we called her, remained alone and raised Clover in the old Doctor Russell Porter Palmer home. Thus began the very strong matriarchal family structure which would become a hallmark of distinction in the Palmer family in which females had to assume not only the role of child bearer and mother but also that of sole provider and father. There were those occasions every summer that Mammy visited Arkansas and I can only surmise that she saw Blue John on those occasions and there was at least one time that Blue John visited Mammy a very long time afterward. Of course, the whole "Blue John" scandal was carefully ignored and most likely no one in the family ever dared mention it while Clover was growing up. Not much was ever related about it from future generations either, until my brother, James Roger Brown, did extensive ancestral research from which I got most of the information for this book. Trying to make any logical conclusions about all of this can lead one in many directions and no true one is to be arrived at. These things happen and the truth lies somewhere between or maybe totally outside of what I have tried to concoct.

Cousins were close in those families back then, and it was fairly common for first cousins to get married and, of course, royalty did it often throughout history. But normally, one would wait to have children until after the marriage and not do the consummation before. There were also instances in Palmer ancestry and in other ancestries in which two brothers would marry two sisters from other families. The resulting children from these marriages would be "double" first cousins. There is the possibility also, that everyone seems to overlook, that Mammy and Blue John truly loved one another. If this were the case, then I can well understand why Mammy made those summer trips to Osceola, Arkansas. They did not have to be married and it was not possible in any case but they could meet and be together during those summer trips that Mammy made.

The stories of Blue John, few as they are, were always captivating and the fact that our relatives were so hesitant to ever bring up the subject, made us even more determined to find out as much as possible about him. Blue John mysteriously returned to Osceola, Arkansas almost never to be seen again. I later found out that he married in Arkansas and had a large family there. The whole "Blue John Scenario" raises many more questions than it offers answers though. Did Mammy and Blue John still have feelings for each other? Maybe they did as there are stories of Mammy going to Osceola, Arkansas and visiting each summer for a week or so. Why was there this sudden urge for Mammy to visit Arkansas so often and without fail when she had never visited there before? Maybe it was because she and Blue John were truly in love and they still wanted to be together even if it had to be in secret. It is true that Mammy had a niece that lived in Osceola, Arkansas named Destie, so she could have used the excuse that she was going to visit her to justify taking her trips there. No one knew that Mammy had any such close ties with Destie though, and besides most everyone knew that Blue John lived in Osceola, Arkansas and they might have suspected her real motive. It would be hard to imagine that Mammy would want to go and visit with Blue John after what had happened years ago unless she were still truly in love with him. Still, those kinds of shenanigans really just do not fit with the upstanding, respectable and staunch matriarchal, image that we all have of Mammy. So what we have here is a real bona fide mystery and there seems, in retrospect, few viable answers to why Mammy took these trips to Arkansas. It is a real puzzle and the pieces do not seem to fit together no matter how one shuffles them around. One final piece to the puzzle is that Blue John made a final trip to Hamilton to see Mammy after he was an older man and no one ever knew what that was all about either. The puzzle still has pieces that will never seem to fit and I will never know what pieces are missing or where to fit the pieces that I do know of.

Even so, the puzzling bit of information about Blue John visiting Mammy one afternoon in Hamilton when he was an older man bears more elaboration. We know this to be true because our Uncle Arthur, who was Clover's fourth child, was older then when he looked through the window of their house and saw an old man walk up from the street toward Mammy's house next door. Arthur saw an old man with a white beard and a cane come to the front of the little house next door where Mammy lived. He had on a dusty and travel worn suit, with white shirt, black coat and dusty baggy black pants with suspenders and he had a long gray beard that made him look even older than his years. The old man then walked over to Cora Lee's house and tapped the porch with his cane. Our uncle Arthur and his mother, Cora Lee, came out and the old man asked (in Appalachian dialect) for "Mer Dizenny" (Mary Dizenia). Arthur told him that Mammy lived in the little house and so Blue John walked next door. When he left Cora Lee said to Arthur "Son, that's your granddaddy". When our Uncle Arthur asked how she knew she said, "He's got Clover Palmer written all over him". At that time Clover had been dead for 15 years so it was truly mysterious that Blue John would be turning up again so many years later. Blue John tapped on the porch of Mammy's little house and Mammy came out. She looked flustered and never smiled or greeted him warmly which was uncommon for Mammy to overlook with her old friends. Blue John never went up on the porch and Mammy talked to him from behind the railing. They talked for a few minutes but no one could hear what they said and Blue John then wandered on down the road. Uncle Arthur later learned that Blue John was staying with a Mr. Carpenter, a cousin of Mammy's, but out of respect for Mammy, Arthur never tried to contact the old man. Mammy and Blue John were communicating for what must have been the first time in many years. No one knows what they talked about or if it was peaceful or heated discussion but I doubt that Mammy really blamed Blue John for what happened to her all those years ago in the "fields of clover". She most likely had accepted partial blame herself and she was so proud of Clover and her family that she probably just told Blue John to be on his way as they were all just fine and needed none of what he might have to offer, be it good or be it bad. One can speculate about what Blue John's purpose for being there might have been and I hope that it was for something positive – maybe showing photographs of his children and bragging on them a bit. I don't think Mammy would've had much interest in seeing them though and all we know is that Blue John left that day and to our knowledge no one in Hamilton ever saw him again and no one ever talked about him again until my brother began doing his ancestral research many years later.

The next chapter will delve further into Mary Dizenia's ancestry including the lives of her father and mother and of their children and of those Palmers and others that came before. As "Mammy" was fond to say:"Experience keeps a dear school, but fools will learn in no other and scarce at that." We did not learn until years later that this was one of many sayings that she got from Ben Franklin's *Poor Richard's Almanac*. Mammy may have believed that Ben Franklin's wise words bore special truth for her own life and with the mistakes that she had made.

Chapter Three

Of Relative Importance

Clover's mother, Mary Dizenia Palmer, was one of four children of her father, Zachariah Gaines Palmer and her mother, Mary Dizenia (Nellie) Armstrong Palmer. The children were Zachariah Gaines, named for his father, George, Margaret Elizabeth and Mary Dizenia, named for her mother, Mary Dizenia Armstrong. Later, Zachariah Gaines, the father, died and Mary Dizenia's mother Nellie married again to George Weaver who became what Mary Dizenia would refer to as "the bad stepfather". One can speculate about how bad he was and how his behavior may have influenced Mary Dizenia's later choices taken with "Blue John". Mary Dizenia's father was Clover's grandfather and my mother Mary Elizabeth's great grandfather and my great, great grandfather. Her mother, Mary Dizenia Armstrong or "Nellie" died about 12 years afterward, so Mary Dizenia (Mammy) was left alone to be raised by stepparents once George Weaver remarried.

Continuing our twisting and turning of the kaleidoscope's lens of ancestral past, we find Clover's great grandfather (my great, great, great grandfather) , and Mary Dizenia's grandfather, Russell Porter Palmer who offered his home to Dizenia and helped to raise Clover. Mary Dizenia's stepparents wanted no part of her after she became pregnant with Blue John's child and Russell and Morning Dizenia, Mary Dizenia's grandparents, took on the role of caring for their granddaughter and her soon to be born child. Russell Porter Palmer married Morning Dizenia Mansell and they had twelve children, including Zachariah Gaines. Morning Dizenia Mansell Palmer was the daughter of Morning Dove White Mansell, a full blooded Cherokee Indian. Of particular interest here is that Elvis Presley was descended from the same Morning Dove White Mansell as well, so that makes my mother, Mary Elizabeth Palmer Brown and Elvis Presley fourth cousins. My brother was always fond to say when he found out all of this, that Lisa Marie Presley and we were fifth cousins and Michael Jackson was our ex fifth cousin-in-law. So you just never know where these ancestral searches will lead. Ancestral searches are as captivating as they are necessary and paramount in revealing the colorful patterns of our past.

The names of their children are relevant to the times and culture that they lived in, so I will list the names of Russell Porter Palmer and Morning Dizenia Mansell's twelve children. The Palmers were fervently patriotic, strongly pro-Union and Republican with strong ties to Classical and Biblical history. Their children were named for American presidents, patriots, Union generals of the Civil War, doctors, and Classical and Biblical characters from ancient history. The eleven sons' and one daughter's names were as follows: Joseph W. Palmer, Benjamin Franklin Palmer, Hezekiah White Palmer, William Russell Palmer, George Flowers Palmer, Thomas Lafayette Palmer (doctor), John Howard Palmer, Zachariah Gaines Palmer (our great, great grandfather), Estern Augustus Palmer, Dizenia Elizabeth Palmer (our great, great aunt), Alexander Sherman Palmer and General Grant Palmer.

These ancestors date from around the period of the American Civil War. They, as Clover, came from the fiercely pro-Union town of Toll Gate (now Hamilton, Alabama) in Marion County or from surrounding communities. Their forebears had brought them here from South Carolina benefitting from federal land grants that they had purchased and received costing about 12 ½ cents an acre. These lands were previously occupied by Cherokee Indians in Alabama, and Chickasaw Indians in Mississippi. It is ironic because their original grandmother was a full blooded Cherokee Indian, Morning Dove White Mansell, who had married William Mansell, an Indian fighter with Andrew Jackson at the Battle of Horseshoe Bend and afterward in the Indian Wars in Florida. Her name was Morning Dove White, named White as all Cherokees loyal to U.S. whites in the Indian Wars were named "White" (Indians loyal to the British were called "Britt" and thus the last name Britt was used for them). She was mother to Morning Dizenia Mansell who married Russell Porter Palmer, our great, great, great grandfather.

There is Cherokee blood that comes from both Clover and Cora Lee's sides of the family and we are fiercely proud of it. My brother was able to verify this in his ancestral searches and was also able to find many accounts about our Cherokee blood from ancestors that lived in Civil War times and before. As my brother wrote in his *Autobiography in the Shape of Alabama II*, Elizabeth Roberts Palmer, who was the mother of Russell Porter Palmer, married Benjamin Hezekiah Palmer in South Carolina and they moved to Calhoun/Benton County, Alabama. They settled for years as farmers in Calhoun County, Alabama. After Hezekiah died and her brothers had all moved to Arkansas, Elizabeth and three of her sons left Calhoun County and arrived at the Mansell's family place outside of Toll Gate (Hamilton), Alabama. Looking at a roadmap, they would have taken old highways 78 and 278 which were then dirt roads and most likely they would've traveled by ox carts. They were familiar with the Mansells, as it is thought they had met them in South Carolina before, so it was convenient to stop over and visit with them on their way. The Mansell's induced them to stay and it was said that Elizabeth's son, Russell Porter Palmer, was taken with Morning Dizenia Mansell, their daughter and was said to have called her "the prettiest girl he'd ever seen". Accounts of the time say that Russell called Morning Dizenia the name "Dove" after the name of her mother, Morning Dove, which could explain why "Dove" was inscribed on her Indian style rock grave many years later.

Further accounts indicated that Elizabeth and her three sons lived in a hut with straw in one corner for a bed and they became "squatters" on the Mansell's land. Eventually, Russell Porter Palmer settled and homesteaded 242 acres adjoining the Mansell farm, married Morning Dizenia Mansell, and they had the twelve children that I listed. This old set of Palmer brothers of Russell's eleven sons were educated people: doctors, preachers and one state senator from Winston County, Alabama (and also another doctor, although a non graduate, according to a document from the Alabama Medical Association). Russell Porter Palmer himself was also a doctor and treated casualties during the Civil War. They were all pro-Union and Russell even named his sons after Union generals, such as Sherman and General Grant. Russell's son, Zachariah Gaines, our great, great grandfather, died a very young man at age twenty two from diabetes (it was rumored to be a drug overdose but likely was a diabetic coma) while at medical school in Memphis, Tennessee about 1882, leaving a widow and three children, Mary Dizenia, Elizabeth, and Gaines. Of interest here is that Elvis Presley had a Gaines in his family and his great grandfather was White Mansell, named after Morning Dove White. Russell Porter Palmer named one son Hezekiah White Palmer after his father's first name and his wife's mother's last name of Morning Dove White. Some of Russell Porter Palmer's descendants were notorious for producing Palmers by second wives who they did not marry. These wives were even accepted by the first wives and the children of the unmarried second wives took the name of Palmer as well. So you see, with this accepting family attitude, there are Palmers scattered all over Marion County, Alabama who are our relatives, unbeknownst to them or to us.

Of great interest to both my brother and myself was our great, great, great, great grandmother, Morning Dove White, a full blooded Cherokee Indian who had been friendly to the whites in the Indian Wars. She met her husband William Mansell sometime after he returned to Tennessee from having served with Andrew Jackson at Horseshoe Bend and in the Indian Wars in Florida. It was common for Indian women to marry white pioneer men as the men far outnumbered the pioneer women. There were many advantages that came from white men marrying Indian women as well. Morning Dove had a superior knowledge of the forests, mountains, rivers and lakes which would be of great value to William Mansell when he acquired and settled his land after the Indian Wars. She also knew about what crops to grow and what game to hunt and how to hunt them, she knew how to design and make clothing suitable for changes in climate, and she knew about medicinal healing plants and she was expert at setting broken bones. Indian tradition allowed for the man to take more than one wife if he so desired as well but William Mansell truly loved and cared for Morning Dove and wanted only her. By marrying William, Morning Dove was giving herself the security that she could not have found alone. She could become a part of white society and avoid the fate of the Cherokees who had been subject to Andrew Jackson's removal and relocation policies. Most Cherokees that remained became Christians and melded culturally into the white communities. Morning Dove had a sister named Mapy who married a white man as well. He was a friend of William Mansell's named Moses Purser and he had fought in the Indian Wars along with William. They had both fought with General Andrew Jackson at Horseshoe Bend in 1814 and later in 1817 they fought the Seminole Indians in Florida. General Andrew Jackson's Tennessee Militia, of which William and Moses were a part, defeated the Seminoles and ended up capturing Pensacola, Florida and ejecting its Spanish governor. Within three years Florida was a part of the United States and Andrew Jackson was its governor. In the spring of 1818, after the Indian Wars ended, William and Moses returned to Tennessee eager to begin a new life.

In the winter of 1820, William Mansell was ready to take advantage of all the inexpensive land in Alabama that had been freed up by Andrew Jackson's relocation of the Cherokees. He and Morning Dove along with her sister Mapy and husband Moses Purser, travelled across the frozen Tennessee River by ox cart. They had joined with other Indian fighters, blacksmiths, wagon makers, machinists and other laborers that were migrating by the thousands into the fertile and inexpensive Alabama territory. Pioneers from all parts of Virginia, North Carolina, South Carolina, Georgia, and farmers from almost every state joined the migration travelling by foot or with their children packed into mule drawn wagons or ox carts along with what meager possessions they could bring. William and Morning Dove settled in Marion County in northwest Alabama close to what was called Toll Gate along with many of the Indian fighters that fought with him in the Indian wars. They had been with Andrew Jackson when he came through there in 1814 and now the land was there for the taking and the soldiers felt it was their due to take "the spoils of war".

In 1820 William Mansell registered his land claim at the courthouse in Pikeville, Alabama and he and Morning Dove settled down and began farming. William was handy as a carpenter and furniture maker and built a large home for them and a workshop for furniture making. They had a beautiful property with rolling hills in back and a gentle rise in front for farming. It was located not far from the main road about three miles from the town of Toll Gate or modern day Hamilton where most all of our Palmer ancestors settled (Russell Porter Palmer would settle there a few years later). The house was a good sized wood frame structure to which William added wings with more rooms as the family grew. William and Morning Dove had three children: John Mansell (the ancestor of Elvis) born in 1828, Morning Dizenia (our great, great, great grandmother and future wife of Russell Porter Palmer) born in 1832, and James L. Mansell born in 1835. It is thought that Morning Dove died in childbirth with James as she passed away in 1835. William lived on for seven years and did not remarry, which was a true testament to his love for Morning Dove.

William had fought bravely and survived the Indian Wars and Morning Dove had lived with nature and was one with it and had much knowledge of Indian medicinal lore. I'm sure that she was the one who taught my Palmer ancestors the medical home remedies that I can remember my great grandmother Mary Dizenia practicing, such as using a tobacco compress to draw out the venom of a bee sting and reduce the pain and swelling. As stated, the children of William Mansell and Morning Dove White were John, Morning Dizenia, and James Mansell. John was the ancestor of the Mansells who moved from Marion County, Alabama forty miles across the state line to Tupelo, Mississippi. This is where Gladys Smith Presley's mother, Doll Mansell, married her first cousin, Obe Smith. So Gladys, who was Elvis Presley's mother, was a product of first cousins just as was my grandfather, Clover. Although it seems unusual to us today, first cousin marriages were fairly common in the south during those days.

My brother, who did much of the ancestral research that I am using to write this book, would never have known of the "Elvis Connection" had he not teamed up with another relative, Joel Palmer, who was doing very extensive Palmer family research of his own. Joel Palmer's research led him to Elaine Dundy (an author and friend of Gore Vidal), who wrote "Elvis and Gladys". While Elaine Dundy was in Tupelo researching her book in the early 1980's, she heard about Joel Palmer's research on the Mansells. When they got together they discovered that Elvis' great, great, great grandfather, John Mansell, was William Mansell's son and our great, great, great grandmother Morning Dizenia's brother. John Mansell had left for Tupelo sometime between the Civil War and 1900 and all contact with him and our Palmer and Mansell line was lost. Thanks to Elaine Dundy's book we were all brought back together again and Elaine Dundy's research helped to fill in many of the gaps in our ancestral history. As interesting as Elaine Dundy's Elvis connection was though, my brother was able to find out many more details and stories about the Palmers from Joel Palmer's research. He was able to share stories of our ancestors from Civil War days and a particularly revealing account of Joel's great grandfather, Private Newton Hubbard Ozbirn, Union Army soldier from Company "D" U.S. Army. I will relate the exciting events of Newton's and our other ancestor's lives during those times in Chapter Four.

Chapter Four

Run for the Hills

Before the Civil War and immediately following the War of 1812, the Indian removal from lands in Alabama and the land grants resulting from it encouraged settlers like my Mansell and Palmer ancestors to migrate into Alabama by the thousands. Alabama's climate, soil, and market conditions encouraged the growing of cotton as a major cash crop. There was extensive settling of Indian lands in Alabama following the War of 1812 and the defeat of the Creek Nation and my ancestors were among the flood of settlers who came from Virginia, North Carolina, South Carolina, and Georgia. In the late 1800's my Driver and Goodson ancestors moved to Alabama from Georgia as well. The lands from the states that they had come from were exhausted because of over cultivation of cotton and the rich soils of the Tennessee Valley and Alabama Black Belt along with the cheap land grant prices of 12 ½ cents an acre were a temptation that was impossible to resist. The more well-to-do settlers brought with them slave labor and the plantation system and established themselves all throughout Alabama's agricultural regions. Most of my Mansell and Palmer ancestors were too poor and did not have or want slaves but farmed their lands with large families of twelve or more children. Around the time of the Civil War most of Alabama's farmers owned few if any slaves and it was mostly the large plantation owners that contributed to the ever increasing population of slaves in Alabama.

Population boomed in Alabama between 1810 and 1820 following the defeat of the Creek Nation by General Andrew Jackson and his troops (my ancestor William Mansell among them). Alabama's population grew from around 9000 in 1810 to around 128,000 in 1820 as a result of settlers from the eastern seaboard moving into previously Creek, Cherokee, and Chickasaw lands. The Mansells as well as the Palmers joined the thousands of farmers who poured into Alabama in search of fertile lands and hoping to become rich cotton farmers. They brought their families which consisted of many children that could farm the land. In some cases, the wealthier families also brought their slaves which more than doubled the population of Alabama between 1820 and 1830. By the beginning of the Civil War, Alabama had almost 1,000,000 residents, nearly half of which were slaves. The Civil War brought Alabama's population growth to a standstill largely because of heavy losses on the battlefield, including the Home Guard skirmishes that my Palmer ancestors were involved with. My Palmer ancestors were among the 2500 white Alabamians that served in the Union Army or were included in the estimated 8000 – 10,000 that acted as Union scouts, deserted Confederate units, or hid from conscription agents such as the Home Guards. Estimates of the number of Alabamians killed in the Civil War range from 25,000 and up.

After the war, tenant farming replaced slavery and provided work for poor farm laborers who had no land and no money to invest in land or equipment. John Thomas Goodson, my grandmother, Cora Lee Goodson's father, had sharecroppers or tenants that worked his land and in the 1930's, Cora Lee, Mammy, and the six children of Clover lived in one of Thomas Goodson's sharecropper houses. This was a short term arrangement though and they soon moved back into town to live in the houses that Clover had built for them. Tenant farming or sharecropping allowed for the landlord to assume the role of furnishing merchant which reduced the tenant's share of the crop and provided the tenant a meager existence at best.

Many early settlers in Marion County, Alabama lived in farming areas known as Shottsville, which was founded in 1839 by John Shotts, or around land on Two Mile Creek, a branch of Bull Mountain Creek in northern Marion County. They also settled in or around another small community named Toll Gate that was formed around 1818 and would later be renamed Hamilton in 1882. Toll Gate as a name is interesting because that is just what the town originally was. In 1821 the Alabama Legislature selected this site for Alabama's first toll gate. Judge John Dabny Terrell Sr. (Marion County's founding father and framer of the Alabama Constitution), was the President of the Alabama Senate during the selection process. Toll Gate was a gate that intersected north/south traffic. A toll was charged for maintaining the road which included 75 cents per wagon and team, 50 cents for each 2 wheel pleasure carriage, 12 cents for each man on a horse, 4 cents for each head of cattle, and 2 cents for each hog or sheep. There was no charge for the U.S. Mail, people traveling on foot, and for those going to mill or preaching. The toll house became a rest station for the stagecoaches going between Washington D.C. and New Orleans. It was located at the intersection of the road to Gin Port (the original county seat of Marion County) and Andrew Jackson's famous Military Road. In 1821 Gin Port became part of the Mississippi territory. Military Road was built by Andrew Jackson's troops (of whom my ancestor William Mansell and his friend Moses Purser were members) from 1816 to 1821. It shortened the route from Nashville to New Orleans by 200 miles making for easier movement of military supply and artillery wagons and was also a safer route than the road to Natchez Trace which was often besieged by bandits. Historically the site is very important as well for being constructed on the site of the hunting grounds of the Chickasaw Indians and being only about a mile north of three Chickasaw burial mounds on the Buttahatchee River. The community that grew up around it was named Toll Gate as well in 1818 and the first to settle the area was a man named William Ragsdale. My Mansell ancestors moved there from Tennessee about two years later. Toll Gate was eventually made the county Seat of Marion County and the name was changed to Hamilton in 1882. The man who petitioned the legislature for moving the county seat to Toll Gate was named Captain Albert J. Hamilton and was Judge Terrell's son-and-law. He also donated 40 acres of his land to the city to be sold in lots to pay for a new court house. So, in his honor, they renamed the town Hamilton.

Hamilton and its surrounds is the area where most of my Palmer ancestors made their homes. They would've built one room or two room log houses that they constructed from timber cut from nearby forests. These were made from cut logs stacked and pegged together with wood pins. Their method was the typical method used by their ancestors from Virginia to South Carolina and eventually used in Georgia and Alabama. Around the time of the Civil War they were clearing land for houses, barns, and farmlands and raising large families, sometimes of twelve children or more to work the land and make their livelihood raising money crops, like cotton and corn for feed and human consumption. Neighbors were few and far between and they too were busy clearing land, building houses and barns, raising families, farming their crops and caring for livestock. Many of these families were farming land that they purchased for 12 ½ cents or so an acre from federal land grants designed to populate the lands taken from the Indians in Alabama, Georgia, and Mississippi during the Indian Wars and after.

In those times in northwest Alabama, there were few newspapers and their common source of news was when someone stopped to talk. They had no clue of what was going on in Washington, D.C. Some passerby along the way said that a Republican, Abe Lincoln, was running for president. People in Marion County had little time for politics and cared little about the slave troubles of the rich plantation farmers. Most farmers in Marion County had no slaves and did not want any as they and their families worked their own lands and did so proudly. So, when my great, great, great grandfather Doctor Russell Porter Palmer came by with the news that Abe Lincoln had been elected and people in the south were talking of Secession (a word they didn't understand), most settlers just kept on working the land as they had always done. The next news they had was that a new government and a new president, Jefferson Davis, had been installed. Before long, the new government began a call for volunteers to defeat the "Lincoln Hirelings". To accomplish this, a day was set for area volunteers to meet at Barnesville to encourage local citizens to enlist in the Confederate Army. There would be free food, drinks and a sharpshooter show to attract settlers from the surrounding area.

My ancestor, Doctor Russell Porter Palmer, was there and later enjoyed telling the tale of a young cowgirl who was supposed to have shot her pistols at dirt clods that were tossed into the air by onlookers while she rode by at full gallop on her horse. Russell always loved to tell a good story, as all Palmers did, and he always laughed when he told this one about the cowgirl. It went something like this, depending on how long Russell wanted to stretch it out: "The cowgirl was putting on a good show shooting cans and bottles off of barrels as she rode by on her old hoss. She was a pretty good sharpshooter with both pistols firing and hitting their marks most every time. Before she could stop firing though, a yard bird flew up on one of them barrels and got shot dead with its feathers flying up in the air all over the place. Old Granny Sims from the restaurant had been watching from her window and came by later and grabbed the old yard bird outta the dirt, took it back to her porch there by the street, and plucked the bird clean. We think it got used in her Sunday chicken pot pie special, although nobody was ever real sure what she would put in that pot pie of hers. By this time, dust was a risin everywhere and bullets was flying left and right, so most of us just tried to lay low and not stick our heads up as the cowgirl rode by, lest we end up like Old Granny Sims' yard bird. The cowgirl took one last gallop around the big oak at the end of the street and spurred her old hoss back up the road to do her dirt clod shooting trick. Just as the dirt clods got pitched up and she started to shoot her pistols, the old hoss throwed his head up and she shot him graveyard dead. You should have seen the dust fly when the old hoss fell flat and spread eagled himself there in the middle of the road! Poor girl's leg got pinned up under the old hoss and we all had to come a runnin out from our hiding spots and pull her out before she got it mashed flat. The cowgirl was real red faced and flustered about shooting her old hoss and once she got her leg free she limped on down the street bawling her eyes out and left the poor critter just a laying there. Hard to say whether she was bawling over her dead hoss or cause her leg was broke, but a bunch of us old Tories got together and pitched the old hoss up in my wagon and we took him out to old Sam Pott's sweet potato field where we gave him a decent burial. Old Sam was fine with it and later said the sweet potatoes growed on the spot the old hoss was put to rest always grew the biggest and sweetest taters in his patch. So it did get downright muddled there at the end but all in all, it was a pretty good show! It was as much excitement as we'd had in these parts in quite a spell!" Like all Russell Porter Palmer tales, this one got embellished a bit more each time it was told and of course the storyteller could make it just as long or short as they wanted depending on their audience and how much time they had. It was a good tale to tell when all of Russell's kids would sit by the fireplace at night and, like other tales Russell told, it made for a colorful bedtime story that the kids always looked forward to hearing. If the kids wanted the story to be longer, Russell could just use his imagination and drag the tale out indefinitely as all good storytellers have a tendency to do.

From the research of our relative, Joel Palmer comes an accounting of Newton Hubbard Ozbirn, Joel's great, great grandfather, and of his treatment and his family's treatment at the hands of the new Confederate government. The new government soon set to law that farmers with twelve or more slaves were exempt from going into the armed forces. That just didn't set well with the small farmers as it was going to be a rich man's war but a poor man's fight. Some of Newton's neighbors expressed their disapproval and one named John Kennedy was hanged at Barnesville for speaking his piece about it. Newton as well as our great, great, great grandfather, Russell Porter Palmer and his oldest son, Joseph, were "Tories" or northern sympathizers which were very dangerous politics to practice in those days. At the beginning of the rebellion, the Rebels had organized a group of men called the "Home Guards" to enforce the laws of the Confederacy. By 1862, there was plenty of bad news to tell and Tories were moving into the Bull Mountain country to escape the Home Guards. Our ancestor, Joseph Palmer's wife, moved there after Joseph stabbed a Home Guard named Robert Whitely and escaped to Glendale, Mississippi. The "Johnnies", as they called them, burned Joe's house a few days later. Joseph refused to join the Rebels saying his grandfather fought the British for the Stars and Stripes and he would not fight against it.

Like Joseph Palmer, Private Newton Hubbard Ozbirn was one of those brave northwestern Alabama settlers that was loyal to the Union and, at the risk of his life and that of his family, served as a Union soldier in the Civil War and refused loyalty to the Confederacy. His ancestors, like Joseph Palmer's, had fought in the Revolutionary War against the British and he would not take up arms against his country. Newton Ozbirn, like his relatives and his neighbors, had a farm in the Shottsville area of northern Marion County. Newton lived there with his wife Mary and their children and had a hard life, but a proud one, consisting of the settling of his property, plowing and seeding his fields, raising his kids and caring for and protecting his family, and standing up for the principles that he believed in and that he would fight and die for if necessary. The Confederacy changed all that though, because he, like most of his friends and family, was loyal to the Union or Tories. Much of Newton's time now was spent avoiding the Home Guards who were out to kill him for treason against the south and many of his friends had been hung for just what Newton believed in and was fighting for. The Home Guards would raid Tory homes and steal whatever food and supplies they deemed necessary for the war effort and would sometimes burn the houses and barns of the families that lived there. Newton and his family were under constant surveillance by the Home Guards and Newton had to hide in the hills and forests with his friends to keep from being caught and shot or hanged. Luckily for Newton, he was a crafty survivor who could anticipate his enemy's strategies and he had learned to think like them and avoid being trapped. He would often sneak back to his family at night and check on them to make sure they were safe. Newton would bring bags of cornmeal and flour strapped onto his horse for them and also chop wood for their stove and fireplaces, plow and plant seeds in their garden so that they could grow beans, potatoes, corn and other food crops and do the necessary repairs on the house and barn while he visited during those nights. During the days he would hide out in the woods with his friends and catch up on his sleep as his buddies took turns and stood watch over him. There were a lot of places that they could hide in those lush green forested hills and bluffs and Newton knew northwest Marion County like the back of his hand.

Toll Gate (Hamilton) and the Shottsville area were located at the southernmost part of the Tennessee Valley Ridge Section and at the southwestern edge of the Cumberland Plateau Section of Alabama. It is a very hilly and heavily forested area with many bluffs, streams, rivers and rich flora and vegetation that are unique to that section of the country. The region is one of the most botanically rich in Alabama and in the Southeast. In fact, after the War of 1812 and the defeat of the Creek Nation, Andrew Jackson declared it as one of the richest and most fertile areas for settlement in the country and encouraged settlers from all parts of the country to migrate there taking advantage of land grants that were being offered by the federal government. In the hilly summits that are comprised of sandstone there is a variety of vegetation and forests of oak, hickory, sourwood, and Virginia and shortleaf pines. In the lower elevations the sandstone is gradually replaced by limestone which supports vegetation such as shumard oak, chinquapin oak, sugar maple, white ash, southern shagbark hickory, redbud, flowering dogwood, and American smoketree. These are but a few examples of the rich plant life to be found in the hills and plains around Toll Gate or modern day Hamilton, Alabama. One cannot blame William Mansell, Newton Ozbirn, Russell Porter Palmer and my other ancestors for wanting to settle there. I can imagine the awesome natural beauty they must have found amongst the ferns and woodland spring wildflowers such as Virginia bluebells, Dutchman's breeches, twinleaf, wood poppies, trilliums, blue phlox, yellow trout lilies and assorted varieties of violets. It would have been breathtaking and as spiritually transporting as those wild fields of clovers might have been much later for Mary Dizenia and Blue John.

Newton would spend much of his young life hiding in these beautiful forests of oaks, hickory, pine and Cumberland seepage bog which is a mixture of black gum (that the pioneers used to make bee hives or "bee gums"), red maples, cinnamon fern, and sphagnum moss. These thick masses of vegetation would hide him and his horse from the Home Guards many a time. One could almost forget the encroaching Confederate danger as one was enveloped within the cinnamon fern, pink lady's slipper orchids, white fringeless orchid, and grass of Parnassus. In the fall there would've been naturally occurring ponds or sag ponds along the upper slopes and summits. The ponds would've been like islands in a sea of trees as Newton rode his horse amongst the gently rolling hills on paths that wound over the forest floor upon layers of hardpan soil. The ponds fill with water in late fall and winter which supports vegetation that grows in rings around them as the water evaporates during spring and summer. The ponds are unique to Alabama and comprise a mixture of woodland vegetation such as swamp black gum, red maple, and button brush. Newton came to know this land well and this land with its thick forests, vegetation, steep hills and bluffs gave him and his friends cover, sustenance, and protection during the years of the Civil War. This was the land that Newton and my ancestors loved and settled, raised their families on, farmed on, hunted and fished on, and fought, at the risk of their lives, to save.

Newton was one of those heroic characters that inspired legends. His courage and strength of character were inspirational and the stories told of his heroic exploits have inspired many generations of his descendents. Newton had the great advantage of knowing the land and how to live there but another advantage that Newton had was his ability to train animals like horses and dogs. Legends must have their heroic characters be they human or animal and this legend has them both. Training animals was something that he must have inherited from his ancestors who fought in the American Revolutionary War and from the Indian tribes that he had lived alongside and farmed and hunted with. With the passing of time the legend grew that Newton had a chestnut colored stallion named "Rex" and a Collie/Sheep Dog mix named "Captain" that he had trained on his farm to do all kinds of maneuvers and tricks. These tricks his animals had been taught would save Newton from the Home Guards and the Rebels countless times. Rex and Captain were extremely loyal to Newton and his wife and family and always let Newton know if any enemy was about to sneak up on them. Captain would bark very loudly and get up a full head of steam, run right at any intruder on foot or on horseback and leap up onto them with the force of a lion, crashing them instantly to the ground. At Newton's command, he would rip into their bodies with his sharp teeth and strong jaws. It was rare that any scurrilous characters dared attack Newton and his family when Captain was around. Rex also had been trained by Newton to rare up on his two hind legs and neigh loudly if he heard anyone approach, and if Newton didn't call him off, Rex would charge at them full speed and trample them under his hooves. These animals were trained to kill if necessary, and with Home Guards constantly on the prowl, it would be necessarily sooner than later. Newton could ride Rex "Indian Style" with no saddle and leap frog onto his back for a quick getaway if needed. Some of these tricks were taught to him by the Indians and others were handed down from ancestors that had trained horses during the Revolutionary War.

Newton had joined the Union Army and belonged to Company "D" that he fought with during much of the Civil War against the Rebels. William Fountain Ozbirn, brother of Newton, joined the Yankee Army after being recruited by my ancestor, Joseph Palmer, Doctor Russell Porter Palmer's oldest son, on September 8, 1862. The Yankees had sent Joseph back to recruit and raise a regiment. The Rebels had organized the Home Guard to enforce the laws of the Confederacy and Captain Stokley Roberts from Itawamba County, Mississippi was in charge of them in this part of Alabama. The Home Guard consisted of two to three hundred guerillas whose job it was to see that local men joined the Rebels and they also were responsible for procuring supplies for the Confederacy in any way they deemed necessary.

Word came to Newton that the Home Guards had raided the road leading to the Shottsville area where his parents and brother's family lived. Newton made a trip by night on his horse Rex to try and help them. He had brought provisions strapped to Rex's back including sacks of cornmeal and flour. When Newton arrived, he found his family alive but pretty shaken up and frightened by what the Home Guards had done. The Home Guards had taken most of their livestock and had tried to capture Henry, Newton's brother, but he had made his getaway and was hiding out in the woods nearby. Newton made sure to chop up some wood for his family and find a proper hiding place for the provisions that he had brought them. He also went around and checked the barn and forked what remained of the hay to the few remaining cows and he scraped up a few of the scattered corn ears and stalks to feed the chickens and pigs that remained. Luckily, his family had an underground cellar that the Home

Guard had not discovered and they still had a supply of food stored there that would hold them over for a while. It felt like to Newton that he was in a hostile foreign country where his family was the enemy and they had to fight for their very existence, and for all practical purposes, he was and they did. What a horrible feeling that must have been to have your beloved country taken away from you and to be surrounded by forces that wanted to destroy your family, your country and everything you believed in.

On his way back home, Newton stopped by Doctor Russell Porter Palmer's place. Russell told him that he and Morning Dizenia were fine and their son, Joseph, was hiding in the woods. The Home Guards did not bother Russell since he was a doctor and tending the sick in the area, and besides, he was too old for the service anyway. Russell told Newton that his son Joseph had killed five deer and that they had cut up the meat, smoked and preserved it, and hid it safely away in their underground cellar out in the woods. Russell also told Newton that he planned to take some of the meat to the Purser family that lived close by come daylight. Old man Moses Purser was ill and so was his daughter-in-law and his son was also hiding in the hills to avoid capture by the Home Guards. Moses Purser was the friend that had moved to Alabama with his Cherokee Indian wife Mapy along with her sister Morning Dove White and her husband William Mansell. The Home Guards had been there a week before and taken all their food, breaking their dishes, and kicking over the "bee gums" (bee hives that they had made from black gum tree stumps). Things had gotten so bad for the Pursers that Russell Palmer had seen seven year old Sara Ann Purser stealing apples from the neighbor Whitt's tree and feeding them to her little brother. Considering how they were treated by the Home Guards, it is no wonder that my Palmer ancestors and their neighbors were loyal to and fought with the Union side in the Civil War.

When Newton returned from checking on his family around seven in the morning, he found his wife Mary worried and watching the road for him. Captain was pacing back and forth on the floor and jumping up to look out the windows, so they could just feel there was danger and ill winds blowing around them. They had been lucky so far as the Home Guards had not caught Newton. Newton's stallion, Rex, was the fastest horse anywhere around and Newton had been able to escape the slower Home Guard horses many times, but both Newton and Mary agreed that it was time for him to go into more permanent hiding until things settled down and life returned to somewhat more normal. So Newton decided to stay in the woods and bluffs for a few weeks and watch carefully over his family from a safe distance. He would leave Captain there to protect them and hope that the Home Guards would not shoot and kill him.

Ultimately, toward the end of this period of watching and waiting, Joseph Palmer signed Newton up with the Union First Alabama Cavalry and he was welcomed as an expert sharpshooter and Rex would be in his element as well being a thoroughbred racing stallion. Newton was given two weeks to help Mary get things in order for his departure scheduled for February 4, 1863 to Corinth, Mississippi. The vegetables from the garden Newton had planted needed to be canned and stored safely away and the chopping of wood for winter had to be finished. Newton boarded up all the windows that he could and left two army pistols and a shotgun with plenty of ammunition for Mary to use if necessary. Mary was almost as good a shot as Newton and they had hunted deer together in their younger days in the north Alabama forests. Newton hoped that between Mary's sharpshooting and Captain's sharp teeth, not too many Home Guards would come around, but would look for easier pickings elsewhere. Anyway, a man has to do what a man has to do and his woman will stand by him every inch of the way. That was just the way things were and people managed to survive that way back in those days.

On February 1, 1863, Newton was chopping wood outside when Captain started barking loudly and Mary and the kids screamed for him to run. This was the day that all that training he did with Rex and Captain paid off. Newton ran like greased lightning and hopped up on Rex, who was grazing unsaddled next to the house. He straddled Rex and gave him a sharp kick with both feet and Rex took off like the wind, jumping over two fences and three hedges before the Home Guards ever had a chance to see what direction he was going. Captain had already charged out of the house and leaped up, knocking Captain Stokley Roberts of the Home Guard off his horse, when Mary came out with two pistols, one in each hand, firing over the heads of the other guerillas. Mary shouted at Captain Roberts who was about to draw his weapon: "Ol Cap is trained to tear yore jugular if you budge another inch. I be you, I'd git up off yore rear end easy like and mount yore hoss and lead them rascals outta here! Ol Cap is short on patience and long on teeth and he's just a waitin on my command, so

I wouldn't tary none about it!" After making her pronouncement, Mary fired her pistols over the spooked Home Guard horses once again as they all did an abrupt about face and started galloping down the road. As Captain Roberts cautiously climbed up and mounted his horse he rode off quickly as well, looking back and shouting to Mary:"We'll be back, and if your man is here, we'll kill him!"

It wasn't easy for Newton to run and leave his family at the mercy of the Home Guards, but Rex, Captain and Mary had valiantly saved his life so that he would live to fight another day. After hiding in the woods and watching over his family from a distance, Newton and Rex headed for Sheeram Creek, praying as he made his way to the home of Harbent Cole, a Union man that had a grist mill near Ball Rock (Rock Bridge Canyon). After getting some sleep in Harbent's barn until sunrise, he was invited to eat a breakfast of eggs and biscuits with sawmill gravy with Harbent's family. Newton discussed his situation with the Coles and the dangers that they all faced from the Home Guards and they all agreed that he should join a group of Union men they knew that were headed, as Newton was, for Corinth, Mississippi. They told him that he could get needed supplies from a Union sympathizer named the Widow Clark who lived not far from them on Beaver Valley Road headed west. Newton saddled up Rex and rode out toward the Widow Clark's home. After about a thirty minute ride through a heavily sugar maple, oak and hickory tree forested countryside, he and Rex arrived at the Widow Clark's home where he was met by a Mr. Murphy who was working outside by the barn. After making the proper introductions and telling Mr. Murphy about the Coles who had sent him there, Mr. Murphy helped Newton with gathering provisions for his journey. The Widow Clark, who had been watching suspiciously from her parlor window, came outside, welcomed Newton and explained, as he and Mr. Murphy were loading the supplies onto Rex's back, that there was an elaborate string of families in that part of Alabama that had established a secret network of Union sympathizers who would help Tories escape from the Home Guard. They would provide places for them to stay overnight, food to eat and provisions that would help them along their way. This is how Newton and others loyal to the Union were able to evade the "Johnnies" and find their way to the Yankee encampments where they could join up with Union troops. Newton's last stop along this Tory network was at Madison Neal's place where he was able to put Rex up in Madison's barn and they both could rest for the night.

By February 4, 1863, Newton had made it to Yankee country where he was assigned to Union Army, Company "D" with Captain George King as his C.O. He was not among strangers as he was to find three brothers, four cousins, one brother-in-law and a nephew in the Alabama Cavalry. William Ozbirn, Newton's brother, was in Company "K" and Newton was able to see him often. Rex seemed happy to have the company of all the cavalry horses as well and he pranced around proudly "strutting his stuff" for the admiring mares. During February, March, and April of 1863, Newton and Rex had many exploits with Company "D" and Rex had been made the Alabama Union Cavalry's official mascot. They called him "King Rex" and they had a flag made up with a stallion head and crown on top that Newton would carry into battle. Newton and Rex always led the cavalry charges with their flag waving proudly in front when they would skirmish with Rebel troops out in the woods, in the open fields, or when they would attack railroad trains that were carrying Rebel weapons and ammunition. Newton was an expert sharpshooter with both his pistols and his rifle and he shot and killed or wounded many a Rebel soldier during these skirmishes. Rex had to jump a multitude of hedges and fences to chase or to escape the Rebels that were shooting at them.

There was one time that the shooting was so fierce that Newton felt sure that Rex and he were goners. Company "D" had been chasing a Rebel platoon through the woods around Bobcat Creek when they realized that they had been lured into a Rebel ambush. Suddenly they were rushed by an onslaught of Rebel horses carrying what seemed to be a whole company of Rebels who were firing at them from all directions. The only alternative was to retreat, racing through the forest, and hope that their horses could outrun the Rebel horses that were now in full pursuit. Tree bark was flying everywhere as the Rebel guns were blazing and their bullets were flying all around them. It was like they were riding the "Horses of the Apocalypse" as Newton dug his heels into Rex and led his troops through what seemed like "The Gateway to Hell". Many of Newton's fellow troops were shot, falling off their horses dead or wounded and others had their horses shot from under them and they were trampled underneath the hooves of the Rebel horses racing behind.

Newton had a counterattack maneuver that he had planned for but never used for dire situations such as this one. He and Rex would create a dramatic diversion but it would take excellent timing and mostly a lot of good luck to pull it off. Suddenly, from over the sound of thundering hooves and crackling of rifle fire emitted a shrill ear piercing, bloodcurdling yell that sounded just like a wild Indian war cry. It was Newton's signal to Rex to spring into action and to perform their killing maneuver. Rex stopped abruptly in his tracks and pivoted around sharply as he sprung up on his hind legs and flared his nostrils and neighed thunderously, kicking his front hooves violently in the direction of the approaching Rebels. Newton kept screaming his war cry and firing his pistols at the Rebels as Rex charged the lead Rebel stallion and crashed into him full speed, knocking him sideways and onto the ground. Newton's death defying sally with Rex had worked as the Rebel horses behind were panicked and terrified by this unexpected attack. Rex must have seemed like the horse from Hell and the Rebel horses began bucking their riders and running off into the woods helter-skelter, knocking the Rebels off their backs as they ran under low hanging tree limbs. As the Rebel horses dispersed in all directions, Rex trampled the lead Rebel stallion under his hooves as Newton fired his pistols and killed about a half dozen of the fleeing Rebels.

By this time, the other cavalry soldiers from Newton's Company "D" had turned their horses around and were now chasing the totally disoriented Rebel troops, shooting them off their horses as they rode into the forest. These men of Company "D" had been trained to ride side saddle and shoot at the same time so that they could avoid the tree limbs and still fire their rifles at the Rebels. This was a trick that Newton had taught them and he and Rex had practiced it with them many times in the woods. This was the day that it all paid off. The Rebels attack had been repulsed and the absolute surprise and boldness of Newton and Rex's maneuver had thrown them into a chaotic and totally confused retreat. The whole concept of what Newton achieved here was what he had learned from the Indians and he had trained Rex to perform the maneuver on his farm years ago. Still, one had to have the attitude of an Indian like Crazy Horse and believe that "The Great Spirit" would protect you and your horse from the hail of bullets flying around you. I don't know if Newton believed this or not, but I do know that he and Rex survived each battle and that Newton lived to be an old man who told war stories just like this one to his grandkids.

During this period of chaos, measles were also killing many men in the camp and eventually, Newton became ill himself. After serving two months and eighteen days, Captain King gave him a leave to go home so that he could move his family to a safer place. Newton arrived home about April 21, 1863. Mary had much to tell him about what had happened while he was gone. Mary and the children had been attacked again by the Home Guards while he had been away fighting with the Union First Alabama Cavalry. Mary told Newton that Captain had tried to protect them but the Home Guards were ready for him this time and they shot him and left him for dead. The Home Guards were able to overcome Mary and disarm her, taking away her pistols and the shotgun and they threatened to kill her and the children if she continued to resist them. So Mary had no choice but to let them pillage and ransack the house, taking whatever they wanted. When the Home Guards were finished, they told Mary the next time she resisted them they would kill her. The Home Guards then rode off on their horses without checking on Captain as he lay motionless on the road outside.

Mary told Newton that after they had gone, she went to see if Captain had been killed and found that he was badly wounded but still breathing. Mary treated Captain's wound as best as she could and put a clay compress on it to stop the bleeding. She and her five year old son, William Washington Ozbirn, picked up Captain and put him in the barn behind some bales of hay so that he would not be seen and they would try to take him to Doctor Russell Porter Palmer in the morning. When Mary went out to the barn the next morning to tend to Captain, she found that he was gone and she went looking for him. After a short walk down the road, Mary's heart sank as she saw Captain lying there next to the fence. He was bleeding from the still fresh wound that he'd received but he was still alive. Mary immediately went and got some damp clay from the field and made a mud plaster that she spread thickly over Captain's wound. She then yelled out loudly to her son William to hitch up the wagon and bring it over to "Cap". William and Mary were able to carefully lift Cap up into the wagon. Mary went back to the house and got the other kids and they all went down the road to Doctor Russell Porter Palmer's place. When they pulled up in their wagon, Russell was out in his garden tending to some freshly planted turnips and he smiled broadly as he saw them approach. Russell could see everyone was panicky, so he hurried over to see that Captain was lying hurt and bleeding in the back of the wagon.

Doctor Russell went and got a stretcher and they put Captain onto it and carried him to the house where Russell had an examination room built inside a "lean to" on the back. He removed the bullet and treated Captain's wound with some medicines that he had in stock and told Mary that Captain needed some stitches and that he would have to stay with him for a while. Captain needed to heal up, rest, and not exert himself for a few weeks until he recovered. He would be OK but he would need to be restrained for a long time at Doctor Russell's. Taking Captain in was not uncommon for Doctor Russell, as he treated all the animals around the Shottsville area, as well as the people.

After telling Newton the story about the raid and Captain being shot, Mary continued by saying that she had other things that worried her, such as another outbreak of the deadly measles and that little George, the youngest child, had become ill. The child was feverish and needed medical attention so Newton went and got Doctor Russell Porter Palmer as he was the only doctor they could trust. There was another doctor named Mangram, but he was helping the Home Guards and reported all Union activity to Hamilton Carpenter, the Home Guard leader. After Doctor Russell arrived with Newton and took as best care of George as he could, Mary discussed with Newton what their options were under the perilous circumstances they were facing. Mary and the kids could not travel as Newton had planned because of George's illness, so Mary suggested that Newton find William (Bill) Whitehead and hide out with him in the woods until they could grow some food and nurse George back to health. Doctor Russell had said that Joseph, his son, was still hiding out and had almost been caught by "Old Stoke" (George Stout) and his gang when he came home to help butcher a hog. Joe hid inside the house while Doctor Russell talked to the men. After that, Joe stayed in the Daniel Davis House while the Home Guards concentrated on the Bull Mountain area.

Between Newton's narrow escapes and his hiding out in the woods and bluffs, he would often check on his family and his neighbors to see how they were all faring during these challenging times when their property, their liberty, and their very lives were being threatened by the Home Guards. He would keep his eyes and ears open and his instincts on full alert as he rode Rex from his hiding places in the woods onto the dirt roads that led to the neighboring farmlands. There were many times that he and Rex would conceal themselves in the hedges as the Home

Guards rode by just in front of them. One move or twitch by Rex or him and they would've been killed by a flurry of Home Guard bullets. Many would say that Newton had eyes in the back of his head because he always managed to escape and live to see another day. Newton believed firmly that one must find a way to stay alive if one wants to fight for his family, his country and for what he believed to be right.

In May of 1863, Newton stopped by Old Moses Purser and his wife Lucinda's (Moses first wife, Mapy, Morning Dove's sister, had passed away from measles years ago) place to check on them and their son, David C. Purser. He was met at the door by Mary Bishop, Lucinda's sister. Mary told him to come in and tell her about his family, who like most were struggling to maintain their homes and farms and keep their children fed while their husbands were either hiding in the woods or had been killed by the Home Guards. Mary told Newton that Moses and Lucinda had passed away during the last measles outbreak and that she and their son David had married and that, now, Mary was in charge of caring for and raising the children. She said that they were eating a lot of poke salad (a thick stemmed, leafy plant that produces berries and grows wild in the woods). The "old wives tale" was that poke salad had to be prepared and cooked carefully as it could be poisonous, but as Mary said:"It shore was good with a little fat back put in fur flavor." Mary had a lot more to worry about than whether the poke salad was safe to eat, and besides, the birds all feasted on the berries from it and God had watched over them. Mary said that they were surviving but that the Home Guards had taken everything and that their lives were in constant danger. Just recently, David's brother had been murdered by an unknown assailant and had paid the price that many in Marion County paid for being Tories or Union sympathizers.

Thankfully for Newton, there was much forested area with lush vegetation and thickets to provide hiding places in the hills around Hamilton and there were many bluffs that provided shelter and observation points that provided panoramic views of encroaching Home Guard guerillas. One probable location in neighboring Winston County was a rock formation that resembled a bridge in stone which arched over an expanse of wooded valley below. It would've made a good shelter from the elements and there was a creek close by that would've provided fresh drinking water and good fishing as well as to attract deer for hunting. They could hunt and fish and use the surrounding caves to cut, dry and cure the meats and then store them for themselves and their families. This spot was called Lodi then but now is called Natural Bridge and is a popular park and tourist site in northwest Alabama.

Newton would've hidden in spots like this and, of course, in those days they were well hidden and guarded with great care. Their locations were kept secret from everyone but themselves, as their lives and the lives of their families depended upon that secrecy as well as upon their sharp wits and instincts for survival. The men would place piles of leaves there in the bluffs where they would prepare makeshift beds to sleep on. One day, as Newton approached one such pile of leaves to get some well needed sleep, he heard a voice cry out to him from the underbrush:"I am Henry Ozbirn looking for Newton Ozbirn!" Once they recognized each other the brothers embraced heartily and were glad to find that each of them had survived the Home Guards. They had both been hiding out in separate parts of the woods and bluffs for months and this was the first time that their paths had crossed. Henry was excited to tell his brother about his plans to join the Yankee army and having done so, this is how Newton responded: "Well", said Newton, "I stayed two months and eighteen days and it's not much better than here. The food was terrible and I was never paid a penny. Mostly a lot of yelling and sickness going on! You're better off here!" They inquired about their families, reminisced over memories of better times and had a good reunion as they enjoyed the cured deer meat and dried fish that Newton had stored inside one of the caves up in the bluffs. They could eat these meats without cooking them, thus eliminating the use of a campfire that might attract The Home Guards attention.

Despite his brother's good advice, on June 10, 1863, Henry joined the 16th Alabama Infantry Regiment, Company "A", of the Union army. The brothers were to hear about two weeks later of the deaths of their two other brothers, Fountain and Chesley, both having died of measles on June 26, 1863. They had gone into battle at Cherokee and suffered a relapse. Fountain left a wife, Mahala Arnold Ozbirn and three children: Judy Ann Ozbirn born September 29, 1853, Madison Monroe Ozbirn born May 17, 1857, and Mary Francis Ozbirn born January 9, 1861. Chelsey left his wife Eva and five children. In the 1860 census, Eva was 38 years old, William 15, Eady 13, Jordan 6, Marshal 4, and Anella 1.

As Newton and his brother were having their reunion, back in the bluffs, a new professed Tory had arrived in Toll Gate. He introduced himself, after being surrounded by a group of ten Tories with pistols drawn, as Drury McKinn and claimed that he had deserted the CSA and now wanted to join up with the Tories. Drury was very suspicious to them though because he was asking a lot of questions about George Stout, who had organized the Tories into a fighting force. Drury McKinn wanted to find George Stout so that he could join up, he said, and they told him, rather reluctantly, that he could be found at the home of two women on Bull Mountain Creek. Drury stayed there and socialized with the men and talked about some of the plans that the Confederates had to attack neighboring Tory encampments and Tory homesteads, so they began to trust and accept him as one of the group. Sometime later that day, Drury left and headed toward Bull Mountain Creek where the two women lived and he hoped to find George Stout there with them. Upon arrival, Drury found that George Stout had gone shortly before and he had left the two women there badly beaten. Seeing this, Drury, confided to the two women that he was there to kill George Stout and that he would avenge their beatings. Drury should have kept his true intentions to himself because one of the women was George Stout's sister, Permilia. Although she had been beaten by George, she knew that her brother would kill her if she kept Drury's plot to kill him a secret, so she wasted no time in spreading the news. Soon every Tory in northwestern Alabama was after Drury McKinn. Drury had been sent by the Home Guards to destroy the unity of the Tories, but now just the opposite had occurred and they were more united than ever.

The Tories found Drury McKinn in Barnesville where he was playing a fiddle for a square dance they were having for the local townspeople. Four of the Tories mingled with dancers and meandered their way up to Drury grabbing him, tossing his fiddle to the side as they led him forcibly outside where they tied him onto the back of a chestnut and white spotted horse. Soon they were all galloping down the dirt road toward Doctor Russell Porter Palmer's house where the pounding of their horse's hooves stirred up the dust and sent the yard birds cackling and flying up in all directions. John Howard Palmer, Russell's son, who was just six years old at the time, heard all the commotion and got up out of his bed to look at the approaching Tory horses. He looked out the window and wondered why the man was yelling and tied to that pretty red and white horse. John Howard watched as the drunken men and their prisoner rode off toward White Rock. They crossed the river at Mixon Ford and headed up to a grove of hickory trees when one of the men discovered that they had forgotten to bring a rope. Someone figured out that they could just cut a stout, limber vine from one of the trees in the woods, so one of the men went to find one. Sure enough, the vine worked quite well and Drury McKinn's feet dangled just inches above the ground as he hung from the hickory tree limb for several minutes before choking to death. So the fiddler had met his tragic end and was buried face down at the edge of what later became John Howard Palmer's field. Animals later dug up the body, eating most of it and leaving the skeleton that some Glasscock girls found and hung up in some bushes as if it were a graveyard spook. The skeleton remained there as no one dared touch it and John Howard Palmer, owner of the field, refused to plow it several years after. This was the stuff legends were made of and the tale would get wilder each time it was told. When Home Guard leader, Hamilton Carpenter, got word that Drury McKinn was in trouble he tried to make a deal with the Tories and exchange Drury for John Meadows, a captured friend of the Tories. But it was too late and the ill fated legend of Drury McKinn had already been born.

Upon hearing the news of Drury McKinn, Newton decided to take a chance and slip back to see Mary and his children for a night. The violent actions of the Tories and George Stout had made him decide to go back to the Yankee Army. George W. Whitehead was planning to go back as well and they could travel there together. Newton stayed in the woods nearby until about midnight and, after checking very carefully, he rode Rex on the side trails back to his home. When he got there he found that the Home Guard had attacked again. Mary said:"They took our mule. They went through the house, got our quilts and anything else of value and they're going to kill you if they find you here. You had better leave tonight!" Mary said that she was glad that Captain had not been there or he would've been killed by the Home Guards. They were both thankful that he had still been at Doctor Russell's recuperating. She said it was likely that he would heal up soon and live to chase rabbits and Home Guards another day.

On this visit of Newton's, Mary told him that she had heard a story that had restored her courage about a woman named Margaret Brown Cooper. Margaret's husband, Columbus Cooper had been killed when a mule kicked him and now, having to face life all alone, Margaret decided to walk from a place near Linden, Tennessee, all the way to Marion County, Alabama where she had kin. Margaret carried her one year old baby, Jim, and a sack of cornbread along with a few personal items the whole trip. The baby was sick most of the way with colitis and Margaret stopped at springs along the way to wash out the one diaper that he had. Several times she thought that they would not make it. One time she found herself in the middle of a battle between Confederate and Yankee troops and had to place the baby in a ditch and lay on top of him. Somehow they managed to escape alive and unseen. When she finally made it to Florence, Alabama, where they had to cross the Tennessee River, she had nothing of value for the boatman's fee. He finally agreed to take as payment the one good dress that she had carried in her sack. They did miraculously make it to Toll Gate, Alabama where relatives, unknowing of their plight, welcomed them with open arms. This tale is one of Joel Palmer's favorite stories as that little baby that survived because of his mother's raw stamina, and pioneer courage was his great uncle.

It was now October 1863 and Newton had gathered the remainder of his small crop of beans, corn, peas, squash, turnips, collard greens, and okra, putting things away for winter and hiding them in the underground cellar from George Stout's gang and the Home Guards. A larger group of Confederates were combing the area for deserters, turncoats or "mossbacks" as they were sometimes called, and Newton had to make a run for it. Mary and the children decided to stay, because safety for them could not be found in the north according to Margaret Cooper and others. Newton rode Rex back to his old outfit, the First Alabama Cavalry, on October 23, 1863. His company commander was not happy to see him after he had been AWOL for four months, but soldiers such as Newton and horses such as Rex were very hard to come by, so amends were quickly made. Newton's timing was such that he was immediately ordered to leave with a force of 650 men for Columbiana, Alabama to destroy the railroad from Line Station to Elyton or Ely's Town, a small community which is now a part of Birmingham, Alabama. Newton left the same day that he arrived riding with Rex at the lead, robbing from Union people as well as Rebels along the way. By this time, there was so much evil going on with each side that it was hard to tell which side was worse.

After crossing part of Winston County, they were ordered to turn back to Corinth, Mississippi, about 45 miles from Camp Glendale. At 11:00 a.m. in the morning near Patterson's Store (also called Jones Crossroads, now Vina in Franklin County, Alabama), they confronted the Rebel pickets, fired a few rounds and drove the Rebels off. After stopping for a break to eat, they moved on to Vincent's Crossroads (Red Bay, Alabama), where they struck the main line of several hundred Rebel infantry forces, that were so strong the cavalry could not hold them back. Newton decided what they needed to do was have more distance between them and the blood thirsty Rebels, so he had Rex lead an immediate sortie to the rear and he kicked his feet to his faithful horse's sides making a dash for it, with what was left of the men in his company. Unfortunately, Newton, Rex and the men were rushing head long into a trap that the Rebels had planned for them.

Upon reaching the Memphis and Charleston road, they encountered about 400 cavalry and about 800 mounted infantrymen who rushed upon them and surrounded them. All Hell broke loose, and Newton saw his cousin, John W. Cross, fall from his horse dead. Shooting his pistol, while at the same time spurring Rex sharply, Newton made a mad dash for it. Rex had received a grazing bullet wound to the neck, but he was still racing like a demon possessed. Rex and Newton managed to clear a thicket and circumvent three or four tall hedges that provided some cover from the overwhelming Rebel cavalry. Newton had not performed this trick with Rex before but while bending his body low and wrapping his arms around Rex's neck, he inserted some of the wet chewing tobacco from his mouth into Rex's wound and plugged it in order to slow the bleeding. To save your horse, sometimes it was best to slide quickly off its back and slap its hind quarters sharply as you slide off so that your animal would run safely away finding its own way to freedom. So Rex, having been trained to do so, went racing off with the First Alabama Cavalry flag still trailing from its saddle holder in the wind. Rex raced away dodging tree limbs and bullets, deep into the forest after Newton had slid off his back. Newton had slid from Rex's back with both pistols blazing and his rifle slung over his back. Newton shot three of the Rebels from their horses with his pistols as he dived into a low thicket of bramble bushes and began to low crawl as bullets whizzed over his buttocks and head. A couple of times he had to jump up and trample and slash his way through Rebels and brush with his 18 inch cavalry knife. The blood of his Rebel victims splashed over his forehead and arms as he ran, leaped, and crawled through the maze of thorns and brush. Although battered, bloodied, scraped, torn by bramble bushes and grazed by bullets, Newton had found safe haven in the thick undergrowth of the forest and, like Crazy Horse who would lead his Indian braves into battle years later in 1876, the "Great Spirit" rode with him again that day.

Newton never noticed the bloody pricks, scratches, scrapes, and flesh wounds as he slithered himself like a low crawling snake through the seemingly endless underbrush of brambles, but he finally scrambled out the other side of it. As he exited he saw several other terrified Company "D" men and they all began "double timing" in unison together toward what they prayed would be a safe haven. After about a half hour or so of this, they slowed their pace and Newton let out a shrill whistle, repeating it several times toward the four directions of the compass and he called out in a melodic Sacred Harp like chanting:"Rex, Rex, come on, come, come on home boy...come on home". They could see the sunlight reflecting from a stream not so far away, and from within the willows along its side, with their limbs swaying in the brisk autumn wind, raced a shining chestnut stallion with a flowing Cavalry flag trailing valiantly from the holder on his saddle. Roaring, jubilant cheers rose from the ranks of the surviving Alabama Cavalry men as Rex pranced up and nuzzled his nose into Newton's embracing arms.

Rex had survived because of his speed, superior intelligence, and training and he, like Newton, would live to fight other battles. Among the survivors was a man from Newton's neighborhood named Robert Brown, who was a medic with the cavalry and was able to treat Rex's neck wound. Luckily, the bullet had grazed Rex's neck and had not penetrated into the muscular tissue and Robert was able to apply a bandage compress to the wound so that it could heal. The group had been miraculously spared from the maw of death and they all decided that it might be best to head back for Toll Gate, Alabama.

On October 28, 1863, Newton and Rex rode up to his home to find Captain all healed and barking excitedly as he raced out to greet them. After catching Captain as he leaped up in his arms and giving him a big bear hug, a lot of head and ear scratching and his heartfelt expressions of joy that he was alive and healthy, Newton went inside his house to receive a raucous reception of adoring kisses and welcoming embraces from

Mary and his kids. They all noticed his cuts, scrapes and bruises and were concerned for his health but very thankful that he had somehow survived the ravages of war and had come home once again. After Newton related to Mary and the kids the harrowing details of what he and his men and Rex had endured, they all gathered around the kitchen table and offered thanks to God that Newton and Rex had both returned home safely. Mary had much news for Newton as well and told him of an incident concerning the wife of one of their neighbors named Stephen Scott. It seems a gang of Home Guards stormed up on their horses and tried to burn down the Scott home. Mrs. Scott, with fire in her eyes, stood her ground boldly right in their path and thrust her bonnet proudly up on her head, loudly proclaiming to the large gang of guerillas: "Steve told me you would come to burn our house and he told me to tell you that he would take care of each of you when he returned. I am remembering all your names: Willy Russell, Stoke Roberts, Joe Roberts, Jim Beckman, Squeal Musgrove, George Harris, John O. Kelly, Whit Hulsey, Sam Nolan, Jim Smith, Hugh Logan, Bob Smith, Sherman Williams, Mike Gaston, Rich Burleson, Cleve Borne, and Bob Reed." An inner strength seemed to overtake her as she stared down these seventeen Home Guard thugs. The men looked at each other with a shared queasiness in the pits of their stomachs and were suddenly overcome by their own squeamish lack of willpower. They all knew that Stephen Scott, a First Lieutenant in the Alabama Union Cavalry, would revenge their deed and they all whipped their horses around and rode away to find more easy prey. After relating this heroic tale about Stephen Scott's wife, Mary anxiously implored from Newton, now that he was again safely home, what he planned on doing next. Newton replied that, with his cavalry weapons, he planned on staying around home for a while, as cutting wood sounded better than returning to Glendale, Mississippi and dodging more Rebel bullets.

His cavalry friends, Robert Brown or "Little Bob" as they called him, and Freeman Drake were staying in the woods up around Red Hill, north of Toll Gate. Both men had good horses and weapons. Mary Jane Mitchell, daughter of James Mitchell Sr. and sister to John Mitchell invited them to come to her house for a good hearty meal. They knew they were taking a chance but it had been a while since they'd had seen a pretty girl's face, let alone, had one cook a meal for them, so they let down their guard and accepted. Little Bob and Freeman arrived one morning about daybreak at the Mitchell place on Red Hill. Mary Jane was cooking and the tantalizing smells of chicken and dumplings, turnip greens with fat back, and hot cornbread were wafting temptingly throughout the house. The men were cleaning up as the meal preparations were being made and Freeman was hanging a mirror on the wall so that he could see to shave when he saw the reflection of Ham Carpenter and the Home Guards approaching on horseback. Freeman yelled to warn Little Bob and they both ran out the back way to their horses. Freeman was shot in the arm as he jumped onto his horse and fell to the ground, catching some blood in his hand which he wiped onto his mouth. Freeman was using an old cavalry trick and lay still there on the ground playing dead as the Home Guards rode up. Little Bob had gotten away when Ham Carpenter looked at Freeman and said: "This one is dead, there's blood coming from his mouth; get the other one!" Little Bob, running his horse as fast as he could, raced down a trail leading to Rideout Falls, outside of Toll Gate, but just before he got to the north branch of Williams Creek, his horse stumbled and fell. Little Bob rolled under a bluff, and still holding onto his pistol, shot two of the Home Guards. Little Bob was outnumbered though, and the Home Guards shot him several times and killed him. The Home Guards rode back to where Little Bob's farm was to tell his family they'd killed him. Ham Carpenter told his wife: "If you cry, I'll kill you too! There'll be a bunch of them 'moss backs' at Bob's funeral and we'll be there to get them too!" The next day a grave was dug at Pleasant Ridge and Old Ham and his gang was ready, but no Tories showed up and neither did Little Bob. The real funeral was held in the woods near Ballard's Mill with friends and family in attendance. Freeman recovered from his wound and lived to tell the story time and time again to his children and friends.

George Stout had gone back to the Yankee Army and the Home Guards were left to step up their dirty work. Newton told Mary that he felt that he had to return to the cavalry, so on December 25, 1863, he and Rex reported back to duty in the First Alabama Cavalry. Captain George King thought that he and Rex had been killed in the Flat Woods fight, so he was glad to have his prized soldier and faithful horse back once again. Newton was ordered to Memphis, Tennessee but his records did not keep up with him and he never did get a pay day. On April 27, 1864, after he and Rex had several more skirmishes with the Rebels, they both rode home one last time, never to be warriors again. The big news upon Newton's return home was that Stoke Roberts and his Home Guard gang had run into a large force of Tories just across Bull Mountain Creek. There were about fifty armed men waiting for him to cross the creek next to the old mill. George Stout had come back with a wagon load of guns and ammunition and when they crossed the creek, the Tories opened fire and killed several of George Stout's men while Stout himself escaped. The last heard of him was that he had ended up somewhere near Fayette, Mississippi.

Mary continued with the news that John Mitchell, Russell Palmer, Edward Flury, Marty Akers, and William Brown were out looking for Home Guards. John Mitchell had already killed Doc Mangram to avenge the death of his wife and Little Bob's killing. They took Doc to the spring where John's wife had died and to the place where Little Bob was killed and shot him in the back of the head while he prayed for forgiveness of his sins. They had also killed Hamilton Carpenter near the prison at White Rock. So the tide was turning and the Tories were achieving the upper hand now. About three months later, William Brown's son was hunting cows when he came upon a pair of boots sticking up out of the ground. He retrieved the boots from their earthly lair, and tried them on. As they fit him pretty well, he decided to keep them and wear them home. His mother inquired about where he got such a nice pair of boots when he returned and he answered: "I found them in a pile of bones". His mother screamed at him:"Take those off! They are Doc Mangram's!" The coroner, Russell Palmer, was sent for to remove the bones and doctor's bag and they were then carried to the Mangram family cemetery and buried next to Doc Mangram's father. Russell Palmer's son, John Howard Palmer, William Brown, Little Bob's brother, and several others assisted and field stones were placed at his feet and head. Unlike Drury McKinn, Doc was given a decent burial and not left out in the woods for animals to drag away.

In large part, the information about Newton Hubbard Ozbirn, his family, the Palmers, and other Marion County neighbors, friends and foes alike, was researched and recorded by Joel Palmer, the great, great grandson of Newton. Joel Palmer's great grandfather was John Howard Palmer, a younger brother of Hezekiah Gaines Palmer, both sons of Doctor Russell Porter Palmer. So Joel Palmer and my mother were second cousins, once removed. Joel descended from Newton and Mary Ozbirn's daughter, Nancy Ann, who later married John Howard Palmer, our great, great uncle, brother to Hezekiah Gaines Palmer, who was our great, great grandfather. Had Newton not survived the Rebels and Home Guards and Doctor Russell Porter Palmer and his sons Hezekiah Gaines and John Howard not survived as well, then none of us, Joel Palmer, Mary Dizenia Palmer, Clover Palmer, Mary Elizabeth Palmer Brown, James Roger Brown, or me, Gregory Hugh Brown would be here to tell the story. How strange twists of fate can be within the kaleidoscope of life.

Joel Palmer goes on to relate from his research that Captain Stokely Roberts of the Home Guard went back to headquarters in Jasper, Alabama and took the oath of allegiance in Huntsville, Alabama in 1865 as a law enforcement officer and served in his home town of Itawamba, Mississippi after the Civil War. In the days and months that followed, Plummer Williams and a Miller man were put in jail in Fulton, Mississippi and a gang of men from Marion County, Alabama, Joseph Palmer included, broke them out. Miller was killed but the others escaped, telling of seeing Stokely Roberts there as a law officer. Newton and Mary moved to the Daniel Davis place (both Davis and his wife died in the war) on the Buttahatchee River in 1865, where Mary died in childbirth in 1866. The baby girl was Nancy Ann Ozbirn, Joel Palmer's grandmother. Newton later married a neighbor, Sally Glasscock (one of the girls that threw Drury McKinn's skeleton in the bushes next to John Howard Palmer's field). Newton and Sally had one son named Henry. Newton lived a long peaceful life thereafter and died in 1900. John Howard Palmer remembered him as a very good man. Legend has it that Newton continued to raise and train horses and Rex was put out to stud and sired many fine stallions and mares. Captain herded cattle and sheep as long as he could and lived to be a ripe old age of 15 which is about a hundred in human years. Rex died not much longer past that and both Rex and Captain were buried in plots of honor in Newton's field next to the Buttahatchee River. On some occasions, legend has it that you could hear old man Newton go out there next to their graves and lovingly sing beautiful old Sacred Harp songs to them both.

Joel Palmer continued to relate that two of his great grandmothers lived to be in their nineties and he remembered listening to them talking about the Civil War. They, like their ancestors, were pro Union and yet they talked of "Old Abe" with hate in their voices. Joel's dad said his father talked of Old George Stout the very same way. I agree with assessments made at the time, "that both sides in the war did a lot of terrible things and that people like Newton Ozbirn had to pay an especially high price as a result. They were exposed to danger every minute and shot at for just sitting by their firesides or walking down the road. They had to leave their families vulnerable to the abuse of the enemy and sometimes the enemy was hard to determine. They had to live like animals in the woods and they suffered all the same hardships, if not worse, as their comrades in the north". Joel Palmer's research was taken from his family's sources including America Cole Lolley (granddaughter of Harbent Cole and Joel's great grandmother), Russell Porter Palmer (Joel's great grandfather), John Howard Palmer (Joel's grandfather and Russell Porter Palmer's young son), Harvey Williams (grandson of Plummer Williams), Jim Cooper (Joel Palmer's great uncle and the baby whose mother carried him and walked from Tennessee to Marion County, Alabama), Margaret Cooper (second wife of John Mitchell), Elizabeth Rye (granddaughter of Margaret Cooper Mitchell).

So ends this chapter of legends of our ancestors who lived before, during and after the times of the American Civil War. As I mentioned at the beginning, much of what I write is based on ancestral research and fact and much is based on legends that have been told over the years and embellished to make for exciting fireside chats and fables. While legends may well be based in fact, one must understand that they are what they are. Legends become more exaggerated as time passes and the imagination of the story teller grows. The next chapter will travel even further back in time to Colonial days and before and facts as well as legend will be intertwined here as well.

Chapter Five

As Legends Grow

We affectionately called Mary Dizenia Palmer "Mammy", as that is what her grandchildren or Clover McKinley's children by Cora Lee Goodson Palmer called her as they were raised during the years of the Great Depression from the 1930's to 1940's. Mammy's pioneer ancestors were of tough stock and they were firm believers in defending their family and country. Mammy was a strong willed pioneer woman as well, who like her mother and grandmother before, raised a family of God fearing children and grandchildren, worked hard plowing in the fields to raise food for her family, and made by hand all the clothing that they wore. Mammy treated her grandchildren's aches, pains, and illnesses with the Indian medicines and home remedies that were passed down from her Cherokee Indian great, great grandmother, Morning Dove White Mansell. The staunch and strict pioneer work ethic had been thoroughly engrained within her by many previous generations of her father's ancestors, the Palmers, her mother's ancestor's, the Armstrongs, and before that, the Mansells. The teachings of these hardy ancestors had prepared Mammy for what she, along with the unwavering assistance of Cora Lee, was about to face with the hardships of raising a family during the depression.

The Mansells were thought to have come from Tennessee from South Carolina where they may have been neighbors of Hezekiah and Elizabeth Roberts Palmer. From Tennessee they moved to Toll Gate in Marion County, Alabama. The name Mansell is thought to have come from the French and the original Mansells came to Scotland during the time of Catholic Queen Mary, Queen of Scots. There were some possible ancestors in Jackson County, Tennessee, and also in McMinn, Tennessee around 1830, which would have been Cherokee territory then. So the Palmers and Mansells had probably moved from the same regions before finally settling in Marion County, Alabama, where Elizabeth Roberts Palmer moved to and settled with three of her sons. They had lived in Benton County, Alabama but then moved to Marion County, Alabama, around 1844 where they met up with the Mansells, whom it is thought, they had known previously. Elizabeth's son, Russell Porter Palmer, married William Mansell's daughter, Morning Dizenia, our great, great, great grandmother. William Mansell had a workshop near his house and he made furniture and wood tools. He made the spinning wheel for Morning Dizenia when she married, that was later passed down to her children and grandchildren and eventually to our great grandmother, Mammy. We still have that spinning wheel in the family. In 1974, my brother was able to retrieve from the Palmer log cabin, a little oak straight back chair with a woven split hickory seat that was made by William Mansell as well. We have a rich history of self made, experience hardened, pioneer ancestors who constructed their own log houses and barns, plowed their own fields with oxen or mules, made their own clothing using spinning wheels and handmade looms, ground their own flour and mill in family or friends' grist mills, hunted and fished for food in nearby forests and streams, and in some cases, made their own furniture as William Mansell did.

Further documentation of Mammy's pro Union background comes from her mother's side of the family. James Stewart Armstrong was Mammy's mother's father and his wife was Mary (Polly) Holt. The Armstrong family came from Ohio and their sons went back there during the Civil War to fight with the Union. Their son, James Stewart Armstrong, was too young to fight though and our great grandmother, Mary Dizenia (Mammy), may have owed her birth to that fact. James Stewart Armstrong and Mary (Polly) Holt were the parents of Mary Elizabeth Armstrong (for whom my mother Mary Elizabeth Palmer Brown was named), who was Mammy's mother.

According to Joel Palmer's genealogy which my brother discovered in 1990, the Palmer's can be traced back to North Cumberland County, Virginia in the 1600's when John Palmer came over with his brother Thomas from England and settled on the lands around the Rappahannock River. John's wife was Sarah and they had two sons and we are descended from the one named Joseph. John died before 1689 and had been born in England in 1633. Joseph was born about 1655 and married Alice Hudnall, the widow of John Hudnall, about 1687. The old stone house which was the Hudnall home near the Rappahannock River was still standing at the time of Joel Palmer's research. Joseph had five sons: John, Joseph, Thomas, Benjamin, and Isaac. Thomas is our ancestor and was born about 1692 and was the third son of Joseph. Thomas had four sons and Elles was our ancestor and was born between 1730 and 1735. Elles was appointed constable in Chesterfield County, Virginia in 1753. In 1777 he sold his land in Virginia and he served in the Revolution and was wounded and in the hospital several times. Elles and his son John moved to Union, South Carolina sometime before 1784 and Elles died in Edgefield, South Carolina in 1801.

So, John Palmer's ancestors first came to this country in the mid 1600's and settled in Virginia. The generations of Palmers that came later moved west with the flow of settlers that received land grants taken from previously Indian lands in South Carolina, Georgia, and Alabama that had been ceded to the United States government. The first known Palmer ancestor was named John as well and came to Virginia in 1649. He had received land as payment for transporting people from England to the Colonies. According to Joel Palmer's research from *the Genealogical Research Institute of Arlington, Virginia,* John Palmer served as a corporal in Captain Lathrop's Company during King Philip's War (1675-1676). Through land deed records we know that he left land to his nine children including John Palmer, born in England in 1640, William Palmer, born in England in 1643, our ancestor Joseph Palmer, born in England in 1645, Edward Palmer, born in Virginia in 1650, George Palmer, born in Richmond, Virginia in 1655, Thomas Palmer, born in Virginia in 1659, Robert Palmer, born in Richmond County, Virginia in 1662, Hanna Palmer, born in Northumberland County, Virginia in 1664, and James Palmer, born in Northumberland County, Virginia in 1665.

Joseph Palmer, our ancestor, and son of John Palmer was born in England in 1645 and came to Virginia when he was four years old with his parents in 1649. Around 1675 he married Alice Hudnall, daughter of John Hudnall, and they had six children including John born in 1677, Joseph born in 1680, Thomas born in 1682, our ancestor Benjamin born in 1684, Isaac born in 1686, and Rebecca born in 1690. Our ancestor, Benjamin, was born in Docomo Parish, Northumberland County, Virginia in 1684 and died in 1735. His children included Robert born in 1718, Alice birth date unknown, William birth date unknown, Judith birth date unknown, our ancestor Elles born in 1725, Benjamin born in 1729, and Sarah Ann birth date unknown. Elles Palmer, our ancestor, son of Benjamin, was born in Virginia in 1725. According to the *Misty Roll Records* in Washington D.C., when he was about 50 years old, Elles

Palmer enlisted in the Revolutionary Army January 11, 1777 for a period of 3 years. He first served in the 10th Virginia Regiment which was later changed to the 6th Continental Virginia Regiment. His pay was 6 2/3 dollars per month. Elles was wounded several times and spent much time in the hospital during the war. He reenlisted at Middle Brook, Virginia on May 15, 1779, a few months before his first enlistment ran out. His bounty was $150.00.

After the war, Elles moved to Union County, South Carolina and settled on Brown's Creek near his son John, who moved there about 1775 with his father-in-law, William Williams. Elles received a land grant November 12, 1787 in Edgefield County, South Carolina and sold his place in Union County in 1788. His homestead on Horn's Creek, South Carolina had 89 acres and his children, Thomas and Elisha, lived with him. Elles made a will in 1800 and he died in 1801. His will listed his 11 children which included Thomas, our ancestor John of Bear Creek, Whitty, Rhoda, Hocky, Elijah, Elisha, Gideon, Judith, Russell, and Sally. The oldest son, Thomas, died in Edgefield County, South Carolina in 1805 and, like his father he left a will in which his brother, John, was named. Rhoda Palmer lived in Union, South Carolina and also left a will. Elijah Palmer moved from Edgefield County to Hancock County, Georgia and lived next to John's son, John Jr., as a neighbor on Shoulder Bone Creek. Elisha Palmer Sr., son of Elles, moved to Greene County, Georgia and lived next door to Amasa Palmer, son of John Palmer, his brother. Elisha received a land grant of 207 ½ acres of land in Lee County, Georgia and he moved there from Greene County in 1829. Elles's son Elisha was a Revolutionary War soldier like several of his brothers and his father. John Palmer Jr. moved to Lee County, Georgia and bought Elisha's 207 ½ acres of land when Elisha died in 1830. Russell Palmer, son of Elles, died about 1800 and left one daughter. There were several Russell Palmers and it is difficult to ascertain which Russell belongs to which Palmer as Hezekiah, John, and Elisha all had boys named Russell. Russell was a very common name with the Palmers as later with Russell Porter Palmer and John Russell or "Blue John" Palmer the father of Clover.

This is the ancestry of John Palmer Sr. who was born September 6, 1753 and died August 19, 1828. John had an unusual request for his children to carry out at his funeral. He wanted to be let down in his grave as the sun went down and his children did as he requested. John Palmer's wife was Martha Williams, born April 18, 1754 and died August 19, 1813, 15 years to the day before John died. The date of their marriage is not known but John and Martha came to South Carolina from Virginia about 1775 with her father, William Williams. They are buried in the family cemetery on Palmer land grant on Buffalo Creek, a few miles north of the town of Union, South Carolina. According to the *South Carolina State Archives, Columbia, South Carolina Revolutionary Records,* John Palmer served as a horseman and 147 days as a footman from May 1, 1780, to March 31, 1781. John Palmer lost a black mare in service of the state that was being used under the command of Colonel Thomas Brandon in General Pickens' Brigade. The value of the mare was appraised by William Williams and John White at a value of 65 pounds. The Thomas Brandon referred to was from Union County and lived about 3 miles from John Palmer. He is buried in the Brandon Cemetery on Brown's Creek.

This ancestral background, as much of the background used for this book, was provided by our second cousin, twice removed, Joel Palmer who did years of research on the Palmer family. This family ancestral background would be especially useful for the ancestral sites in Union, South Carolina that my brother would visit as part of his own research. On March 8, 1990 my brother, James Roger Brown, visited Mrs. Marcelle Palmer Cannon of Union, South Carolina. She was 83 years old and lived in a large two story house built around 1900 by her mother on Palmer land about two miles north of Union. Her father Ellis died at age 49, when she was five, of heart failure or stroke. She was born in the house that Ellis Palmer, her great grandfather and brother of Benjamin Hezekiah Palmer (our great, great grandfather), built which was originally a one story house. A second story was added by her grandfather, William Palmer. Slave houses were on the property at one time, slaves are buried there, and slaves stayed on after the Civil War and lived on Palmer land. The property went back to Buffalo Creek in the rear to where an old log cabin built by John Palmer, our ancestor, was located. The property may have gone as far as Brown's Creek.

Mrs. Marcelle Cannon referred to "Friday", John Palmer's slave, who helped build the original log house of John Palmer. My brother was able to visit the remains of this house on his visit and took pictures of the site and house. John Palmer built his log house there in Union, South Carolina, around 1784. After the Revolutionary War, he moved there to the land granted him on Buffalo Creek. Court records show that he bought small tracts of land at the time. When he bought his first horse, he also bought a bell for the horse to wear, so if Indians led the horse off, he could locate it again later when the bell rung (of interest here, the bell cost more than the horse). When John Palmer and "Friday" built the log home they practiced the same traditional method of construction that early settlers had used for centuries. Because there were two of them, the house could be made larger with taller walls than when just one person alone would build a house. They didn't need many resources, just an axe or saw and the choice of the tallest, straightest trees in the nearby forest. Of course, they needed a horse and a wagon to transport the trees to be cut and prepared for assembly to the site of the house. Working together, John and Friday first cleared a plot of land where the house would be built and also an area where they could have a garden and build a barn to keep animals like oxen, horses, and pigs. They would have to cut down the existing trees on these plots and remove the stumps to clear the land. This was good though because they could use these trees in the construction of the house, barn, and in the building of fences. After clearing the land, John and Friday cut down all the additional trees needed to build the house and barn. They looked for trees with straight trunks that would make the best logs for building with. Once the logs had been hauled in the wagon to the site, they cut them to the right length and cut notches at each end so that the logs would fit together at the corners. The bark also needed to be stripped off to prevent the logs from rotting. Once the logs had been prepared they would build all four walls by building them up a log at a time. The notches at the ends had been cut to allow the logs to fit tightly together at the corners of the walls when stacking them one on top of the other.

If John hadn't had Friday, he would only have been able to build the house six or seven feet tall and also, it would've been extremely difficult to cut and move all those logs alone. John could only have lifted the logs so high, but with Friday's help they could lift them higher and the walls could be twelve feet tall or more. When the walls were completed they would build the roof and place handmade split wooden shingles on the top, leaving an opening for the chimney and an entrance until they could later cut the doors and windows. The cracks between the logs were sealed with mud or clay with a technique that John called "mud daubing" or "chinking". John and Friday built a large house, so they constructed a big stone chimney with double fireplaces that had opening hearths facing toward each end of the house. The chimney was placed in the middle so that the heat would circulate and would keep the family's rooms warm in winter as well as provide fire for cooking meals. They cut the windows and doors in last and covered the windows with greased paper, as glass was hard to come by. At first, the floors were packed earth, but later, John's son Elles added split oak logs for flooring and, at that point, they added three additional rooms. Furniture was scarce and what they had usually was handmade, but sometimes talented friends and neighbors would make chairs, tables, beds, and spinning wheels (as William Mansell did). They had rugs, whale oil lanterns, and chests from their ancestors containing personal items, clothing, and quilts.

As for the barn, the building method was the same, but it was made higher with a loft for storage of hay or corn which they would dry and shuck for the animals to eat. There could be a "lean to" added for enclosing a pen for pigs, cows or mules. Mostly the chickens were "free range" and they roamed about the yard pecking at bugs and kernels of dry corn all day. Beside the barn was their garden, which they tilled with an iron plow pulled by mules or oxen and they would plant corn, beans, peas, sweet potatoes, okra, collards, turnip greens and other vegetables that could be canned or dried for food during the winter. There was a shed in back of the barn for smoking and curing pork or deer meat as well. It was a hard life but they were self sufficient and they, on purpose, had plenty of children so that they could work the land. They awakened early in the morning with the crowing of the roosters and would have a healthy breakfast of biscuits and gravy, eggs with fatback or bacon, and then head to the barn to hitch up the mules or oxen for plowing the fields, or planting or harvesting the crops when the time came. Cotton was a big money crop and many times they would spend all day picking it and filling their cotton baskets until their fingers were rubbed red and raw. After a lunch of cornbread, turnip greens, black eye peas or butterbeans they would go back to the fields and return later in the afternoon to milk the cows, feed the chickens, gather the eggs and shuck the corn to feed the mules. There were plenty of buckets to fill with water from the river for taking back to the house for use in the kitchen, bathing, or for the livestock troughs in the barn. There was never idle time during the day and at night they were tired and turned in early.

The nights were for sleeping but occasionally the kids would sit around the fireplace and listen to one of their father, John Palmer's tales. One of his favorite stories was the one about his slave, "Friday", riding a deer as if he were riding a horse. It went something like this as he would explain to them: "We had horses that were through bred and trained to race, work in the field, as well as help round up cows and sheep, and sometimes they would chase after deer that we hunted in the forest. Friday trained these horses to jump hedges, duck low under tree limbs, and skillfully round up animals into their stockades or pens. Friday would ride these horses bareback, Indian style. He had trained the horses to stand still while he ran up behind them and leap frogged onto their backs while straddling them tightly between his legs. This was quick and efficient and Friday was able to race away holding onto the mane of the horse. Friday didn't use a saddle but did rely on reins and a bit to control the horse and turn them in the direction he wanted them to go. He could pull the reins and kick the horses a certain way and was able to lower the head and neck of the horse so that he could lean his body on the horse's back for quickly running under low hanging limbs or small openings like doors or cave entrances. Friday could hang sideways off the horse as well if he wanted to avoid being seen or shot at. Of course, Friday trained them to jump high and they could clear any fence at full gallop anywhere and make a quick getaway. Friday had some close calls with Indians chasing him in those days and the horses helped him to escape every time. This type of training came in real handy back in Colonial days and after during the Revolution when we were fighting the British and were running for our lives on the backs of horses such as these. I remember losing one of my best black mares in battle when she was shot out from under me by the British." John would continue with his story and of course the kids were on the edge of their seats with anticipation as they sat anxiously by the fire listening closely to what tall tales their father would tell.

"Well", continued John: "We were real proud of our horses and really proud of the way Friday trained and cared for them. This is a tale about Friday and what a good rider he was that I have told around many firesides. I was off tending my fields one day making sure that my workers was plowing straight rows and that the seeds were evenly spaced out in the fertile soil. Friday was busy minding the cattle at the far end of the pasture close to the fork of the rivers when he spied an Indian sneaking up at the edge of the woods with a rope in his hand. The Indian was quick as lightning and jumped the fence, and before you know it, he had thrown a lasso over the neck of one of our cows. At the same time, Friday's attention was caught by something moving fast on the other side of the pasture. A ten point buck was running right at him and the thieving Indian. Without even a second thought, Friday jumped up on the back of the buck as he ran past just like he was a horse. Friday grabbed onto the antlers of the buck like he was a bull and kept on holding on for dear life as the buck kept running toward the Indian and our lassoed cow. That old deer bucked Friday like a prize bull but Friday hung on and pulled his antlers over to the right toward the Indian and I'll be danged if the deer didn't charge right at the Indian and knock him flat on his back. Friday kicked the buck like he was a horse and made him turn around and go back after the Indian who was now running like crazy toward the fence. The Indian was so scared that the deer would gore him with his antlers that he shot over the fence like a cannonball and almost set the woods on fire as he tore through the brush. That sure was spectacle enough and you'd thought that the show was done but Friday wasn't done yet. The cow was standing dumbfounded in the middle of the field with the Indian's rope still around his neck when Friday rode hanging sideways off the buck up to the cow and reached down and grabbed the rope. It was a sight to behold as Friday rode that buck across the pasture with the cow being pulled behind by that Indian's rope. I was standing watching it all from the field as Friday rode by on the buck and let go of the cow up close to the rest of the herd. Finally, Friday waved to me and jumped off the buck as he came back laughing his head off and slapping his thighs. We both laughed until we cried and our bellies shook and we both agreed that we wouldn't be seeing that thieving Indian or that ten point buck again."

There were many stories like this that John Palmer would tell his kids by the fireside and they would get passed down and exaggerated more and more as the years went by. The kids always wanted him to tell the stories over and over again because he would change them around and make them more exciting each time he told them. Legends are born like this and they just keep on improving the more that they are told. There was a slave named Friday and he did train horses and one time he even rode a deer. There were also Indians that would steal John Palmer's cows, so the story was based on fact but sometimes a story teller will exaggerate to make things more interesting. As John Palmer's kids sat by the fireside their beaming faces were lit up by the light of its flames and by the light of their smelly whale oil lanterns which would sometimes blow out when the wind came in through an open door or a crack in the log walls. The flickering of the fireside flames and the intermittent shining of the whale oil lamp's magical glow must have provided a dramatic backdrop and mood for John Palmer's tales that enriched his family's lives and fed their imaginations. In pioneer days, storytelling like that was very important to one's entertainment and well being as, I believe, it still is today.

After the tales were told though, it was off to bed to get a good night's sleep, as another round of hard work awaited them come daybreak. The oil lamps were their only light to see with at night after the fire went out and sometimes the wind would blow them out. At these times, everyone would be stirring around bumping in to one another trying to find the matches to relight them. For the kids that had schoolwork to do for the next day, permission was granted to stay up and do the English, literature, history, and arithmetic with quill pens on their parchment or to do simple exercises with chalk on their slate boards that were made there on the farm. They would have to make do with the flickering light of the lantern as it danced fitfully across the pages of their school books. From time to time they would have to trim the lamp's wick to make the lamp shine brighter. They were many generations away from the invention of electricity and kerosene lamps, which made for a more efficient and brighter flame. The times were challenging and even the more basic needs and simplest of tasks were made difficult by the limitations of the technology of their time period, but their love of family, country and faith in God gave them sustenance and kept them all going. I think today that if we had a little less technology and a little more love of family, country and faith in God that we might all be the better for it.

Other than storytelling, there were occasions for entertainment when their work schedule permitted it. Sometimes on Saturdays or holidays they would have barn dances in one of the neighboring towns or in a neighbors large barn where there would be square dancing to the tune of fiddles, banjoes, mouth harps, and guitars. On Sundays they would go to church and many of them would have all day Sacred Harp Singings, the practice of which had been passed down to them from their ancestors in England, These were choral assemblies in which the people would form a square and face each other as they sang very structured gospel songs consisting of invented shaped notes of do, re, mi, fa, so, la, ti, do. The Sacred Harp was an ancient society founded to help teach the new Protestant how to sing and keep harmony. Christians had been used to having choirs do the singing and the new congregations did not know how to keep tune. They invented shaped notes that they could all read and understand as they sung in square formations inside the churches. These Sacred Heart Singings would sometimes last all day and are still practiced today in many parts of the south such as Hamilton, Alabama where Clover later became an accomplished Sacred Harp singer and song writer. These were very powerful and uplifting performances designed to praise the glory of God and afterward there were very often church picnics at which the congregation would have dinners on the tables behind or to the side of the churches. These were good occasions for people to get together and share good times with their families, and neighbors or to meet new people or possibly meet a future wife or husband to be (my father met my mother at one of these church picnics in Marion County, Alabama in 1940). Then there were always the passing politicians making their political speeches at town halls or courthouse squares with their endless promises of better times, but at least free food and drinks were to be had at these events. Additionally, there were the passing medicine shows with their medicine wagons where the quacks would try to sell their "miracle cures" to an unsuspecting populace. So, there were some diversions for these early pioneers, some good, some not so good. But, for the most part, it was much work with little play. Only the rich partook in the pleasures of life and very often, they took advantage of the less fortunate everyday citizen. Sounds familiar, doesn't it?

It is of interest to note that John Palmer's log house was at least partially intact until the 1990's when my brother visited it outside of Union, South Carolina. Mrs. Marcelle Cannon allowed him to take a small piece of log from near a window which is now part of the collection at *the Roger Brown Study Collection of the School of the Art Institute of Chicago.* My brother also visited Mrs. Marcelle Cannon's house while in Union, South Carolina. She was a descendant of Ellis Palmer who was the brother of Benjamin Hezekiah Palmer, our ancestor. In his own words, my brother described the place in this way:"William Palmer or her father Ellis planted aspens along the long drive up to the house which looks a little like Mt. Vernon. Old pear trees grow nearby. Two magnolia trees, about thirty feet high, were planted by Marcelle's sister. The drive is now lined with native wild cedars (junipers). The Palmers descended from Ellis seemed to have been a cultured southern family. Marcelle's house is furnished with many Victorian antiques. There is an old organ that belonged to her mother similar to the one Clover Palmer owned. The old back door to the present home was taken from the old Ellis Palmer house where she was born. The house she lives in is about ½ mile south of the old Ellis Palmer house, which is another ½ mile south of the old John Palmer log house built around 1784."

Elles, the son of John Palmer, added three rooms to the John Palmer house just before he got married. The lower floor is built entirely of oak logs. When Elles married Nancy Long of Union County, South Carolina, he brought his bride home to their first home together on horseback. She rode in front of him. Elles was born March 22, 1792 and died February 4, 1865. Nancy was born December 8, 1794 and died in 1866. Elles inherited the place from his father, John Palmer. When Elles got ready to marry he added three rooms to the house with the help of a bachelor slave named Bill. They cut the trees from a nearby forest and hewed the logs for the new rooms. The logs of the second story were of pine and the entire house was "mud-daubed". Bill also cooked and did all the housework for Elles and his father John and continued to do so after Elles got married to Nancy.

When John Palmer died August 19, 1828 he left a lot of land records and a will listing his children as heirs. His children were: Amasa Palmer born July 22, 1774, William Palmer born July 16, 1776, our ancestor, Benjamin Hezekiah Palmer born November 9, 1778, John Palmer Jr. born February 13, 1780, Nancy Palmer birth date unknown, Sally Palmer born August 15, 1786, Elles Palmer born March 22, 1792, Rhoda Palmer born April 17, 1796, and Rebecca Palmer born February 1, 1789 and died August 1, 1855. Rebecca Palmer married Isaac Goings and lived on John Palmer's old place on Brown's Creek which they bought and made deed for on October 27, 1829.

After John Palmer's wife Martha (Patty) died on August 19, 1813, John married a widow named Hannah (White) Cole. They made a prenuptial agreement on October 19, 1813, two months to the day after Patty, his first wife, died. This shows just how careful they each were to insure that their children were well taken care of upon each of their deaths.

I include it here:"Attested agreement between John Palmer of the first part and Hannah Cole, widow of the other, witness that they have agreed to live together after the holy order of marriage and that each one shall keep his or her property and that whatever the said Widow Cole brings with her to the said John Palmer of her property the same shall the said Widow have at the death of the said John Palmer and she shall not be entitled to any part of the said John Palmer property but his children shall have all his property and the said Widow's children shall be entitled to all her property as she sees fit. The names of the children are: John Cole, Richard Cole, Rebecca Cole, and the said John Palmer shall do his duty in the raising of her children and the said John Palmer, by this agreement, shall not be entitled to pay any debts and lawful contracts and the said John Palmer shall not waste or make way with any part of the estate of the said Widow so that she nor her children suffer thereby." Subscribed to and published before marriage in the presence of James Lake, and S. Cole, the agreement was signed by John Palmer, and Hannah X. Cole. It was recorded April 28, 1828 in an old deed book T page 8, Union County Courthouse, Union, South Carolina.

Our ancestor, Benjamin Hezekiah Palmer, third son of John Palmer, was born in Union County, South Carolina near Brown's Creek on November 9, 1778. He married Elizabeth Roberts, daughter of Obsolom Roberts, a Revolutionary War soldier who lived near Elles Palmer (Hezekiah's grandfather) on Horns Creek, Edgefield County, South Carolina. It was said that Elizabeth was a small woman with dark eyes. Hezekiah and Elizabeth married about 1800 and lived near Buffalo Creek in Union County, South Carolina until 1816. On November 19, 1815, Hezekiah sold to his brother, Ellis Palmer, 118 acres of land on Buffalo Creek, and in 1816, he moved to Greene County, Georgia where he bought 20 acres of land from John Oslin on February 27, 1816 on the waters of Richland Creek. On November 14, 1817 he bought about 100 acres from Edward Woodham that adjoined the 20 acres that he had previously purchased from John Oslin. Hezekiah's brother, Amasa, and his sister, Nancy, who married William Edwards, had moved to Greene County and were living on Richland Creek before January 7, 1811. Hezekiah sold his land to his older son, Elijah, on August 10, 1819 and moved to Hancock County, Georgia on Shoulder Bone Creek and Oconee River. Hezekiah was a farmer and a preacher and lived very close to the Indians who lived across the river. About 1829 Hezekiah moved up to Walton County, Georgia and in 1831 he moved to Benton County, Alabama where he lived among the Indians once again. When Hezekiah moved to Benton County, Alabama, he left all his children in Georgia except our great, great, great grandfather, Russell Porter Palmer, Joseph Palmer, and Benjamin Palmer. Hezekiah died about 1839 and he had about twelve children (about because we think William and Willis may have been the same person). His children included: A.H. born in 1800, William born in 1802, Willis born in 1803?, Elizabeth born in 1805, Elijah born in 1805, an unknown girl born in 1808, John born in 1809, two more unknown girls born around 1814, David born in 1817, our ancestor, Russell Porter, born in 1818, Joseph born in 1827, and Benjamin born in 1829.

Doctor Russell Porter Palmer born September 5, 1818 was Hezekiah's son and is Clover's great grandfather and our great, great, great grandfather. He moved from Benton County, Alabama to Marion County, Alabama in about 1844 with his mother and two brothers, Joseph, and Benjamin. This is where Russell met Morning Dizenia Mansell, the daughter of William Mansell and Morning Dove White Mansell. Russell Porter and Morning Dizenia were married and, like Russell's father Hezekiah before them, they had twelve children. Their eighth son, Zachariah Gaines Palmer, was born on February 17, 1860. He married Nellie Armstrong, the mother of our great grandmother, Mammy, or Mary Dizenia, who was the mother of Clover McKinley Palmer. Zachariah and Nellie had three children: Zachariah Gaines Jr., Margaret Elizabeth, and Mary Dizenia. Zachariah Gaines died on October 14, 1882, at the young age of 22 while in medical school and it was rumored that he died of a drug overdose. Afterward, Nellie married again to George Weaver, the "bad stepfather" that Mammy always referred to.

This ancestral history brings us from the first Palmers that moved from England in the early to mid 1600's all the way up to Mammy and her son Clover as we have journeyed back to when the Palmers first settled in Virginia. In the next chapter we will begin the ancestral journey back in time of Cora Lee Goodson, Clover's bride who he married on the side of the road next to the little pine tree on March 29 of 1919.

Chapter Six

Goodsons and Drivers

My brother, James Roger Brown, researched for over thirty years into the ancestry of both my mother's and my father's side of the family. This book deals with my mother's side beginning with her father, Clover and her mother Cora Lee. Having explored Clover McKinley Palmer's family roots, I now turn my attention to Cora Lee Goodson Palmer and her ancestral history.

From my brother's, *Autobiography in the Shape of Alabama II,* he wrote:"My grandmother Cora Lee Goodson Palmer (Foy, Wright) and Aunt Rhoda wrote to me about the Goodsons and Drivers. I received documents from the National Archives and Georgia State Archives showing Cora Lee's grandfathers, Michael Goodson and Allen Berryman Driver in the Civil War. It was said that Michael Goodson married Mary Hurt and that her mother was a Quaker. Uncle Oscar Goodson said that Michael's wife owned slaves. He was against the war and ran away at Shiloh and swam the Tennessee River and got back to Villa Rica, Georgia where his store had been. He was almost hung, but the mule they sat him on with a rope around his neck kicked one of the hanging men. He got away and was never hung. It was said that Michael Goodson was from England (as our Palmer ancestors) and landed in New York, making his way south by working on a boat. It was also said that his father had left the house one day and never came back. They did not know if Indians got him or he fell in a hole. They lived in Carroll County, Georgia not far from Atlanta. "

In the book, *Carroll County and Her People,* by Private Joe Cobb on page 67 it says:"There lived in and around Villa Rica before the new town was laid out, some before and some after the Civil War, many good men, some of whom were Michael Goodson, Nicholas Sheets, William Sheets, Allison Chever, and F.M. Fielder". In *Georgia's Last Frontiers* by James C. Bonner on page 89, it says:"A sizable Republican organization was formed in Carroll County after the end of Reconstruction. A group calling themselves Union Republicans met in the courthouse in May, 1872 and adopted resolutions endorsing the administration of President Grant.

William McDavid was chairman and Michael Goodson was secretary."

These references, especially the later one, are confusing because, before deserting, Michael Goodson was a first lieutenant in the 37th military district of Carroll County, Georgia, militia, under Lt. Colonel Ely Benson of the Confederacy. This is a contrast to the strongly Republican families of Palmers and Armstrongs, who left Winston and Marion Counties in north Alabama and fought on the Union side in southern units of the U.S, Army. The confusion may be somewhat cleared up if one considers that Michael Goodson's loyalties could well have changed after the Confederates tried to hang him for desertion and he may have become a Union sympathizer. It was amazing that any of our ancestors survived long enough to produce heirs that would tell their stories. Michael Goodson was an original settler of Villa Rica, Georgia in 1826 when there was a minor gold rush in the area. When it was learned that there wasn't enough gold to make mining profitable many settlers left but Michael remained and later became a justice of the peace and a travelling salesman. He and his wife, Mary Hurt from Atlanta, had two sons, John Thomas and Bob, and a daughter, Laura, who later married a German man named Wasaman. As quoted from my brother's autobiography earlier, Michael's father had a strange ending as he left the house on an errand one day and never came back. His family did not know whether he was killed by Indians or had an accident someplace and no one was around to help him. In any case he survived long enough to produce Michael, and Michael produced John Thomas Goodson who married Mollie Driver.

Mollie Driver was Cora Lee's mother and also came from Carroll County, Georgia, although John Thomas Goodson met and married her in Anniston, Alabama. My brother continues with his statement about the Driver side of the family:"Cora Lee's mother was Mary (Mollie) Driver who also lived in Carroll County. It was believed they originally came from North Carolina. Allen Berryman Driver was her father. One of his sons, called Uncle Tobe visited us when I was five years old. He lived in Tyler, Texas. Mary (Mollie) Driver died when my grandmother was a small child. I have her tombstone in my collection (it had been replaced with a new one) which is now in the *Roger Brown Study Collection of the School of the Art Institute of Chicago.* When I was in Carroll County in 1974, I visited the Reverend Leonard Driver. He remembered hearing about Mollie Driver when she was a girl and before she left Georgia.

There was a dance where "Mouse" his father, Robert Driver, was to be the fiddler. All the boys were going to the dance and she wanted to go. Her father would not let her because the weather was getting bad. It was getting dark and looked like a tornado was coming. After the brothers left they had to hurry back home because a tornado did strike and they rushed home to see about the horses. Everything was all right though and nothing had been damaged." All that is known about Mollie is that she had red hair and family history states that she was ¼ Cherokee Indian which would have made her grandmother a full blooded Cherokee. It is thought that her grandmother's last name was Britt and that indeed could have been an Indian last name as Cherokees loyal to the United States were called "White" and those loyal to Britain were called "Britt". We have old photographs of Mollie and she does look very much like an Indian.

If Mollie had gone to that dance my brother spoke about she might have met someone other than John Thomas Goodson and married them instead. Of course there is the other possibility that she could have been killed by a tornado. The tornado twisted the kaleidoscope of life in another direction though and we are all here as a result to tell the story. Mollie did meet John Thomas Goodson later and got married and had two children, Cora Lee our grandmother, and Oscar, our great uncle. Mollie died shortly after Oscar was born after getting pneumonia as a result of rain leaking through a leaky roof. Cora Lee grew up with a step-mother for a while and with foster parents, the family of a Baptist preacher named "Preacher Watts".

Ironically, tornadoes played a tragically powerful role, years later in Cora Lee's life, as she was plagued by them in Hamilton, Alabama. One of her best friends was killed by a tornado along with four family members and thereafter Cora Lee was terrified of tornadoes for the rest of her life. She had storm cellars built beside all of the places that she lived and she would always rush to them with her children or later when the children had grown up, she would rush to them by herself at the slightest hint of a storm. I can remember her having an expensive pre-fabricated storm cellar installed underground behind her apartment in the early 1960's, when I was a teenager. She must have spent her entire savings on it, but this was the only way that she could feel secure.

My brother did a lot of research by 1971, but had not gotten any further back than just before the mid nineteenth century despite receiving a wealth of information from our relatives. In the meantime though, he received a letter from Nell Driver Suarez of Tyler, Texas. She got my brother's address from Vachel Driver, who he had visited in 1974 in Carroll County, Georgia. Vachel owned a farm outside of Carrollton and my brother looked his name up in the phone book and called him. This what my brother related of their meeting:"He knew very little of family history but he put me on to a cousin, Louise Gilbertson, who lived way out in hilly country in a house well over a hundred years old at the time. Her father had built the house. Again, it was a weathered clap board building with a large porch and fieldstone fireplaces. It was beautiful and it did not take much imagination to see Allen Berryman Driver there in the late nineteenth century dressed in baggy black broadcloth suits or the women in long paisley print dresses and sun bonnets, a French Neoclassic fashion influence, just the way my great grandmother, Mammy, dressed went she went out to work in her flowers; four o'clock's, zinnias, cockscombs, verbena, sweet William, thrift, and more. I was able to get a list of Drivers names which didn't connect us to their Drivers, but we were there all the same. There was a Goodrich / Goodridge Driver and that name appears often across the later generations of Drivers. In the 1850 census, a Goodrich Driver owned a hotel in Lafayette, Alabama. He was probably the brother of Allen Berryman Driver. His daughter was married in the hotel in the 1850's."

Lafayette is only about twenty miles or so from my brother's and my home town of Opelika, Alabama. So it would not be hard to imagine that our relatives on my father's side, the Browns, and relatives on his mother's side, the Owlsleys, might have frequented the hotel and might have even attended the Driver wedding. In fact, our great grandfather, Lafayette "Fate" Brown was from the Lafayette area and had farmland somewhere in the vicinity of Beulah, Alabama where we now own a historic 1850's period stone house that would've been built around the time of the Driver wedding. It would be interesting to speculate how our ancestor's paths might have crossed and how they all might have shared corn whiskey from a jug as they sat around the hotel's fireplace or sat at the bar spinning old yarns about themselves and their friends and families. I know that "Fate" had a passion for drinking and there are stories that abound about him riding his horse and wagon through town "three sheets to the wind" many a time. "Fate" would have been just the kind of character to hang out at that hotel and to party with his pals on Saturday nights. When I write my next book on the Brown side of the family, I'm sure that I will explore his legend more fully.

My brother goes on further to relate:"Vachel did not know the name of Allen and pointed out what was supposedly an old cemetery in a clump of trees high up on a hill overlooking a pasture next to his house. I walked back there and sure enough there was an old rounded stone stuck oblong into the ground. Very faintly was carved an "A" over a "DRI" over a Christian Cross into the stone. I took rubbings of it using some red clay rubbed over a piece of paper from my notebook. I got a very faint impression but it convinced me that this was some "A" Driver's final resting place. Allen had been a very prosperous farmer with slaves and property before the Civil War. The war liberated the slaves but destroyed prosperity for nearly everyone. On May 2, 1974, in Anniston, Alabama, at 320 South Allen Street, I met and talked with Carrie Driver, 88 years old. She told me that her husband's father, Phillip Driver (called Philmore), had been a slave for Bill Driver's grandfather who would have been Allen B. Driver's father. Philmore was 7 years old when the war ended, so he had been born into slavery and when the war was over, his family took the name Driver. He had a sister named Mollie. During World War One, when he needed some certification of age for age benefits, he had gotten information about his date of birth from Chambers County, Alabama (where Lafayette is located). Carrie Driver had cared for him when he was an old man and someone had suggested that since Bill Driver (Mollie's brother), had so much money, they should tell him about Phil's condition, but Carrie's husband said no, they would make out themselves. Bill Driver owned a great deal of land when he died and was said to be worth half a million dollars. After the war, the Drivers dispersed from Carroll County and headed west. Some went to Anniston, Alabama. Others moved off to Texas and settled around Tyler."

The floodgates began to open now with the Drivers as my brother received more information from Nell Driver Suarez in Tyler, Texas. She had compiled a history of the Driver family going back to 1650 in Isle of Wight, Virginia and even beyond that, to England. After my brother's visit to Vachel Driver in 1974, Vachel had become inspired to go on his own quest for family history, and after about 17 years, my brother benefitted from his research. Vachel's research matched closely to what my brother had found in the North Carolina Archives except that it had a missing link in the early Drivers in Virginia before they moved through Tar River Basin, North Carolina and then on into Georgia.

According to what my brother found these are his words as written in his *Autobiography in the Shape of Alabama II* on pages 9 and 10:"The first Driver in our record is Giles Driver of Ashton/Aston in Gloucester, England and died there in 1639. He married Dorothy Bagley of Wheatenhurst (or Whitminster). His eldest son, Robert, was born in England and died there in 1676. His other son, Giles, is our ancestor and immigrated to Virginia before 1657. John Driver, his brother, married Elizabeth Bridger, daughter of Lawrence Bridger, in England. His son John owned large estates which continued in the family for several generations. Lawrence Bridger had a son, Samuel, who had a son, Colonel Joseph Bridger, who immigrated to America in 1655 and some Drivers came along with their uncle. He brought Giles Driver, Robert's son, to help in the finished woodwork of St. Luke's Church near Smithfield, Virginia. Giles Driver married Olive Hardy, daughter of John and Alice Johnson Hardy. Giles died in 1676. He had four sons. These sons were Robert, Charles, John, and Giles. Evidently, Charles and a relative, Thomas, were brick masons and did further work adding a bell tower to Old St. Luke's Church. They carved their initials, "CD" and "TD" into two of the bricks high up on the tower and they are visible, as I photographed them when I visited the church. At this point, John Driver moved to Edgecombe, North Carolina or his son, John Driver, moved there. Giles, Jr. died in 1677. Charles died in 1727. He had a son Giles who died in 1748. There is a John Driver in Nash County in 1782 and is thought to be the son of Giles who died in 1743. One of these Drivers, but we do not know which one, had a son, Charles Giles. Charles Giles is our ancestor. Charles Giles married Susan Williams. He is listed in the 1800 census in North Carolina. He came to Jones County before 1807 and settled in an area near Round Oak in northwest Jones County. A corner cabinet, 'a fine piece of furniture he brought with him', according to Vachel Driver, still exists in the possession of B.S. Harvey of Clem, Georgia. The original Drivers had strong ties to the Church of England, and there were Anglican ministers in the family. When the English settled in America, however, it was difficult to maintain the ritual and doctrine unless Anglican ministers came along from England. This was not always possible, so many of the clergy were American born and gradually lost the adherence to the strict ritual of the Anglican Church. This gave rise to the many denominations of Episcopal, Methodist, and Baptist. As the frontier spread, the Primitive Baptist movement became a faith of choice by many. It is said that Charles Driver donated the land for the New Hope Primitive Baptist Church about five miles south of the county road from Forsyth to Juliette to Round Oak in the U.S. Wildlife Preserve. Charles Giles and Susan had eleven children: Ichabod (Bud), Martha, Mary, Sarah, John, Elizabeth, Julius, Giles Jr., Goodridge, Berry, and Allen. Charles' son, John, born in North Carolina in 1786, was our ancestor. John came to Jones County, Georgia with his father and married Mary Ann Isham Ussery on October 23, 1812. They had ten children: William Wright, John M., Goodridge H., Mary Ann, Allen Berryman, Luelza M., Julius L., Martha, George Washington, and David Franklin. John moved through Monroe and Pike Counties before settling in Carroll County in 1849. Some of his land still belongs to C.B. Driver, whose great grandfather was John M., second son of John. Allen Berryman Driver, born October 24, 1821, married Martha Britt (this is the ancestor that we think was Indian having the last name Britt), who was our ancestor. Allen probably lived on land that was originally bought by his father. That is a familiar pattern in southern migration, and when one finds it in one family, it can be applied to the next and see what happens. Nearly all our ancestors came through South Carolina and Georgia and on to Alabama because of land grants. The Owlsleys (on my father James Gordon Brown's mother's side), the Palmers, and I have discovered, I believe, the Browns came to South Carolina the same way."

So my brother's extensive and laborious research finally paid off and he was able to determine, with a reasonable degree of accuracy, that the Drivers had come from England to Virginia, to North Carolina, to Georgia and to Alabama where Cora Lee eventually met and married Clover in Hamilton, Alabama on March 29 of 1919. Cora Lee's mother was Mollie Driver who married John Thomas Goodson, September 19, 1894. John Thomas Goodson and Mollie moved to Hamilton, Alabama, where on January 2, 1902, Cora Lee Goodson our grandmother and wife of Clover McKinley Palmer was born. Cora Lee's brother, Oscar was born in January of 1905 and his mother, Mollie, died soon after.

Thanks to my brother's research and that of Joel Palmer and the research of the Driver family and many other relatives, we have a very good understanding of where Clover and Cora Lee came from and how greatly their lives were influenced by those who came before. The tales our ancestors have told and passed down add to the enrichment of the legends that I write about.

Chapter Seven

Cherokee Blood

The stories handed down about our Cherokee Indian ancestors are probably the most fascinating to our family and we hang on to every bit of information that we can obtain and listen with captivated curiosity to each tale about them. The Cherokee Indian aspect has always been interesting in the Palmer family and was equally important to Cora Lee as her father, John Thomas Goodson, always told her that her mother, Mollie Driver Goodson's grandmother, Mary Britt, was half Cherokee Indian. That would've made Mollie's great grandmother (unknown) a full blooded Cherokee. This could very well be true as her last name Britt was the name the British used for Indians that were loyal to them, so then we would have Cherokee blood from both Clover and Cora Lee's side of the family. However, this is one of those dead-ends in Driver family history because we do not know who Martha Britt Driver's mother was. We are all proud of our Cherokee blood though and we choose to believe, as Cora Lee did, that her father told her the truth.

It is ironic that the lands that our ancestors purchased and lived on, in almost all cases, were obtained from government land grants that they purchased from formerly Cherokee or other Indian lands that had been as much as robbed from the Indians by the U.S. government. In most cases, our ancestors had paid 12 ½ cents an acre or less for the land that their Cherokee ancestors may have lived and hunted on. In some cases, the lands were purchased before the Indians were forced to give up their lands and move out west to reservations, and in some cases after the Chickasaw Boundary Line was established. On May 28, 1830, President Andrew Jackson signed into law the Indian Removal Act. Under its terms, all tribes east of the Mississippi River were to cede their lands in exchange for territory in the west. The Chickasaws made removal treaties in 1832 and 1834, insisting provisions by which a commission of Chickasaw Councilors would pass on the competency of any tribal member making a private sale of property. In 1837 they moved west. The states principally involved, Georgia, Alabama (created in 1819 mainly from Creek and Cherokee country), and Mississippi (created in 1817 mainly from Choctaw and Chickasaw country), passed legislation outlawing tribal governments and placing the Indian Nations under the jurisdiction of state laws. This was in violation of securities granted the Indians by treaties with the U.S., and the Indians appealed to the federal government for protection.

Our ancestors who lived during these times, in many cases, lived on lands claimed by the Cherokees, and sometimes married Cherokee women, as did William Mansell. Moses Purser, a good friend of William Mansell, married Mapy, the sister of William's wife, Morning Dove. The Cherokee's journey through ancestral history resulted in their eventual settlement in Tennessee as did the ancestral journey of their white neighbors, William Mansell and Moses Purser. Although their journey started many hundreds of years before, I will relate their more recent history of the 18th and 19th centuries as that more closely corresponds to our own family's journey from England to Virginia and westward toward Alabama. In the early 18th century from 1710 to 1715 the Cherokee and Chickasaw allied with the British and fought the Shawnee, who were allied with the French. Cherokees fought alongside the Yamasee, Cattawba, and British in late 1712 and early 1713 against Tuscarora in the Second Tuscarora War. So, contrary to what we may have believed, the Cherokees were truly a nation of warriors and fought in many battles with other tribes as well with the French, and Americans. Even their relationship with the British, which remained strong for much of the 18th century, would see disagreements arise and battles result in some instances.

The relationship between the Cherokees and Creeks saw many conflicts as well, and many battles were fought between them over the years. In 1716, a delegation of Muscogee Creek leaders was murdered at the Cherokee town of Tugaloo, which marked the entrance of Cherokees into the Yamasee War which ended in 1717 with peace treaties between South Carolina and the Creeks. The Yamasee War (1715–1717) was fought between British settlers of colonial South Carolina and several Indian tribes including the Yamasee, Muscogee, Cherokee, Catawba, Apalachee, Apalachicola, Yuchi, Savannah River Shawnee, Congaree, Waxhaw, Pee Dee, Cape Fear, Cheraw and others. Some of these tribes played minor roles whereas others launched major attacks against the colonists. Hundreds of colonists were killed and many of their settlements were destroyed. The colonists were forced to abandon their settlements and flee to Charles

Town where they faced starvation as supplies ran low. The South Carolina colony faced destruction during 1715 until the Cherokees sided with the colonists against the Creeks who were their traditional enemy. The last of South Carolina's major Indian enemies withdrew from the conflict in 1717 which brought a tenuous peace to the colony. The Yamasee War was one of the Indians' greatest challenges to European domination and was bloodier than King Philip's War which is often thought to be the bloodiest of the Indian wars. This was about the period that our own ancestors, such as the Palmer families and Driver families were having to deal with Indian attacks in Virginia, North Carolina, and South Carolina, and for all we know they could have been involved in these battles. The treaty did little, as is true with most treaties, to stop the skirmishes and there were sporadic raids between the Cherokees and Creeks for decades to come. In 1721, the Cherokee ceded lands to South Carolina that may have been land granted to some of our ancestors. In the years following the Yamasee War new confederated Indian nations emerged such as the Muscogee Creek and Catawba.

In 1730 at the Cherokee town of Nikwasi in North Carolina, Sir Alexander Cumming convinced the Cherokees to crown Moytoy of Tellico as "Emperor". Moytoy agreed to recognize King George II of England as the Cherokee protector. A Cherokee delegation traveled with Cumming back to England and signed the Treaty of Whitehall. Moytoy's son, Amo-Sgasite (Dreadful Water), tried to succeed his father as emperor, but the Cherokees instead elected Standing Turkey as their leader. After this the Cherokees remained independent and formed what was estimated to be 64 towns and villages with about 600 warriors. In 1738–1739 a smallpox epidemic broke out among the Cherokees, who like all Indians, had no immunity to the disease and nearly half of them died. As many as 100 of them committed suicide due to the pock marking scars caused by the disease.

From 1753 to 1755 more battles broke out between the Cherokee and Muscogee Creek over disputed hunting grounds in North Georgia. The Cherokees were victorious and their British allies built forts, including Fort Loudoun near Chota (present day Chota Falls, Georgia) and in 1756 the Cherokee fought alongside the British in the French and Indian War. Disagreements arose between the Cherokee and British however and this resulted in the 1760 Anglo-Cherokee War. A Royal Proclamation of 1763 was issued by King George III that forbade British settlements west of the Appalachian crest but it proved difficult to enforce. In 1769-1772 mostly Virginian settlers began squatting on Cherokee lands in Tennessee and I suspect that William Mansell's ancestors may have been a part of that group. Also, at that time, Daniel Boone and a group of settlers tried to create a settlement in what would become known as the Transylvania colony. These settlements led to the beginning of Lord Dunmore's War fought with the British against Shawnee, Delaware, Mingo, and some Cherokee in 1773-1774. This conflict was between the colony of Virginia and the Shawnee and Mingo Indians and could well have involved my ancestors from Virginia, the Palmers and Drivers. The governor of Virginia at that time was John Murray, 4th Earl of Dunmore – Lord Dunmore and he asked the Virginia House of Burgesses to declare war on the hostile Indians and to create a militia. The conflict started when British colonists, in accordance with previous treaties, began exploring and moving into land south of the Ohio River or modern day West Virginia, Southwestern Pennsylvania, and Kentucky. War was declared in order to counter Indian hunting and war band attacks upon the settlers. The war ended after Virginia's victory in the Battle of Point Pleasant on October 10, 1774. The Indians lost the right to hunt in the area and agreed to recognize the Ohio River as the boundary between Indian lands and the British colonies. Not all Indians agreed with the terms however and fighting continued and when war broke out between the colonials and the British in 1776, the Indian war parties quickly gained power and mobilized the various Indian nations to attack the colonists during the Revolutionary War. These were the circumstances that my ancestors lived amidst for much of their lives as they settled the lands they had moved to in Virginia and later in South Carolina. So when John Palmer spoke of having his cows stolen by Indians in South Carolina those incidents would have been a decade or so past the time of these Indian wars.

The Chickamaugas were a diverse group of Cherokees, Creeks, and African Americans who resisted white settlement in Tennessee for about 19 years. On March 19, 1775, one month before the American Revolution, Richard Henderson signed the treaty of Sycamore Shoals with the Cherokee Indians led by Attakullaulla, or Little Carpenter. The private treaty ceded Central Kentucky and northern Middle Tennessee to Henderson. Little Carpenter's son, Dragging Canoe, led the opposition and vowed a bloody resistance to white settlement. In 1776 the Shawnee chief Cornstalk came south to try and get support from the Cherokee and other southern tribes and to get them to join the British and resist American settlement. In 1776, allied with Shawnee led by Cornstalk, Cherokees attacked settlers in South Carolina, Georgia, Virginia, the Washington area, and North Carolina in the Second Cherokee War. European-American militias retaliated destroying over 50 Cherokee towns in 1777. Most of the surviving towns signed treaties with the states but the Cherokee, Dragging Canoe, Bloody Fellow, Young Tassel, and Hanging Maw moved into several abandoned towns including Citico and Chickamauga Creek and began calling themselves the Chickamaugas after the "river of death". The British provided the Chickamaugas with 2000 pounds of supplies early in 1779 in preparation for a major raid on the East Tennessee settlements. However these supplies were seized in a surprise attack by Evan Shelby and 900 Virginia and North Carolina troops that had descended the Tennessee River by boat. The troops under Shelby burned the villages and took the supplies but produced few Indian casualties and Dragging Canoe moved the group to an area near present day Chattanooga, Tennessee and established the five Lower Towns of Running Water and Nickajack in Tennessee, Lookout Mountain in Georgia, and Long Island and Crowtown in Alabama.

By this time the Chickamaugas included an assortment of Upper Creeks, Shawnee, French "boatmen", African Americans, and Scots traders. Daniel Ross settled with them by 1785 and the Shawnee warrior Cheesekau and his younger brother Tecumseh had also settled with them. There were several skirmishes from the 1780's on including an attack in the fall of 1780 on the Cumberland settlements where Mansker's Station in Goodlettsville was destroyed. The following April of 1780 they attacked Fort Nashborough but lost the Battle of the Bluffs. In December 1780 the Chickamaugas lost 80 men to troops under command of John Sevier at Boyd's Creek, near the Little Tennessee River. The Chickamaugas kept the Cumberland settlements isolated in 1787 and attacked Fort White (Knoxville) in 1788. In 1792 they attacked at Buchanan's Station, four miles south of Fort Nashborough. Travelers between East and Middle Tennessee were forced northward to the Wilderness Trail and lost 100 people from the attacks of Chickamaugas. On February 29, 1792, the day after a great victory celebration, Dragging Canoe died unexpectedly and the leadership of the Chickamaugas passed to Young Tassel. The beginning of the end of the Chickamauga period came on September 12, 1794 when a Southwest Territory militia unit under Major James Ore and led by former Chicamauga prisoner, Joseph Brown, crossed Monteagle Mountain and defeated Nickajack and Running Water. By the end of the year the remaining Chickamaugas had joined the Overhill Cherokees to make treaties with the white Tennessee settlers. The Cherokee-American Wars was ended by the Treaty of Tellico Blockhouse on November 7, 1794, but Indian resistance continued at the towns of Lookout Mountain, Long Island, and Crowtown as they aligned themselves with the Upper Creeks. There were numerous raids into southeast Middle Tennessee and the area from Murfreesboro to Beech Grove could not be settled until 1800. Warren County opened to white settlement in 1806 and Sequatchie County was settled between 1807 and 1810. No true white settlements reached Chattanooga, except the trading post of Daniel Ross, until 1817. The Chickamauga movement finally ended with Andrew Jackson's victories over the Red Stick Creeks in the 1813-1814 Alabama campaign that my ancestor, William Mansell served in.

The Cherokees organized a national government led by the three chiefs, Little Turkey (1788-1801), Black Fox (1801-1811), and Pathkiller (1811-1827). The seat of the Upper Towns and also the Nation was at Ustanali, near Calhoun, Georgia and was led by the former warriors, James Vann, The Ridge or Pathkiller, and Charles R. Hicks, who were known as the "Cherokee Triumvirate". These Cherokees were the most progressive favoring adoption of European culture, formal education, and modern farming methods. In 1815 the U.S. government established a Cherokee Indian Reservation in Arkansas and the Lower Cherokee were the first to move west. The group consisted of The Bowl, Sequoyah, Spring Frog, and Tatsi (Dutch) and their bands were known as the "Old Settlers". John Ross became the Principal Chief of the tribe in 1828 and remained so until his death in 1866.

John Ross led the battle to halt removal of the Cherokee. His party known as the "National Party" was opposed by the "Ridge Party" or "Treaty Party". The Treaty Party signed the Treaty of New Echota that resulted in removing the Cherokee Nation from lands in the East for lands in the West in Indian Territory. Cherokees were displaced from their ancestral lands in northern Georgia and the Carolinas during a period of rapid growth in white population. A big cause of this expansion was a gold rush in Dahlonega, Georgia in the 1830's (roughly during the time that my ancestor, Michael Goodson and his family lived in the area). President Andrew Jackson said removal policy was to protect the Indians from the fate the Mohegan, the Narragansett, and the Delaware had suffered. This seems contradictory however as the Cherokees were adapting to modern farming techniques and were succeeding to become an economically and culturally viable part of American society. In June 1830, Chief John Ross brought forth a delegation to discuss tribal grievances to the U.S. Supreme Court. In the case, Worcester v. Georgia, the U.S. Supreme Court held that Cherokee Native Americans were entitled to federal protection from the actions of state governments. This case is considered one of the most important decisions in law dealing with Native Americans. Despite the ruling in their favor, the majority of Cherokees were forcibly relocated westward to Indian Territory in 1838-1839, a migration known as the "Trail of Tears". Many Indians did not survive and died from malnutrition and disease along the way. This took place because of Andrew Jackson's Indian Removal Act of 1830. Some Cherokees were able to evade removal and became the East Band of Cherokee Indians. William Holland Thomas, a white storeowner and state legislator from Jackson County, North Carolina, helped over 600 Cherokee to obtain North Carolina citizenship which exempted them from forced removal. Another 400 Cherokee either hid from federal troops in the desolate Snowbird Mountains or belonged to towns that had negotiated with the state government to stay in North Carolina. An additional 400 Cherokee stayed on reserves in southeast Tennessee (where Morning Dove's people were), north Georgia, and northeast Alabama as citizens of their respective states as mostly mixed bloods and Cherokee women married to white men (as with Morning Dove). Altogether these groups make up the Eastern Band of Cherokee Indians from whom we are proudly descended.

This historical background provides the backdrop for our ancestors William Mansell and Morning Dove White. This chapter will tell of William Mansell who fought under command of General Andrew Jackson at The Battle of Horseshoe Bend and of his wife Morning Dove White who was a loyal Cherokee or a "White". This battle was fought during The War of 1812 and led by Andrew Jackson who commanded the militias of Tennessee, Georgia, and the Mississippi Territory against the "Red

Sticks" or Upper Creek Indians. The Creek Indians were divided into two factions: the Upper Creek or "Red Sticks" (of note here the name Baton Rouge comes from the French "red stick"), and the Lower Creek. The Red Sticks were in the majority that opposed American expansion and sided with the British and colonial authorities of Spanish Florida during The War of 1812. The Lower Creek were friendly toward and tried to adopt the culture of the Americans and had a stronger relationship with them that they wanted to retain.

The Shawnee leader Tecumseh visited Creek and other Southeast Indian towns in 1811-1812 in order to recruit warriors for fighting against American expansion. The Red Sticks were sympathetic to his cause and had already been organizing resistance of their own. They began raiding American frontier settlements and were met with resistance from U.S. forces and the Lower Creek Indians who assisted them. The Red Sticks captured and punished the Lower Creek Indians who had joined with the Americans. The Red Stick raids continued and in 1813, militia troops attacked a Red Stick party returning from obtaining arms in Spanish Colonial Pensacola, Florida. This became known as "The Battle of Burnt Corn" and in August of 1813, the Red Sticks attacked an American outpost at Fort Mims in retaliation. After the Fort Mims massacre, frontier settlers appealed to the government for help. As Federal forces were being used against the British, Andrew Jackson was called upon to organize the militias of Tennessee, Georgia, and the Mississippi Territory, which fought against the Red Sticks along with Lower Creek and Cherokee allies.

On March 27, 1814, General Andrew Jackson and his forces won The Battle of Horseshoe Bend. This was the major battle of the Creek War and culminated an effort by Andrew Jackson to clear the Mississippi Territory for American settlement. He commanded an army of Tennessee militiamen, of which my ancestor, William Mansell, and his friend, Moses Purser, were members. Andrew Jackson had spent much time and energy training these soldiers to be a professional fighting force. In addition, Jackson had the 39th United States Infantry and about 600 Cherokees, Choctaws and Lower Creeks that fought against the Red Sticks. So, on March 14, 1814, General Andrew Jackson led 2600 American soldiers, 500 Cherokees, and 100 Lower Creeks to begin his attack on Red Stick fortifications near a bend in the Tallapoosa River called "Horseshoe Bend". Horseshoe Bend is located in central Alabama close to what is now

Dadeville, which from an ancestral point of view is ironic because my hometown of Opelika, Alabama is only about 25 miles from there.

General Andrew Jackson sent General John Coffee with the mounted infantry and the Indian allies, of which William Mansell and Moses Purser were a part, south across the Tallapoosa River to surround the Red Sticks camp, while he stayed with the rest of the 2000 infantry north of the camp. General Jackson led his troops up a steep hill near Tehopeka, the Creek's village, and began his attack from this higher vantage point. At 6:30 am he split his troops and sent about 1300 men to cross the river and surround the Creek village. At 10:30 am, Jackson's troops began an artillery barrage consisting of firing from two cannons that lasted for about two hours. The Red Sticks had prepared for this and had built 400 yard long, log and dirt fortifications. Andrew Jackson was so impressed with their strategy that he later wrote:"It is impossible to conceive a situation more eligible for defense than the one they had chosen and the skill they manifested in their breastwork was really astonishing."Taking into account his lack of success with the cannon barrage, Jackson ordered a bayonet charge led by Colonel John Williams of the 39th Infantry that was able to breach the breastwork and engage the Red Sticks in fierce hand to hand combat. Sam Houston (the future statesman and leader of Texas) was a third lieutenant in Jackson's army and was one of the first over the barricade. He suffered a serious wound there that he suffered with the rest of his life.

By this time, the troops under command of General John Coffee had successfully crossed the river and surrounded the Red Sticks. There was intense fighting and William Mansell and Moses Purser were among the many soldiers charging the Red Stick fortifications with their bayonets fixed and ready to kill the surrounded but savagely fighting Indians. William slashed violently at several of the attacking Red Sticks and managed to kill or wound about half a dozen according to legend before he himself was wounded by a Red Stick arrow. He fell bleeding onto a pile of wounded warriors and soldiers and pretended to be dead. Soldiers continued to rush over him as they charged the remaining Red Stick warriors and Jackson's infantry rushed the fortifications from the other side. The Red Sticks were surrounded now and almost 800 out of 1000 of them had been killed by Jackson's and Coffee's troops. Chief Menawa had been seriously wounded but somehow managed to lead his surrounded warriors to the river and swim across to the relative safety on the other side where they eventually retreated to and joined the Seminole tribe in Spanish Florida.

During this time, Moses Purser had been savagely fighting in the trees and thickets not far from where he had seen William Mansell fall with the Red Stick arrow still sticking from his body. Moses always carried a medicine bag slung over his shoulder and he had treated arrow wounds such as these before and had brought along the medicines and compresses that were necessary to treat William's wound. It wasn't a pretty sight but the Red Stick arrow had entered William's shoulder missing his vital organs but passing all the way through to his back and there was a lot of bleeding that had left William weak and on the verge of passing out. Moses immediately broke the arrowhead end off where it had passed through William's shoulder and quickly pulled the arrow out of William's body from the front. The pain of this was excruciating and caused more bleeding but Moses immediately shoved an herbal compress into both the front and back opening of the wounds which slowed and soon stopped the bleeding. Moses applied compresses on the exterior and held them down to apply pressure until the army medic could arrive and treat William and evacuate him to a field hospital. Thanks to Moses, William did recover and they both eventually returned to Tennessee where they remained until the campaign against the Seminole Indians began in 1818.

General Andrew Jackson had fewer than 50 killed and 154 wounded, including William. The fighting had been savage and lasted for over five hours with the Red Sticks refusing to surrender. Before they finally retreated with Chief Menawa almost 800 had been killed. History leaves a brutal account of what Jackson's troops did after the victory. They made a body count by cutting off the noses of the dead warriors and cut strips of their skin to make bridle reins for horses. The Indians clothing was sent to the "ladies of Tennessee" as souvenirs. There had been atrocities on both sides during the Indian Wars, but these acts defy all comprehension. "War is Hell". The result of General Andrew Jackson's victory at Horseshoe Bend was that on August 9, 1814, he forced the Creek to sign the Treaty of Fort Jackson. The Creek Nation was forced to cede 23 million acres – half of central Alabama and part of southern Georgia to the United States government. This also included some of the lands of the Lower Creek and the Cherokee who had to cede 1.9 million acres. The Indians learned the hard way what their loyalty meant to Jackson and the United States. After Horseshoe Bend, Andrew Jackson sent his friend John Gordon, Captain of the Spies, to secretly go to the Spanish Fort at Pensacola, Florida to see if the British were using it as a base to arm the Red Sticks. John Gordon found that the British were aiding the Red Sticks and this eventually led to Andrew Jackson's taking of Pensacola and to the future battles with the British at New Orleans. The victories at these battles led to Andrew Jackson's public popularity and to his eventual election as president in 1828.

After all of William's and Morning Dove's experiences during the Indian Wars, it is easy to understand how their attitude toward their place in this raw and wild frontier might have been a complex and most confusing affair. There were the inevitable split loyalties that would lead to heated family discussions and arguments on both sides but there was always the unwavering loyalty and love that they had for each other that won out in the end. Morning Dove had made her choice after William and Moses returned from the Indian Wars in Florida and she along with her sister married white men. They would become assimilated into white culture and they would be saved from the relocation policy of Andrew Jackson. After a harrowing experience of crossing the frozen Tennessee River with ox carts where at any miscalculation they might go crushing through the shards of ice, William and Morning Dove made their way to Toll Gate in northwestern Marion County, Alabama where they built a homestead and started a family. Moses Purser and Morning Dove's sister Mapy would build a homestead and start a family on land not too far away from them. William farmed the land that he had purchased through land grants and also built a workshop where he could make furniture. They had three children together named John, James, and Morning Dizenia who would later marry Russell Porter Palmer, our great, great, great grandfather. From their union came the descendants that eventually produced my mother, Mary Elizabeth Palmer Brown and her fourth cousin, Elvis Aaron Presley.

One cannot be thankful enough for the courage, dedication to family and country, and iron will of these ancestors. It gives me faith that we, having come from their DNA, will survive the trials that face us. As well, I hope that we as a people will have the capacity for love and understanding that previous generations lacked in their treatment toward the Indians. The Indians were the first Americans and they have never received the respect and honor that they deserved. They fought bravely for their land and lost it but they lost the basic rights due all human beings as well.

Both my brother and I have done works of art dedicated to them and my brother did his "*Autobiography of Alabama II*" based in good part on their lives as well. One of my linocut prints that I did in 1992 was entitled "*Thanks to Morning Dove*". People have often asked me why I chose to give thanks to a dove. I always answer, "Morning Dove was my Cherokee Indian grandmother whose bravery and strength of character saved her family. I would not be here today to talk about my art, let alone produce it, if not for her and the man she loved." In chapter eight, I invite the reader, who has journeyed with me through the stories about our Indian ancestors, to now twist our kaleidoscope lens widely open in order to reveal the legends inspired by the descendents of our ancestral past.

Part II
Legendary Fields

Chapter Eight

Tall Tales and Taller

This chapter offers the reader tales of bygone days that are stories my relatives told which, although they may have originated from true events, have been embellished into "tall tales" or "taller" over the years. The main characters are fictional and may or may not have been based on actual people. The storytellers chose fictional names to use for their stories mostly to protect the individuals who actually perpetrated the actions within them. Our main characters in the stories or "tall tales" I present here are Jedidiah and Joshua which were both Biblical names given to them by their devout Primitive Baptist parents. Of course everybody called them Jed and Josh and I will refer to them by those names as I tell their stories.

Jedidiah was always a good boy growing up and Sarah Ellen was his very proud and dedicated mother. In fact, she would become quite possessive of him and this would manifest problems for her later relationship with his future wife and foster resentment within Sarah Ellen for her daughter-in-law. Jedidiah's mother remained aloof with her daughter-in-law after her son's marriage and lived in a small clapboard house not far away from her son and daughter-in-law. She worked hard along with her son's wife to help raise the kids they had but communication between her and his wife was minimal at best. He was her only child and she did not want anyone else to have him. One can understand, as Jed's father, was missing from their lives after he ran off with another woman years ago. Sarah Ellen had to be both mother and father to Jed. For obvious reasons, we know that Jed's father was seldom mentioned and very rarely seen again. Sarah Ellen's in laws had abandoned her after their son married the "other woman" and had a new family in faraway Texas. Sarah Ellen was forced to move in with her parents who were elderly farmers in Hamilton, Alabama close to where Sarah and Jed lived. Her parents helped her as much as they could and provided a home for them. After her father passed away in 1909 and her mother passed away two years later in 1911, her parent's home remained for them, but Sarah Ellen bore the burden of having to raise Jed almost completely on her own. She raised her son as if she was a widow, and for all practical purposes, she was. There must have been very strong emotional trauma associated with what had happened years ago with her uncaring and irresponsible husband. Considering the traits of his father, one might well expect that Jed would inherit those traits both good and bad.

Then, keeping in mind from whence he came, it is not surprising that Jed would have inherited some of the same wild DNA that his father possessed. Most bright, energetic and imaginative young boys find plenty of mischief to get into as they grow into young men – I know that I did. There are many escapades that Jed took part in throughout his youth and I will relate a few of them to you. There were plenty of times that he would neglect his chores and run with his friends to steal watermelons from the local farmers' patches or run off to explore the northwest Alabama hills and forests in search of "wildcat" stills ("wildcat" is what the folks called moonshine in those parts). The woods were full of them and some most likely belonged to his relatives. No one in these parts paid too much attention to Prohibition and, besides, they had always made their own whiskey anyway. Some of the best copper stills to be found were in these woods and they were very cleverly hidden from the prying eyes of the Revenuers who searched for them. My uncles have told me stories about them that I will recall when trying to imagine how Jed would've reacted to them as a youth. He was a very clever and attentive child and he had I'm sure overheard many times when the old timers would talk about wildcat and what still it had been made from. He played in and hunted deer and rabbits in the hills, bluffs, and forests and knew the local landscape well. So when they talked about their stills, Jed, like most young boys, would've been all ears and would've committed to memory the locations of their wildcat stills.

Jed and his friend, Josh, would've met at their favorite spot up around Red Hill and spent their lunch breaks and sometimes longer periods of time searching the Hamilton hills for those stills his relatives talked about. It had to be very exciting and also very dangerous for these two young daredevils, because you could get shot at by the owner of the still if they thought you were a Revenuer. Jed, like most boys in those parts, had Cherokee Indian blood in him and he just instinctively knew how to sneak up on deer and rabbits and, as well, on unsuspecting still owners. I know from my own experience from exploring the Alabama backwoods as a child, that the still owners would often leave some sample jugs for customer tasting, laying about close to the still. Jed and Josh could've sneaked up on the still and made sure that nobody was around guarding it and they most likely could've each run up and grabbed a jug and scampered off like scared rabbits for the cover of the woods. There were a couple of times when shotguns were fired over their heads but that just made it all that much more fun. How do I know? I was young once, myself.

I will continue by telling the stories of this chapter using the past tense of possible history and embellish the stories to my liking and hopefully to yours. Jed and Josh had a hiding place inside a cave up in the bluffs where they would hide the jugs and sometimes they would drink a few little chugs from them before going back to work in the cotton fields. Although they stole watermelons in summer time from Dan Boyette's and other farmer's patches, stealing the wildcat was a lot more fun and really sent chill bumps up their spines. Sometimes later, when Jed went to the Sacred Harp singings at the local churches, he would bring a watermelon that he had stolen and he would spike it with some of the stolen wildcat. You could cut a neat little cylindrical, cork like plug out of the melon and pour some wildcat into the melon to your heart's desire and then just put the plug back in and no one would be the wiser. After the singings the church goers would always have food on the grounds and serve fried chicken, pork chops, ham, sweet potatoes, turnips, potato salad, black eyed peas, corn on the cob and many other southern delicacies including watermelon, if it was a hot summer day. It was great fun to go to those Sacred Harp Singings and Jed was quite good at singing. It was also great fun to watch the church goers get drunk on the watermelons that he had brought. They would break out in song as they sat and ate and Jed would always remark how well they sang and how they were truly filled with the "spirit". They all seemed to look forward to those outdoor picnics on the church grounds tables and they always praised Jed and his watermelons. Dan Boyette himself would remark how he wished that he could grow them like that. Well it was all in fun and no one ever got hurt and besides most everyone knew what Jed and Josh were up to anyway. They mostly just kept quiet and "let boys be boys".

There was one time though that really "took the cake". It seems that Jed and Josh were tired of pulling the same old pranks and decided that they would do something really creative. It was inspired by an incident that occurred at the White House Church of Christ Sacred Harp Singing and food on the grounds celebration one Sunday afternoon. One of the local farmers that visited from Red Bay, Alabama participated in the festivities and enjoyed himself immensely by eating his share of food and more; in fact you might say he gorged himself to the limit. It seemed that just having a free meal wasn't good enough for him though and he began to complain that he had tasted much better at other church outings. He also began to voice suspicions about those watermelons and how everyone seemed to get drunk after eating them. He called himself "Hog Higgins" which was a nickname he got from the fact that he was a pig farmer. Could be the name had to do with his fat belly and pudgy red face, as well as the fact that he "ate like a pig". Even though Hog couldn't sing worth a hoot himself, he would constantly butt in to criticize those who were singing and enjoying themselves. Hog pointed out to everyone at the picnic how bad their singing sounded and how they sounded like a bunch of drunks. Of course, no one likes a "smart ass" so everyone went off and left Hog to "stew in his own juices". They all decided if the watermelon had wildcat in it, then so be it. The spirit that was brought forth by it made their singing all the better, so Hog and everyone else should just "let well enough alone".

Old Hog Higgins was so beside himself that he left in a huff and swore that his wagon wheels would never grace the path of the White House Church again. "Besides", he said, "My pigs squeal better for their slop than you all do with your do, re, mi, fa, so, la, ti, do". This was almost as big an offense as Hog could have perpetrated on the grounds of the Sacred Harp, so no one was upset when Hog left in his wagon and they all wished him "good riddance". Old Hog's actions got up "under the skin" of almost everyone, but especially so with Jed and Josh and that is what inspired them to come up with their most daring and creative prank of all. They would get even with Hog and his words, "My wagon wheels will never grace the path of the White House Church again", reverberated in their ears as they plotted their revenge. The harshness of Hog's insensitive tirade struck a chord within Jed's poetic and musical soul and was the key element that inspired his plan to even things up with the pig farmer.

Jed had always been good with his hands and he could take most anything apart and put it back together again. He was doing that with his mother's old alarm clock when he was just four years old and Sarah Ellen would often tell her grandkids the tale of how she would patiently wait while he would put it back together in time for her to set the clock for the morning. Later on he would repair all the farm machinery and tools. So taking things apart was not a problem for him, but now he was planning on taking a wagon apart and putting it back together again. His plan was to take Old Hog Higgins' wagon apart and put it back together again on the roof of his pig barn. He was sure that he and Josh could do it together and that they both would be up to the challenge. If they could do it, Old Hog Higgins would think that it was divine providence that his wagon had gotten put on the roof of his barn because of his speaking such blasphemy about the White House Church and its Sacred Harp music. How else could such a heavy wagon get put up on the roof of his barn except by the hands of providence? Well, Old Hog would soon learn that the hands of providence work in strange ways sometimes and it might be a lesson to treat your fellowman with love and respect and not be so critical of their joyful singing, especially when your own isn't worth a hoot.

Jed found out easily from neighbors where Old Hog lived and he and Josh planned a visit there the next night that there was a full moon. They would be able to see everything well by moonlight at night and besides they said a full moon makes you crazy and, in Jed and Josh's case, they might have been right. So, the first full moon night, they gathered up all the necessary tools, ladders, and rope and loaded everything up on their old wagon for a trip to Hog Higgins' place. When they got there they pulled the horse and wagon up behind a hedge of thick trees and brush not far from Hog's barn. Hog's pigs were all inside the barn and resting easy as Hog was inside his house not far away. The moonlight was splendid and Jed could see Old Hog's wagon parked in front of the barn. Josh went and unhitched "Hack", their old horse, from their wagon that was hidden behind the hedge and led him slowly and carefully to the front of Hog's barn. Jed watched closely for any signs of Hog waking up and catching them and Josh hitched Hack up to Hog's wagon. They then led Hack with Hog's wagon up the road to a nearby field where they could begin disassembling Hog's wagon. After stopping by their wagon to get their tools, they led Hack to the field and began taking apart the wagon's sides, front and back, seats and floors, leaving them in big enough sections so that they could easily be put back together again. It took some time and good old pioneer knowhow, but they got the wagon apart and then removed the axles, springs, and wheels. They were far enough away so that the noise of taking the wagon apart would not disturb Hog or his pigs.

Now came the tricky part. They had to hitch Hack back up to their wagon, lead him over to the field and then put all of Hog's wagon parts into their wagon and then lead Hack and it back to the front of Hog's barn without waking up Hog or disturbing the pigs. Josh had already thought of how to handle the pigs and had put a jug of wildcat into the pig's drinking trough and watched diligently as they greedily gulped it all down without as much of a squeal. Soon all of Hog's pigs were passed out on the hay inside the barn and were dreaming of brighter days rolling around in the cool Red Bay mud. This took care of the pigs but they would just have to hope that Hog was a heavy sleeper and would not hear them lifting the wagon's sections up with the ropes and putting them back together on top of the barn roof. They took the sections of Ham's wagon out of their wagon, carried them one at a time over to the side of the barn, and then propped them vertically against the side of the barn so that they could be lifted up with ropes. Josh used the tall extension ladder they brought and climbed up onto the top of the barn where he tied a long rope around a steeple that was in the center of the roof. He then dropped the rope to Jed who carefully balanced and tied the rope to each section of the wagon one piece at a time. Jed then walked the sections up the ladder as Josh pulled them up from above. As each piece was lifted up, Josh tied them down and secured them to the steeple to keep them from sliding off the roof. This took about an hour but eventually all the wagon's wheels, sections, and pieces were lifted up and secured onto the barn roof.

So far, they had done all of this without making much, if any, noticeable noise. Now the challenge was to reassemble the whole wagon back together again by softly tapping the hammers and driving in the nails and screwing in the needed screws into their respective holes without dropping the screws, nails or tools. All of this had to be done while balancing each section and holding it place with the ropes while another section could be attached to it. This was a very tricky operation and one false move would end up with everything plummeting off the roof and crashing to the ground below. It was a balancing act worthy of "Barnum & Bailey" but there was no determination like self determination and no better help than having a good friend like Josh by your side. Just before sunrise and the crowing of Old Hog's rooster, Jed and Josh had done "God's Work" and Old Hog's wagon was back in one piece and firmly wedged into place on top of the pig barn. It rested at an angle that aligned with the pitch of the roof and remained firmly fixed there as if some grand gravity defying force had monumentally frozen it. Jed and Josh had placed wooden wedges under each of the four wheels and braced the front harness arms as well to keep the wagon from rolling off the roof. After testing to be sure the wagon was secure, they removed the ropes and dropped them off the roof, gathered all their tools and placed them back in their tool boxes, and carefully carried everything as they climbed back down the ladder to the ground. They then lowered the ladder and put it along with their tools and the ropes back into their wagon, after which, they ever so gently led Hack and the wagon onto the dirt road that would lead them jubilantly back to Hamilton, Alabama. They howled with laughter the whole way back and shared the last of the wildcat from one of the jugs.

Their wagon got back just in time for them to unload everything and return things to their proper places. When it was time to use the wagon to load the hay that morning it was back in place and no one ever knew that it had been missing and used in the grand plot against Hog Higgins. Of course Jed, having never gone to bed, was still up and just told his mother that he'd gotten up early to do his chores. Josh managed to sneak back to his home through the woods and got back just in time for breakfast. Sarah Ellen and Josh's mother were suspicious as to why Jed and Josh were so sleepy and tired out that morning but, other than that, no one but Jed and Josh's friends were ever the wiser. With the crowing of the rooster, Old Hog Higgins got up that morning got dressed and went out to the barn to check on things. The first thing he noticed was that his wagon was missing and when he rushed inside to check on his pigs, he found them all still sleeping on the hay beside the trough. Hog thought that this was unusual but he was in such a rush to check on his horse, he just let them be. The horse was still there and Hog thought that it was strange that whoever stole his wagon never even bothered his pigs or stole the horse to hitch to his wagon. By this time, Hog's face was so red and he was cussing so loud that he woke up all his pigs and they started squealing and running around in circles inside their pen. Hog threw his saddle hastily onto his horse which was also panicky because of all the noise and it took all Hog's strength to hold him steady enough to tighten the saddle. The old horse wasn't used to being saddled either because normally he was hitched to Hog's wagon. Hog jumped up on the horse and rode him right through the barn doors nearly trampling the free range chickens that were also going berserk, cackling up a storm, and running everywhere outside. During all of this animal chaos Old Hog never once looked up at the top of his barn as he rode his horse off in the direction of town and the Sheriff's office.

When Old Hog tore into town hanging sideways off his poor old horse, the noise and dust they stirred up got the attention of the shop owners who were just opening up along the street and all of them rushed out to the sidewalks to see what the ruckus was about. By the time Old Hog and his horse made it to the Sheriff, half of the townspeople were running behind them trying to get close enough to see what was going on. The Sheriff popped out the door of his office with his pistol drawn and ready to fire when he saw that it was just Old Hog Higgins about to ride his poor old horse to death. The Sheriff yelled at Hog, "What's going on with you Hog, you been hitting that wildcat jug again?" Hog was so flustered and red faced that he could barely talk but he managed to stutter out that someone had stolen his wagon. Hog got up his stamina and yelled back at the Sheriff, "I want justice and want you to find the varmints and hang the lot of them!" The sheriff immediately deputized two of the townspeople and after giving Old Hog some time to calm down and give his old horse time to rest a bit, they all saddled up their horses and rode out to Hog's pig farm.

A few other townspeople came along on their horses as well just to see what was going to happen with the case of Hog and his stolen wagon. As they all rode up to Hog's farm, the first thing that everybody saw was Hog's wagon perched sideways up on the top of his pig barn. The Sheriff and his newly appointed deputies all dismounted and pointed in unison to the top of Hog's barn. The Sheriff called out to Hog who was following in the rear with his tired old horse "Is that your wagon up there on the roof?"Hog rode up and jumped down off his old horse and was so flabbergasted that he began squealing like one of one of his pigs "My wagon's on the roof. How in Hell did it get up there?"The Sheriff and his deputies slapped each other on the backs and laughed until tears rolled down their cheeks and they, along with all the other townspeople, finally jumped back on their horses and rode laughing uproariously all the way back to town. The story of Hog and his stolen wagon quickly spread and he became the laughing stock of Red Bay and all of northwestern Alabama from that day forward. After that fateful morning when the pigs slept late and the wagon rode high, Hog Higgins never criticized another living soul. No one in Hamilton ever knew for sure who put that wagon on Hog's roof but they all knew that "boys will be boys".

Well that story as well as the other stories I will tell was inspired by actual pranks that were told to me by my uncles. I have embellished the stories and adapted them to Jed's time period with Jed and his best friend, Josh, substituted as the main characters. These stories, like most stories, get expanded upon to the extent that the storyteller desires. My uncles told me of many pranks that were played by friends or relatives and I will proceed as before and keep Jed and Josh as the main characters while keeping the gist of the stories intact. This next story had to do with a prank pulled on the site of Hamilton High School, which during Jed's time would've been West Alabama Agricultural School.

Folks around Hamilton never expected Jed would be a part of such shenanigans and partially that is why he was able to get away with pulling off these brilliant pranks of his. Like I said at the beginning of this chapter he was a good boy. He took care of his folks, especially his mother, and he was a faithful churchgoer and prized Sacred Harp singer. He was well respected around town and was always helping his friends and neighbors and he was a handsome, and intelligent young man who always did well with his studies in school. In fact he was appointed by the principal of his school to head a committee that was in charge of investigating untoward student activities such as cheating on tests, smoking cigarettes or drinking alcohol on school grounds, committing vandalism on school property or destroying or stealing school property and the like. Jed was a very even tempered, well mannered and very respectful young man who never got in trouble or challenged authority in any way. He was one of the most popular boys in town and he had the good looks to go with it. So if ever there was anything underhanded, unscrupulous, mischievous, or of moral depravity being perpetrated around Hamilton Jed would have been the last young man that anyone would have suspected to be involved in any way whatsoever.

Now, this is not to say that disassembling Hog Higgins' wagon and putting it back together on top of his barn was such a heinous crime, but the spectacle of it did ruin what was left of his credibility and good name. No one really knew how that wagon got up there on that roof or who could've done it but they did know that it had to be someone smart enough and bold enough to get away with doing it. There were a lot of pranks that were carried out successfully in Hamilton like that and no one ever found out who the perpetuators were. Mostly people just thought they were pranks pulled by bullies or overzealous teens with too much time on their hands, but they generally would not have suspected that a nice young man like Jed would ever be a part of such a scurrilous affront to social order. That's why he was appointed by his school principal to head the committee for investigating such abuses. He would work with students and teachers to gather information and report back to the principal who in turn would report to local authorities when something was found to be amiss. There were two such events of such a scandalous nature that they make for grand storytelling. Both events concern the vandalizing of properties that were of such magnitude that they indeed required the full investigative capacity of the school committee of which Jed was head. His school was West Alabama Agricultural School with around 100 students from grades 9 through 12 and it was one of the regional schools for Marion County School District. It was a two story, wood frame clapboard structure and had been built in 1895 and was equipped with steam radiator heating in each of its 16 classrooms, with 2 additional radiators in the auditorium, 2 in the lunchroom and 1 in each of the 4 administrative offices. That made 24 radiators in all and these details were of particular importance to the planning of the first prank that I am about to relate.

Jed was an exceptional student and always kept up with his studies, was always attentive to instruction and was respectful to his teachers. However, there was one English teacher who was abrasive to students and always demeaned them in front of their peers if they did not perform well in his class and Jed found his behavior to be callus, offensive, and totally reprehensible. Usually the trouble arose when proper pronunciation of words was involved with class oral reading assignments. The teacher's name was Mr. Walter Skinks and of course the students all nicknamed him "Mister Stinks (like a skunk)". Many people in northwestern Alabama spoke with an Appalachian drawl that put heavy emphasis on the letters "A", "H" and "R", and this came from using the old English that had been passed down to them from their English ancestors. The way they saw it, their pronunciation was the correct way because it originated from the original English and they were proud to speak the dialect of their ancestors. So words like "there" would be pronounced "thar", "your" would be pronounced "yore","sure" would be pronounced "shore", and "are" would be pronounced "air" and so on. In other words, "They sure were tired." would be "They shore war tarred." or it would sound that way when spoken. "Mister Stinks" was educated up north so he would have none of this "Old English" spoken in his presence and that made for a bona fide predicament and a totally dysfunctional student teacher relationship that was bound to eventually spiral out of control. It had gotten to the point that many students did not even want to attend his classes and be insulted and made fun of because of their accents. Some students would even skip his classes altogether. Of course, skipping classes was totally unacceptable and would result in the suspension of the guilty student or students.

Jed was not among the students who skipped class and were suspended but his best friend, Josh, and several others that were his friends had skipped and had been suspended. This called for drastic action and Josh asked Jed to schedule a caucus with all the parties concerned. One day, after school had been dismissed, they and their other friends met out in one of the caves in the northwestern Alabama hills and had a priority caucus to discuss plans of action. Josh was first to comment on how unfair their treatment had been by teacher Skinks and started everyone chanting out loud the words "Mister Skinks really stinks!" over and over as they sat in a circle inside the cave. After a while of sitting there and chanting and chugging wildcat from the jugs Josh had hidden there, Jed came up with a jewel of a plan. He announced his plan in this manner: "If Skinks really stinks like the skunk he is, then let's make the smell rub off some!" No one really understood at the time what Jed meant by this but by the time he sat with them and explained his plan they were all stunned by the brilliance and justice of it all.

Jed began by telling them all about an old man he knew that lived up in the bluffs around Red Hill who lived in a one room log cabin with dirt floors. The old man had built the cabin years ago and had lived there with his wife until she passed away from consumption. He had buried her there under an old Indian style grave with stones piled up pyramid like on the top of it. He had vowed never to leave her alone even in death and he remained there as a guardian angel of sorts until his old age. He remained alone and became a hermit and avoided human contact and company of any kind with humans but loved to have the company of his animals which included squirrels which he had trained to perch on his shoulder and eat hickory nuts and wild apples from his hand. He also had won over the trust of forest creatures such as raccoons, woodchucks, rabbits, and deer. He never harmed the animals and never hunted them for food but had a vegetable garden next to his cabin where he grew vegetables of all kinds and would can them and create all kinds of dishes including soups and stews which he would serve up for himself and for the animals that would come looking for a meal. As Jed related, he was a strange old bird but he was kind to animals and did no human any harm as long as they stayed away from him.

Jed went on to say that he had met the old man while hunting rabbits one day and the old man had sprung out of some bushes as Jed was about to draw a bead on a rabbit with his shotgun. An awful smell emitted from around the bushes as the old man jumped out toward him and began slinging an old soiled rag violently in all directions around his body. What he was acting out seemed to be some kind of wild Indian war dance and it really took Jed by surprise. The smell became more pungent as the old man came closer and Jed had to turn away and run for cover. He had experienced that smell before when he had accidently come up on a skunk in the woods while hunting, so he knew what the old man was slinging at him with that rag. It seemed unbelievable but the old man had somehow managed to extract the spray that skunks emit when they are threatened and he was slinging it toward him in order to make him run away and leave the rabbit alone. There was something familiar about the old man though and Jed watched him carefully from a safe distance until he went back into the woods. Just then it struck him who the old man was. His mother, Sarah Ellen, had told him of a peculiar cousin of hers who she hadn't seen in many years whose wife had died and she believed that he had passed away as well. No one ever saw him much after his wife's death so they thought he had moved off somewhere or he had been killed by wild animals or murdered. Jed knew that this had to be that cousin and he was determined to try and follow him and explain to him who he was and find out more about him. Of course the smell would've been enough to keep most people away but he was determined and once he set his mind to do accomplish something, he most always did.

Sure enough, Jed managed to trail the old man up to his cabin and he called out to him explaining that he was Sarah Ellen's son. The old man's ears immediately perked up when he heard this and he called back:"it must be true, cuz you be the splitting image of yore Pa". It turned out that he and Sarah Ellen's husband had been friends and even related and according to his story, the old man was the child of one of Sarah Ellen's grandfather's unmarried, second wives. This seemed to fit with what he had heard about this peculiar cousin before, so Jed humored him along with his story. The old man continued by saying that Slim was a bright young man but was born under a bad sign and was always finding trouble or trouble was always finding him. He said that they were good friends though and that he knew Sarah Ellen back then as well and that they too were cousins. Sometimes he, Slim, and Sarah Ellen would see each other and share each other's company at family outings or church singings but he never imagined back then that Slim would get Sarah Ellen with child and then go off and leave her to raise the child on her own. "Yet you be the proof of it son, there can be no denying it." The old man reiterated.

Jed had wanted to inquire more into why his father, Slim, was born under "a bad sign" and why the old man thought that he always found trouble or that trouble always found him, but he really just wanted to get back to hunting rabbits so that his mother could "cook up a mess" of her delicious rabbit and dumplings for Sunday's Sacred Harp Singing. Jed didn't want to expound too much on his family relations' quirks amongst his friends either, so he went on to explain what the old man had told him about the skunk smell he had stirred up earlier in the woods. It seems the only animal that the old man could not abide was the skunk. No matter how much he tried to tame them he always got sprayed and it took a good long time for the smell to go away. So this is when he got the idea to use the skunk's smell to his advantage. If the smell of the skunk would keep him away then it would keep everyone else away too and so he devised a way of extracting the fluid from the skunk's glands. Pretty soon he had trapped and killed enough of them to cut open and collect the fluid in jugs that he would cork up and store in a safe place out in the woods. Jed didn't want to know the exact technique of how the old man managed to do this, but he did find it fascinating and kept the memory of his encounter with the old man and his stories fresh and accessible for later reference should the need arise. There wasn't much that escaped Jed's intellectual capacity and he would store an infinite amount of information in that bright mind of his.

Sure enough, Jed had now found a use for the old man's skunk fluid and as defiling a use as it was, a perfect subject had been presented as a recipient of its foul odor. However, it was not his plan to imitate the old man and dip an old rag into the skunk fluid and pounce through the door of Walter Skinks' classroom slinging the awful liquid in all directions. Jed devised a much more clever method of achieving his final result. Walter Skinks was always assigning work to students that refused to conform to his wishes and that mostly consisted of putting a fresh coat of paint onto the walls of the classrooms and onto the radiators which had a tendency to rust over time. Jed knew where Walter Skinks kept his paint cans and it would be fairly easy to divert Mister Stinks' attention away from the classroom long enough for Jed to sneak a bottle of skunk fluid into the can of radiator paint. Once the paint mixed with the fluid the smell would lie dormant enough until it was painted onto the radiators and dried. Mister Stinks was proud of his radiator paint and would always brag of its protective qualities to the principal. In fact, the principal was so impressed that he suggested that the students paint all the radiators in the school during Christmas vacation so that they would be ready for use in time for cold weather after the break. Being the head of the school committee, Jed knew of this plan and thus his diabolical plan to get even with Skinks was born.

Jed explained to Josh and his friends in the cave as they sat in a circle rapt with awe and admiration, the dastardly deed that they were about to perpetrate. First there was a blood pact of secrecy during which they pricked their fingertips with knives and shook hands swearing, as their blood mingled, that they would never tell anyone of what they were about to undertake. Jed would visit his eccentric old cousin in the woods and see if he could obtain some of the old man's vile skunk sauce. Jed had a metal pocket flask that he normally kept his wildcat in that would work perfectly to store the skunk sauce in until they were ready to use it. It was going to be a pretty foul plot but it could be done if they were careful and acted as if nothing untoward were underway. Jed explained how Mister Stinks or Walter Skinks, the English teacher, had an arrangement each Christmas break with the principal to have a student work crew come over during the break and paint the school walls, do minor repairs, scrub out the toilets, or just anything that needed doing around the school. The principal liked

Walter Skink's arrangement because he got a lot of free labor out of it and Walter Skink's liked it because it was a good way to discipline his problem students - it was like KP in the Army. The students were forced to do hard manual labor during the holiday under supervision of Mister Stinks who kept a constant watchful eye over them, lest they try to sneak off and avoid their disciplinary duties. Of course, the work crew this time would be Jed's best friend Josh and all his pals. Josh and his pals smiled broadly as Jed pointed out that he was head of the school committee investigating disciplinary abuses, vandalism, and insubordination among student population, and he would be put in charge of these work crews to act as an advisor and student representative.

It seems that Mr. Walter Skinks was always trying to brownnose the principal and would bend over backwards to get on his good side. Mr. Skinks had recently ordered 6 cans of extra insulating high preservative silver radiator paint that was just going to be the best ever paint for the school's steam radiator heating system and the Christmas Holidays would be the best time to have it painted on each and every radiator in each and every room. Besides, they had these unruly set of juveniles who needed a lesson in responsibility taught them, so it would a good time to accomplish both missions. The unruly students would make up the time they had skipped by working during the holidays at the school painting the radiators. So it was all set up and those radiators would be a bright shade of silver and shiny like the silver bells decorating the school windows during the holidays.

Jed made a trek up to his old cousin's cabin on the weekend before the Christmas break. He took his shotgun as before telling Sarah Ellen that he was off to hunt rabbit for Sunday dinner. It wasn't long before he had shot enough rabbits to make for a big mess of rabbit and dumplings that his mother would cook up for Sunday and take to the Sacred Harp Singing and dinner on the grounds afterward. Jed had a good hiding place there in the bluffs where he had a cage that he could hang the rabbits until he would come back later in the afternoon to pick them up. All the shooting had stirred up the animals in the woods and by the time he got back from the bluffs his old cousin showed up rustling limbs and bushes and slinging that old stinking skunk rag of his over his head. "What air you back up hare agin fur, Jed? I'd a thought you'd had enuff of my skunks stank by now!" yelled the old man. "I came to ask a favor of you" Jed responded.

"Well, git on wid it!" the old man responded. "I need for you to loan me some of that skunk sauce as I got some evening up to do with a high brow brownnoser in the flatlands."

Jed told the old man how Mr. Walter Skinks had demeaned Josh and the others for using the old northwestern Alabama dialect when reading aloud in class. The old man got really riled up when he heard how the teacher had made fun of the boys and then had them suspended just for skipping his infernal class and speaking the King's English, as he called it. Jed went on to describe his plan to his old cousin as they began walking back in the direction of his old log cabin. "The way I figure it", Jed said, "I can put this skunk sauce in with some paint and brush it on the radiators at school. Once it mixes with the paint it should calm the smell down long enough for it to be painted on the radiator and as long as the radiator is off, the stink shouldn't be all that bad. The paint will dry and mask the smell of the skunk sauce as long as the heat is off. When the heat comes back on, Katy Bar the Door, because ain't no living soul gonna be able to stay within a mile of that place." The old man cackled like an old witch as he listened to Jed's plot and said "You be the dead ringer of yore Pa, Slim. It be jus that kind of devilment he would a done!" The old man said it should work though. It would smell bad mixing it up but the smell should calm down when mixed with the paint. He had an idea of how to disguise the smell while brushing it on the radiators as well. He said that he'd give them one of his freshly killed skunks and put it in a bag to take back with him. The old man said:"You can throw that ol skank under the school where ol brownnoser can see it and he will think the smell is coming from it. Don't worry none cause I done removed the stank from that skunk and it be sweet as a turtle dove for you to carry it back in the bag."

Now all that was left was to get some of that skunk sauce and pour it in the metal flask that Jed had brought with him. "Old Cuzz Monk", as Jed now called him, directed him to follow him down a path outside his cabin toward the bluffs and he followed Old Cuzz Monk alongside a stream until they came to a small waterfall on the side of a craggy hill. It was all bushy there by the waterfall and hard to negotiate a path through the maze of vines and brush but Jed kept following and could see that there was an opening in the craggy rocks just behind the waterfall. "I be leadin you to my secrit scank cave so git ready for sum powurful polecat aire inside!" Old Cuzz Monk was right and the stink made Jed gag as they went inside the cave. There were torches placed in the cracks of the cave's walls and the old man took some matches laying there in the rocks and lit two of them so that Jed could see a slaughter table and some makeshift shelves built up against the cave walls. "This is wher I skin em and takes out the stank glans for my skunk sauce!" the old man said to Jed who was barely able to breathe the dank and putrid air of the cave. Jed's eyes had begun to water but he could see some jugs on the shelf behind the table and he surmised that they contained the skunk sauce that they had come for. The old man grabbed one of the jugs and reached over and grabbed a freshly killed skunk from the bottom shelf saying:"I wuz jest about to skin this one when you come up. I done took the juice outta him so he won't be a stanking none now." The old man explained that Jed could take this skunk in the bag he gave him, sneak it over to the school and throw it up under so that it could be easily seen. Before starting their painting project, Jed could point out the skunk to Mr. Walter Skinks and tell him that a skunk had died under the school and that the smell may have gotten inside.

The plan sounded good to Jed and he agreed that it would be a good way to explain why there was a skunk smell coming from the school as the students opened the cans and began to apply the paint. Old Cuzz Monk nodded his approval and then took a funnel and poured the skunk sauce into Jed's metal flask and sealed it up tight. "A long as you keep this corked up tight, the stank will stay in thar and when you pour it don't shake it none. Jest pour it slow like in the paint can and shut the lid tight so the stank stays in the can. The stank will mix all by itself and all that paint will be full of it". The old man explained that there was enough stank in that flask a plenty for six cans and that Jed should divide it in even parts as he poured it into each one. So Jed had what he needed to execute his plan and now he headed back with his skunk bag and skunk sauce to his hiding place in the bluffs. His rabbits that he had killed were still hanging there in the cage and he put them in a sack for the trip back home. He took his shotgun out from under the brush he had hid it and slung it over his shoulder and grabbing the sack of rabbits with one hand and the skunk bag with the other, he headed for home. The flask with the skunk sauce was tightly sealed up and safe inside his pocket and when arrived home, he would take it out and hide it along with the skunk bag up in the loft of their barn where he would retrieve them later.

Sarah Ellen was proud to see the rabbits that her son had shot and happy to have him back home but she couldn't help but notice the awful smell coming from his clothes when he came into the house. "Laud, Laud, Laudy what have you done got yoreself into!" Sarah Ellen implored. "Git them clothes off and let me warsh them quick like before you stank up the whole house!" Jed explained to her that he had come up on a polecat in the woods and couldn't get away fast enough to keep from getting sprayed. This mission was going to be a challenge and getting around the skunk smell was going to be the most challenging part of it all. Sarah Ellen was satisfied with his explanation though, even if she was not at all happy about having to clean his clothes and get rid of the smell. Still though, he had brought home some nice rabbits and they would make a fine meal for a lot of churchgoers at the Sacred Harp Singing on Sunday. So thanks to the rabbits, all was well on the home front that evening.

After washing up and cleansing himself of the skunk smell, putting on some old work clothes, and having a tasty meal of cornbread, black eye peas, turnip greens with hog jowl, and a slice of Sarah Ellen's fresh apple pie, Jed left for what he said was a scheduled meeting of the school committee in preparation for the school painting project and told his mother not to worry about him messing up his clothes. He knew he was going to get dirty doing some chores over at the school so he on purpose put on some old clothes. Of course he had really planned to meet up with Josh and execute the initial phases of their plot against Mr. Walter Skinks or "Mister Stinks". Jed went outside, climbed up to the barn loft, retrieved the skunk bag which was now no longer as sweet smelling as a turtle dove, and grabbed his flask with the skunk sauce. Within just a few minutes he had arrived at Josh's place where Josh had planned in advance to meet him outside by his barn. Jed didn't have to show Josh what he had in the bag, because they both had to hold their noses to keep from smelling the day old skunk inside. After hearing the plan about throwing the skunk up under the school to make it look like it had died there, Josh agreed that it would be a good ploy and would seem to explain the smell that was going to be stirred up when they painted the radiators. The following Monday was when the holidays started, so the skunk would've had a couple of days to get really rank up under that school by the time they all began their painting project. Jed showed Josh his flask with the skunk sauce and explained to him how he would divert Mr. Skinks and have Josh pour the sauce into the six paint cans while Mr. Skinks was away. Jed had a hiding place figured out for the flask up under the school and he would be able to retrieve it on Monday morning. Tonight though, all they would do was to sneak up to the school and throw that old skunk up under the floor by the front entrance steps and let nature take its course.

Jed and Josh's plan worked well and they were able to approach the school from a thick growth of trees and hedges in back of it without being seen. Josh stood guard as Jed ran stealthily up to the back of the school with his bag in hand and belly crawled up under it until he reached the front steps on the other side and "let the skunk out the bag". He let it slide out and lay there on the ground as if it had died and was laying there on its belly and was careful not to brush up on it as he didn't want that smell to get on his clothes again. Jed got the flask from his pocket and put it up on top of one of the pillars that held up the front steps so that it was behind the steps and concealed from view but it was still easily accessible for when he needed it. He then crawled on back under the school and jumped out to join up with Josh who was hiding close by in the hedges and then they both ran through the woods and back on home.

Now the first phases of the diabolical plot had been accomplished and they only had to wait until Monday morning to begin executing the rest of the plan. Sunday, though, was a day of worship and celebration of the Sacred Harp Singing with a joyous gathering on the grounds afterward to eat all the good vittles that the women from the church had prepared. Sarah Ellen's rabbit and dumplings and apple pie were a big hit with the churchgoers as always and she was proud to tell them all that Jed had nabbed the rabbits just yesterday when he went hunting in the woods. The women all bragged on how well she cooked the dumplings and how tasty they were and how delicious the apple pie was and they all had to have the recipes. All the men were so busy eating and smacking their lips that they just smiled and praised the food between bites and bragged on how good a shot Jed was to have gotten so many nice plump rabbits. Jed just thought to himself "if you only knew what I went through to get those rabbits and how much of a stink I had with the polecat". It was church time though and not a time to bring up unpleasant conversation, so Jed just smiled his best smile and thanked the men as they all laughed and sang and enjoyed one another's company. They all agreed that Jed was such a nice young man and how proud his mother must be of him.

The holidays had begun in earnest. It was Monday morning and school was out and for most kids it was a joyous time to spend with family and friends and enjoy all the blessings of the season. But for Mr. Walter Skinks it was a time for retaliation and he would punish those students who had dared to challenge his authority. He would deprive them of their holidays and make them do manual labor at the school to make up for the time they had skipped from his class. He was so proud of himself, not only for enforcing the strict discipline he thought the students needed, but for coming up with free labor to paint the school's radiators with the new paint that he had so highly recommended to the principal. The students would have to paint all 24 radiators in the school and Mr. Skinks just smiled as he thought to himself how brilliant he was to have come up with this idea. Little did Mr. Skinks know, but his plan was about to backfire on him in ways that he could not have possibly anticipated.

Jed was waiting with Josh and all the other boys in front of the school when Mr. Skinks arrived with the keys to open up. He had told the principal to have all the steam radiators cut off so that they would save on heat and besides they needed to be painted and needed to be off anyway. It was December and it would be cold inside the school but he just told the principal the boys would have to work even faster to keep warm. They both had a good laugh about this at the students' expense, but this was really just as Jed and Josh had hoped for and had devised their plan accordingly. Mr. Skinks was impressed that all the boys were waiting for him this morning and that Jed was there as well to help direct everything – maybe his brand of discipline was beginning to pay off, he thought. Mr. Skinks noticed a foul odor as he led the group up the steps and into the school but didn't think much of it at the time. He led them to a closet where he had stored the radiator paint, brushes, pans, rags and other supplies needed for the project. He then walked them around the school, pointing out all the classrooms, as those would be the rooms that they would begin the painting of radiators. The auditorium, lunchroom, and offices would be toured at some other time as they would be painted later during the final days of the break. Jed was following Mr. Skinks along all the way and assured him that the boys understood their mission, would do a good job, and that he would always be there to watch over them. Jed also pointed toward the entrance of the school and said that he had noticed something as they were coming into the school that Mr. Skinks might want to investigate. What Jed did not tell Mr. Skinks, though, was that he had gotten his flask from behind the steps and put it in his pocket before Mr. Skinks had arrived.

While Mr. Skinks head was turned away toward the front door, Jed passed over his flask to Josh and winked his eye for Josh to start the next phase of the plan. Jed said that he had noticed a peculiar odor when they were coming up the steps and he asked Mr. Skinks if he wanted them to go and check on it, Mr. Skinks said that he had noticed it too and so they both went back to the entrance to see what could be found. This gave Josh the opportunity to open all six cans of radiator paint and pour equal portions of skunk sauce from Jed's flask into them. He deliberately measured and slowly poured the toxic potion into the cans and then firmly placed the lids back on the cans and tapped them down with a hammer. Luckily not much of a smell had escaped as of yet but there was a trace of it in the air when Jed and Mr. Skinks returned from their reconnaissance of the front of the school. "Aha", Mr. Skinks said as he returned, "There is an odor here of what we found under the front steps!" They had found the dead skunk under the steps and Mr. Skinks said to just leave it there as the smell would be gone by the time everyone came back from break and besides, it wasn't a good idea to stir up the carcass as that would make the smell worse. Of course Jed agreed with Mr. Skinks saying that his assessment was correct and that this was the best course of action to take.

"Well, let's not worry about a little foul odor and a cold place to work, but instead get to work and get these radiators painted", instructed Mr. Stinks. So they each grabbed a paint can and departed for a classroom of Mr. Skink's direction to begin their work. Josh had carefully instructed the boys to open the lids with care and brush on the paint delicately with what would appear to be the greatest of attention to detail and delicacy of touch. In this way, the least amount of odor would be stirred up and additionally it would impress Mr. Skinks that they were so attentive and deliberate in their efforts to do a good job, In any case, there was no hurry, as Mr. Skinks had said they were not going anyplace these holidays except here to paint those radiators. The boys all thought to themselves and smiled ear to ear as they applied the paint:"He wants the radiators painted and painting them we will do!" At the pace they were going it was going to take a week just to do the 16 classrooms and another week to do the rest of the radiators in the school. Mr. Skinks kept a close tab on them the whole time and made sure that they were diligent in their efforts and did not try to sneak away undetected and of course Jed was there to see that all went as it should as well. The only thing that bothered Mr. Skinks was the smell of the skunk and how it apparently got stronger by the day instead of fading away as he had thought it would. To the great delight of the boys, the smell was disagreeable to Mr. Skinks and he would go outside to get some air on many occasions throughout the course of the project.

The boys had spent their entire holiday with the exception of Christmas day painting those radiators at the school. It was true that Mr. Skinks was a mean spirited and heartless soul, but at least he let the boys have Christmas day off. One might conjecture that he figured even Charles Dickens' Scrooge had let Bob Cratchit off for Christmas, so he, like his favorite writer, could do the same. By this time, most of the families in town were appalled by Mr. Skinks and what he had inflicted upon the school boys at Christmas time and some of them had vehemently protested his actions to the principal. Things were already getting uncomfortable for Mr. Skinks before school started back up and things were about to get a whole lot worse. The day before school started Mr. Skinks assured the principal that all was finished, the radiators looked splendid, and so it was alright to turn all the heat back on at school. He had checked on the skunk carcass and had the bones and remains removed and taken off to be buried in the woods behind the school where whatever odor was left would go totally undetected. Of course, he assigned this task to Josh as he wanted to inflict one last indignity on the student that he so disliked. Josh was proud to do it though because he knew what was coming up for Mr. Skinks if all went according to his and Jed's plans.

When the heat was turned on Sunday night before school opened on Monday morning, the hot steam pipes released fumes as a result of all the skunk sauce that had been meticulously painted onto all 24 radiators inside the school. The odor was so overwhelming and the air was so thick with putrefaction that habitation by human life forms had become impossible. No living thing, animal or human, could walk inside those once hallowed but now horrific halls. The smell permeated the entire school like thick clouds of sulfur leaking out into the surrounding environs where it began polluting the breathing air of the entire town. School had to be cancelled and students all had to be sent home until officials ascertained what the problem was and were able to rectify the situation and make the school safe for human habitation once again. A special student, teacher and administrative caucus was called for to investigate the incident and try to determine what the problem was, how it could have occurred, and what action was needed to correct it.

Being the head of the student commission, Jed was naturally called upon to organize a student investigative body that would inform the representatives and be responsible to the caucus as a whole. Jed took his responsibilities with an air of great seriousness and dignity and began to organize the students into an investigative body. Special protective gear had been provided by the state so that an assigned group of students and administrative staff could enter the building and determine the nature of and the source of the oppressive smell. With gas masks in place and their protective jump suits and rubber overshoes put on to protect them, the group went boldly inside the school on a quest for clues that might reveal answers to the questions the entire town's population had about this noxious attack that had been inflicted upon them. Once inside, Jed offered his observations about what had taken place the days before with the radiator painting project and how that it seemed to him the radiators had a bad smell to them when the students brushed the paint on. He further observed that there had been a dead skunk found just under the steps at the entrance and that everyone just assumed that the bad smell was a result of the skunk having sprayed underneath the school. Mr. Skinks was happy to confirm this as he had been there with Jed when they discovered the skunk. Mr. Skinks went on to explain that they had deemed it best not to disturb the skunk and just let it lay until it could be removed later. Mr. Skinks, when asked by the committee why the skunk had been allowed to remain there for so long, stated that stirring up the remains of the skunk would've aggravated the situation and would've spread the odor throughout the school. Jed respectfully agreed with Mr. Skinks that this was the best course of action to pursue. Having heard this news of the skunk and the rationale given by Mr. Skinks for leaving the animal in place, the principal stated his observations about what should have been done. He firmly believed that the skunk should have been removed at once and that the painting project should have been cancelled immediately. Additionally, it was obvious to him that the skunk had entered the school at night, become threatened in some way, and sprayed the schools radiators as it ran from room to room. The principal related in a very authoritarian manner that anyone should have noticed the smell and known better than to have painted over the radiators as that would've permanently sealed over the offensive spray. Suddenly, it was apparent to all and the mystery had been solved. The principal had come up with the answer and everyone agreed that this had to be the way it all happened, except, of course, Mr. Skinks who had just had the blame of it all laid completely at his feet.

Mr. Skinks was in no position to argue as those "between a rock and a hard place" are prone to say, and his fate had been sealed by the very astute observations of the principal. That solved to everyone's satisfaction how the situation had occurred but now they had to resolve how to rid the school of that awful smell. The principal offered Mr. Skinks an ultimatum: "You can take whatever time that is necessary to strip all that paint from the radiators and scrub them clean of the skunk scent, or you can turn in your resignation to me tomorrow morning!" To the great jubilation of most all the students, especially Jed, Josh, and their friends, Mr. Skinks cleaned out his office and turned in his resignation promptly the next morning. As far as anyone in Hamilton ever knew he never showed his face there again and no one ever learned about, or cared about his whereabouts. Thanks to an eccentric old man and his brilliant cousin, justice had been done at West Alabama Agricultural School and eventually a maintenance crew came to strip the paint and scrub away the foul odor from the radiators. The school opened back up about two weeks later and everyone enjoyed their extended holiday break. The legend of Mr. Skinks or Mister Stinks and his stinking steam radiators had been born.

Again, there was an incident at Hamilton High School where someone had maliciously painted all the radiators with skunk fluid and the school had to be evacuated when the heat was turned back on. My uncles told me about it and who did it, which will be kept secret, but I think you can guess there were relatives involved. I've changed the characters and embellished the plot as before but the legend lives and grows more interesting as time passes. There is one more prank that my uncles loved to tell about and I will tailor it a bit for a better fit as well.

You'd think that this would be enough for Jed and his pals to laugh about and celebrate for a long time, but there were more malicious pranks to come and I will tell the story of one more before ending this chapter. I will call this prank "The Billy Goat's Revenge" and, as before, I will describe the events that led up to its execution by Jed and Josh. It all started the day of a school competition between West Alabama Agricultural School and Pottsville High School which was about 25 miles south of Hamilton. Every spring during the spring break the schools from northwestern Alabama would have an annual field day event with competitions between the high schools in that area of Alabama. The events included tug of war, three legged races, pitching horseshoes, bobbing for apples, slingshot competitions, barrel rolls, relay races, broad jumps, wrestling matches, tag football, softball and many other activities and events. It was coordinated with the farmers in the area, and they called it the West Alabama Farm Festival. As well as the sporting events they had animal events such as horse races, rodeos, livestock competitions with prizes awarded to the local farmers and in many ways it was like a state fair. There was a big barn square dance in the evening for local students and their families to attend and there were plenty of tables outside for families to bring food that they had especially prepared for the festival. They had homemade cooking, pie, and cake judging contests after the dance that local women could enter and be awarded cash prizes and a prize ribbon. So the festival was a big event and people came from all around to celebrate, compete in sporting events or cooking contests or just dance, sing and have a great time in the comfortable spring time weather.

This festival was looked forward to by the schools and the families in the area and most all the schools attended and competed against one another. The local farmers loved it as well as they could show their prized livestock, race their horses and learn about new farming techniques from area agricultural representatives. Jed and Josh liked to compete in the horseshoe throwing events, tug of war, and tag football. Sarah Ellen liked to enter her prized rabbit and dumplings and her homemade apple pie in the cooking competitions – she won first prize most every year with both entries. Jed and Josh would represent West Alabama Agricultural in the horseshoe pitching, and tag football along with the other students who signed up to compete from Hamilton and they would do the tug of war as part of the competition, but mostly just for the fun of it. So West Alabama Agricultural would compete against other local schools such as Pottsville High and this was an arch rivalry for both schools. In fact the competition between them was so fierce that it became downright nasty and fights would break out between the competitors and even their families at times. This year someone had greased the tug of war rope just before the event started between West Alabama and Pottsville and West Alabama ended up losing because they got the greased end of the rope and lost their grip. Of course the result had to be negated and a new rope provided for another contest, but West Alabama never got over the jeering that came from the Pottsville fans and they lost the event on the second attempt as well. It was just this sort of prank that got Jed and Josh riled up and it didn't take too much more aggravation from the Pottsville fans to inspire them to get even.

The next prank pulled by the Pottsville folks was the last straw for Jed and Josh. They both were horseshoe pitching champions and always would win or place second or third in the competitions each year. It was mostly just a lot of fun though and they enjoyed the good natured joking and jostling around with old friends and new ones to be. It seemed the Pottsville crowd was always up to no good though and they were determined to make Jed and Josh look bad and keep them from winning the competition this year. Jed should have known better and checked the poles to make sure they were hammered into the ground securely because when he pitched his first ringer it knocked the pole over and his horseshoe ended up about two feet away from the pit. Someone had pulled the pole up just enough so that it would stand, but if a horseshoe struck, it would fall to the ground. As usual, the Pottsville crowd started to jeer and heckle at Jed and it was all he could do to keep from pitching his horseshoes at the unruly bunch. The judge must have been from Pottsville, because he allowed the missed ringer to stand and Jed ended up losing third place to a Pottsville contestant. Josh did manage to place fourth but no prizes were awarded for fourth place and they both "were fit to be tied".

As mad as they were about being cheated by the judge, Jed and Josh took a break and had a serious caucus in one of the tents where they kept the livestock entries. Jed noticed while there that one of his cousins had a prize Billy Goat there in one of the stalls. An idea began to brew inside his head as he watched the Billy Goat angrily butt the sides of the stall with its horns. His cousin, Walt Langley, came up to say hello and inquired why Jed was so downtrodden. Jed explained what happened with the horseshoe competition and Walt declared that they should get even with those Pottsville people and he offered to help in any way he could. Jed called Josh over and they all discussed what could be done as Jed continued to watch Walt's Billy Goat butt the sides of his stall. Suddenly Jed had an inspiration and he announced his strategy to Josh and Walt:"You know that cider chugging contest they have later in the afternoon? Well Pottsville is entering an old man named Fox Fairley that brags he can chug more cider than anyone in northwestern Alabama. I know where they store the cider for that contest because I helped my mother take some of hers over to the tent today and they have them all separated out for the different contestants – each contestant has their own batch to drink made by one of their friends or family. My mother made up some for Harlon Boyette to chug and we put it in a big box with his name on it. I know you're both trying to figure where I'm going with all this, but here goes. My mother always has some powdered Indian herbs with her to cure constipation and I don't know what's in it but it really does the trick. If you take some of that stuff with a drink of water, you'll be 'messin like a goose' within 5 minutes. I know I can get a hold of the bag of it that she carries in her purse while she's getting her pies and dumplings ready for the competition. If she does notice me getting it, I'll tell her my stomach is cramping and I need some of her herbs. I think you know where I am going to put that powder now, don't you boys?"

Walt and Josh were ecstatic with joy upon hearing Jeb's idea but wanted to know more about the end result he had in mind. "Well", Jed said, "you know that I am going to have you pals guard the tent for me while I go in there and pour the powder in each one of Fox Fairley's jugs. Now this is where you come in Walt. I need for you to let me borrow your Billy Goat while the cider chugging contest is going on. I want you to walk him around the grounds to calm him down some as I noticed he's mad about being penned up in that stall. When you notice that Fox Fairley begins his chugging, I want you to take your Billy Goat up to the outhouse behind the tent at the chugging stand and put him inside and wedge the door shut with one of those corn cobs (this was before the days of toilet tissue) that they keep inside – just jam it under the door and it should keep the door shut until Fox Fairley comes running up the hill. Fox will have chugged enough of the powdered cider to make him explode by the time he runs to that outhouse and he will jerk that door open to get inside. Your Billy Goat will run out like a scalded pig and butt him over as he charges back down the hill back toward the livestock tent. You can get your goat back and put him back in the stall with all the other goats before anybody realizes what has happened. I don't think Fox Fairley is going to be in any hurry to get up and protest to everyone what has transpired because he is going to be "purty messed up"!!

That was the plan and the three of them swore that it could be carried out and all agreed that justice would be done and that the Pottsville crowd would for once be silenced by the horrendous spectacle that would occur with their contestant. As it happened, no one ever found out what goat had done the damage or who had put him there in the outhouse, but Walt Langley did win first prize for his Billy Goat later that day. No one said anything about that judge being from Hamilton and possibly biased toward Walt's goat, but a resounding chorus of raucous cheers arose from the Hamilton fans when the blue ribbon was placed around the neck of Walt's goat. Incidentally, Harlon Boyette from Hamilton, who chugged down 4 jugs of Sarah Ellen's apple cider, won the apple cider chugging competition and got a blue ribbon as well. Old Fox Fairfield from Pottsville had just started on his fourth jug when all of a sudden he had to bolt off and run like a wild boar to the outhouse. People heard the commotion when Fox jerked the outhouse door open and the goat came busting out and rammed into him. The goat ran off before anyone got a good look and no one saw Walt Langley grab hold of his horns and lead him back to the livestock tent – or if they did, no one ever said so. The plan was executed just as Jed had detailed it and Fox Fairley and the Pottsville crowd became the laughing stock of the West Alabama Farm Festival. Old Fox had to get one of the barrels from the barrel rolling contest and put it around him in order to cover himself and get back to his wagon so that he could get someplace quick that had a creek he could jump in to wash himself off. After this horridly humiliating experience, he and the Pottsville folks were not seen anywhere around the festival for the rest of that day and their participation in future annual events was lackluster to say the least. So this day justice was done and the legend of Fox Fairley and "The Billy Goat's Revenge" was born.

These are but a few of the many tales that could be improvised upon that were told me by my uncles. They all have an element of truth in them but like a good pair of socks have been stretched to make for a better fit. I know the true participants will pardon me for substituting Jed and Josh as characters because they probably want to keep it all secret. Suffice it to say, my relatives when necessary, could mastermind plans that were designed to leave their enemies' lives in total disarray, but only if they were deemed guilty of having desecrated the honor of them, their family, or their friends. Woe unto them that dared to do such dishonor. The guilty parties were fortunate in that they were never suspected of being the "ring leaders" that perpetrated these deeds but remained "above it all" and fooled everyone by acting as shocked by it all as everyone else. Diabolical pranks like the ones I've related and expanded upon were told to me by close relatives as we would sit around their living rooms late at night and share each other's company and re-engage in the art of storytelling and I can only hope that their telling brings as much joy to the reader as they have brought to me. Again, the more legends like these are told, the better they get! There are many more stories and family history recollections to come in chapter nine which includes many letters sent to my brother and other relatives about our ancestral past.

Chapter Nine

Letters from Home

This chapter is about the family letters that were sent to my brother during the time that he was doing his ancestral research and the impact that their content had on family history. Their importance has to do with what is written but, just as important, is by whom they were written. The letters presented in this chapter were those written by family members that had at their very core the utmost love and concern for their families and for their ancestors that came before. It is important that I record their stories here but it is just as important that I make these relatives "come alive" on these pages. My family was rich with relatives that have shared their letters with my brother when he wrote to them and requested them to relate their knowledge of family history. In many cases they were able to establish a link between our 20th century ancestors and those of the 19th and 18th centuries and sometimes even further back than that.

Included in these pages is a choice selection of letters that will expand upon the ancestral history of the Palmers, Goodsons, Drivers and other families from our ancestral past. Most of our Palmer ancestors loved to talk and were great storytellers and most of them loved to write letters as well. My mother, Mary Elizabeth Palmer Brown, loved to write to all of her friends that she grew up with that had moved far away and she was especially devoted to her oldest son, my brother, who had moved to Chicago and wrote to him two or three times a week. She wrote at least twice a week to her friends and also to her sister, my Aunt Iva Louise Palmer Gamel, who lived in Dixon, Illinois. There were also the letters that she wrote to her mother, Cora Lee Palmer, and to her grandmother, Mary Dizenia (Mammy) Palmer. My mother always kept the letters that she received back from these friends and relatives and I have boxes and boxes of them stored in my garage.

Mostly what I have in this chapter though are the letters that our relatives have written to my brother, James Roger Brown. There are letters from our Aunt Iva Palmer Gamel, from Cora Lee Goodson Palmer, our grandmother, from Rhoda Goodson Boyette and Rowena Goodson

Porterfield, our great aunts, and from other relatives from different parts of the country that my brother discovered as a result of his ancestral research. Rhoda Goodson Boyette and Rowena Goodson Porterfield was our grandmother, Cora Lee Goodson Palmer's half sisters by John Thomas Goodson's previous wife, Mary Ragan. Cora Lee was very close to these sisters and they wrote beautifully and richly informative letters to each other throughout their lives. Both Rhoda and Rowena passed away in 1974. I have included select letters from them to my brother in this chapter.

There are examples of other relatives' letters included and deemed necessary to further enrich the story of my ancestors. In some cases I have included pertinent newspaper clippings that tell of events that were important in the lives of my relatives that were included in the letters sent by them to my brother or to other relatives. My Aunt Iva and my Grandmother Cora Lee were especially prone to send clippings in their letters and the combination of their writing and clippings added a dimension to my story that could not have been achieved by any other means. I start the transcription of these letters with a number of letters from our grandmother, Cora Lee that she wrote to my brother. Included with these letters are also letters written by her half sisters, Rowena and Rhoda.

As stated earlier, Rowena and Rhoda were Cora Lee's half sisters by her father, John Thomas Goodson's, previous wife, Mary Ragan, who passed away after the birth of their last child. Sometime after the death of Mary Ragan Goodson John Thomas met Mary Elizabeth (Mollie) Driver in Anniston, Alabama where he had recently moved. Mollie Driver bore him three children, one of whom was my grandmother, Cora Lee. Rowena and Rhoda loved and watched over their little sister throughout their childhood and were very close to Cora Lee throughout their adult lives. Mary Elizabeth (Mollie) Driver Goodson was a very good wife and mother to her children but she passed away from pneumonia after the birth of her third child, Oscar Goodson, Cora Lee's little brother. After Mollie's death John Thomas married again and moved to Hamilton, Alabama where he bought farm land and built a home. During this time, Cora Lee and Oscar were raised by their step mother for a while until they were taken in by her brother, Thomas Goodson's, mother-in-law, the Preacher Watts' wife. They were raised by Mrs. Watts until they were school age and Cora Lee became very close to the Watts family, especially with Mary Ethel Watts Goodson, Thomas Goodson's wife.

So Cora Lee and Oscar lived in Hamilton, Alabama where their father, John Thomas, had moved but Rowena and Rhoda, who were older, remained in Anniston, Alabama, where they had been raised. Cora Lee would later visit with them when her father and her brother, Oscar, returned to Anniston to work at a factory there in the winter. They would farm their land in spring, summer, and fall but return to Anniston in winter to earn money in order to provide for their family. They would take Cora Lee with them and they would all stay at Uncle Bill Driver's apartment while Cora Lee's father and brother worked. Cora Lee's half sister Rowena got Cora Lee, who was a teenager by now, a job at Woolworth's during World War I. That way Cora Lee could work in the day while her father worked at day and her brother slept, so he could work the night shift at the factory.

I believe Rowena regretted the marriage of their father to his third wife, Jane, because it split the family up and they didn't get to see Cora Lee and Oscar as often as they would've liked. At this point, Rowena and Rhoda still lived in Anniston, Alabama where John Thomas Goodson had moved with his family from Georgia. Eventually, John Thomas moved to Hamilton, Alabama because the land was fertile for farming and didn't have as many rocks in it as the land around the mountains in Anniston. Rowena and Rhoda remained in Anniston where they eventually married and started families of their own. John Thomas bought farm land outside of Hamilton, Alabama, and built a house up from Taylor Road on a little hill close to Harlon Boyette's family (the future in-laws of Rhoda).

When Cora Lee and Oscar reached school age (after spending their youth with the Watts family) they moved back in with their father and Cora Lee lived there until she met Clover and got married on the side of the road next to the little pine tree not far from her father's house. From the time of their marriage on, Rowena and Rhoda kept in touch with Cora Lee and Clover and helped out as much as they could with the raising of Clover and Cora Lee's six children. The Goodsons and Palmers were very close and we have a photograph of Clover and his oldest son, Harrison, sitting alongside John Thomas Goodson and his children and Boyette neighbors in front of John Thomas Goodson's house.

The following letters are from Cora Lee and have included with them some letters from Rowena and Rhoda. As you will see from their letters, Rowena and Rhoda were very helpful in giving aid and comfort to Cora Lee and her children after Clover's death and also very helpful much later in providing ancestral information to my brother as he researched the family's history.

Much of what we know about Clover McKinley Palmer was learned through the stories we heard as children from our mother, from our aunts and uncles, from our grandmother Cora Lee, and from his mother, our great grandmother, Mammy. The many letters that were written to my brother from them in answer to his requests for ancestral information, help to enrich and add personalities to the total ancestral picture. Cora Lee wrote about one of the first pictures of her and Clover in one of her letters. The picture was taken by his mother, Mary Dizenia or Mammy. Cora Lee was going through some of the old photographs that Clover had put away in a box and she wrote this about them:"I have looked at them all day. We look so natural sitting there. This was our first picture together. Clover was the <u>Best</u> looking boy in Hamilton, a good father and good husband. It was hard for me to go through life without him. But I had our children and that has helped me to stand up. I tried to do the things we planned for our children (I mean to bring them up right) and all of them are good children." Cora lee's children were Harrison Roe Palmer, Mary Elizabeth Palmer (our mother), Iva Louise Palmer, Joseph Arthur Palmer, Herbert Hoover Palmer, and Horrice Edward Palmer.

Clover died on September 11, 1930 three days after receiving a serious head injury as a result of a head on collision on a dangerous curved road in northwestern Alabama. It was Cora Lee and Mammy that were left to raise the six children during the beginning phases of the Great Depression. These strong female figures had to hold the family together and assume all the responsibilities of raising their family. Mammy had already experienced what it was like not having a loving father as she had lost her father, Zachariah Gaines Palmer, when she was just nine months old and was raised by her mother Nellie Armstrong Palmer and her new husband, George Weaver, "the bad stepfather". As she grew up with her younger brother Gaines, there was really no loving father figure that she could turn to. After her mother Nellie Armstrong passed away when Mammy was 12, she felt more alone and unloved than ever. Mammy's grandparents, Russell Porter Palmer and Morning Dizenia Palmer, kept and cared for her and her brother as best and as often as they could but they were aging pioneers and could not assume the task all by themselves. Mammy and her brother had to move from "post to pillar", as Mammy put it, and stayed with whatever relatives as would accept to have them. So early on she had to assume the role of caregiver and assume adult responsibilities whether she was ready for them or not. Of course, with Clover's death, Mammy and Cora Lee both had to assume the role of sole parents to Clover's children and thus a strong matriarchal bond was established between them by necessity. Both Mammy and Cora Lee knew what it was like to have been raised by step parents and they had both become strong and self reliant as a result, but they did not want Clover's children to ever experience the often uncaring family environment and undue hardships that they had to endure.

From the same letter, Cora Lee refers to another photograph of Mammy, Gaines Palmer, Mammy's brother, and Taft Palmer, her nephew and writes:"That was good of Mammy, Gaines, and Taft standing by the old fireplace. I could see the wooden window and also the door. There are lots of memories in that old house." This would've been the old Doctor Russell Porter Palmer house that I have written so much about previously and was the house that Clover was born in as well as his son Harrison and daughter, my mother, Mary Elizabeth. If that house's walls could talk what stories it could tell. I will do my best to use my crystal ball though as our story continues.

Cora Lee reminisces about her relatives in many of her letters as when she writes of a cousin whose name was Benjamin Franklin Driver who had recently passed away. One of the brothers of "Frank", as they called him, was George Washington Driver, who they called "Pete". As one can see, it was quite common to name children after presidents and American patriots in the Driver family as it was in the Palmer family. Both families were extremely loyal to the Union as many of their ancestors had fought in the American Revolution against the British.

My brother made copies of all of Clover's photographs that he could obtain and made several prints so that he could send them to all Clover's children and other living relatives. As I wrote before, Clover had taken a correspondence course in photography and taught himself to take pictures and develop them from glass plates inside a makeshift darkroom that he had improvised in his barn. Of these photographs that my brother sent to our Aunt Iva, mother's sister, she related in her letter to Cora Lee:"I always wanted to know who Roger (my brother) looked like." Cora Lee responded in her letter back to Aunt Iva in this way:"Roger didn't look like the Palmers much, but your face was just like my mother's (Mary Elizabeth, Mollie, Driver). Mary Elizabeth also looks a lot like the Drivers and so does Horrice (Clover's youngest son). Harrison (Clover's oldest son) was tall and always looked like Uncle Bill Driver that lived in Anniston, Alabama. Roger (my brother) always seemed quiet natured like the Drivers. Harrison always wanted to sit by himself and study and was a smart man like Clover and the Drivers." Cora Lee relates in the same letter that the Drivers never drank whiskey (very unlike the Palmers who did) or smoke. This is probably why they lived to a ripe old age, such as Uncle Bill Driver who lived to be one hundred and seven years old (this is great but I myself would hate living all those years without having a good drink of whiskey).

My mother, Mary Elizabeth Palmer Brown, observed when she looked at the photograph of Mammy, Gaines, and Taft that the clothes they had on were probably made from cloth that was "home spun" on the old spinning wheel inherited from William Mansell and that they were all "homemade". Indeed, our Palmer, Goodson, and Driver relatives were still self sufficient in the early 20th century and made their own houses, barns, furniture, and much of everything else, including their clothes, just as their ancestors had done before them. One can get an idea of what it must have been like in those days by reading a letter of Cora Lee's to my brother that relates information about the old Doctor Russell Porter Palmer home where Clover was raised. Cora Lee writes:"I was going through some old pictures today. This little picture of Harrison was made at the old Russell Palmer's place where Harrison, Clover and your mother (our mother) was born. The little picture of Harrison is cute with the pigs and chickens all around him. He was feeding the chickens corn and these were the mixed kind of chickens of old time chickens." One can imagine Doctor Russell Porter Palmer and Morning Dizenia feeding their free range chickens, with pigs running about in just about the same way during Civil War days because, at this point, with Harrison feeding the chickens, not all that much had changed.

What I have related earlier in the book about Cora Lee's earlier life was largely taken from one of Cora Lee's letters to my brother that I will include here to provide a more personal view. Cora Lee writes:"Roger, my father left Georgia and Anniston (Alabama) because of so many rocks. He was a real good farmer, one of the best farmers, I guess. So he wanted land that wasn't rocky. Mr. and Mrs. Coffield left Georgia and came to Alabama with my father. Mr. Louis Coffield was our postman. When I was small he came by in a hack. They used hacks and buggies in those days. His oldest boy, John Coffield, was also Postmaster but he was using a car to run his route in Hamilton, Alabama. I used to wash for Mrs. Bertha Coffield, John's wife. Harrison knows their children, Doll, Kitty, and Dona. Dona was Elizabeth and Iva's first schoolteacher. They live in Florence (Alabama) now, but the old ones have passed away, so has my father (John Thomas Goodson) and Uncle Bob his brother." We know the how and why of Cora Lee's coming to Hamilton, Alabama by what she writes in this same letter:"Roger, my father and brother (Oscar) went to Anniston to work in the winter time and took me with them. Rowena (her half sister) lived there, so I got a job in Woolworth's during World War I. Rowena met this Porterfield man in Anniston and they married and went to Birmingham, Alabama. He was a railroad man and had a route up to Chicago, but he is not living now. My father worked on day shift and my brother on night shift. So, you see, I worked to get out so they could sleep. Uncle Bill Driver let us live in one of his apartments, but we went back to farm in spring. We lived then, close to Hamilton."

According to this same letter from Cora Lee there were some Drivers that lived in Tyler, Texas that might be of help with family history and she recommended that Roger try and contact them. As she wrote:"These lived in Texas: Jeska Driver, Fannie Driver Still. Fannie married a Still and she is mother of Helen Still that came to Hamilton with my mother's brother, Uncle Tobe. Her sister is Margaret Still. I don't know what place in Texas they live (we later found out it was Tyler, Texas). I think all my mother's (Mollie Driver) brothers are dead. Mother (Mollie) was the only girl and there was Uncle Tobe, Uncle Bill, Uncle Frank, Uncle Silas, and I don't know the other's names." My brother was able to make contact with these Texas Drivers and eventually find out more about the Driver ancestry.

In another letter Cora Lee tells more about her father and mother and relates information written by her half sister Rowena Porterfield:"Mary Elizabeth "Mollie" Driver was my mother. My father (John Thomas Goodson) was the one that said my grandmother (Martha M. Britt) was half Indian and said he could see it in my children." The later part of this letter is probably what led to my brother's further research on the Texas Drivers. Cora Lee refers to what her half sister has written:"Rowena said we might write to Marion Wesley Driver in Arp, Texas. He is Uncle Silas Driver's son. She said he was a nice person. She said some of them lived in Tyler, Texas. A lady said to write to the Postmaster at these places and ask about Drivers."

Cora Lee's other half sister, Rhoda Boyett, was able to give some more in depth information on the Goodson side of the family. Rhoda wrote to Roger:"Michael Goodson (my grandfather and your great grandfather) sold goods in Atlanta. I don't know if he lived there but John Goodson and Laura Goodson was born and raised in Villa Rica, Georgia. Michael Goodson's mother lived somewhere within a mile or so of him. I don't know what her name was. She was a Quaker in belief. My great grandmother, Mary Hurt, lived somewhere around 10 or 15 miles away. My father said she could walk it in a day. There were three Michael Goodson children: Laura, John, and Bob. Bob was a baby when his mother died and a family named Harper took him and cared for him. His father sent him clothes and things and this family finally moved to Randolph County, Alabama. His father and John would visit him and that is where John Goodson met his first wife and married. He bought land and lived there until she died and he later married Mary Elizabeth (Mollie) Driver (our great grandmother) at Anniston, Alabama. Laura Goodson didn't have any children. She married a man named Wasaman (I don't know his given name) and lived on grandfather's old place in Villa Rica until she died. Bob Goodson had 6 or 7 children but they all died but around 2. I don't know their address but they live around Heflin, Alabama. They always said my great grandmother Goodson and her family came from across the water. I don't know where, but they always said they were part Irish. It was John Goodson born 1855 and not Michael. I don't know when he was born – I guess around 1825 (1821). Michael Goodson's father left one day (the ancestor they said fell in a hole) to go see about something and never came back. They think he got killed or died – there was no way of finding out anything much them days. Michael Goodson was Justice of the Peace. I don't think he lived in Atlanta. He sold goods there and might have lived there for a while, but he owned land in Villa Rica and lived there when he died."

Rhoda Boyette was also able to further inform us about our Palmer ancestry as she wrote additionally in the same letter:"William Russell

Palmer married Susan "Sook" Nichols and they had five children. He quit her and married a Lewis girl. One of them five children (of William Russell and Susan Sook) named John (the infamous "Blue John") was supposed to be Clover's father. Susan "Sook" Nichols was Cobe Nichols girl. Her mother was a Cole before she married Cobe. If Sook Nichols had any other name, I can't find out what it was. Old man Russell Porter Palmer was born in Georgia they say. I am sending you a picture of Uncle Tobe Driver. He is Cora Lee's mother's brother, your great, great uncle – it is a good picture and just like him. I have a door stop (I am sure that you never saw one) that my father John Goodson made some time, when I see you or some of the family, I will give it to you. It is made of wood to fasten to the floor to stop the door from going back too far. Oscar (Rhoda's half brother) left your letter here for me to tell what I know about the Goodsons. I am a bit older than he is. I am 84 years old and awful nervous so don't be surprised at this letter being no better." I am sure that my brother was happy to get such a fine letter from such a loving and knowledgeable source as our great aunt of 84 years of age. Would that most of us could have the great recollections from the past and presence of mind to relate them that she possessed. Rhoda was old enough to remember many of our ancestors and was able to link the 19th and 20th centuries together for us. It was also enlightening to learn how similar we all are to the ancestors that we came from. There are really no better words or no better documentation than the letters of surviving relatives who can remember and are articulate enough to write their memories down for their descendants to read. Rhoda's handwriting may have been shaky but her memory for recalling the past was as solid and as firm as an old oak.

Cora Lee wrote many letters to Roger and among them was this one which included some additional family information. Here she states that the old set of Palmers (Doctor Russell Porter Palmer's family) had 12 boys and 1 girl, which I believe is incorrect as records show 11 boys and 1 girl, 12 children in all. I include her words here:"I know about the old set of Palmers. There were 12 boys and 1 girl. The girl married a Cooper (the same Cooper whose mother carried him as a baby from Tennessee to Marion County, Alabama). We went and visited her when Clover went to the King Church House to sing (this would've been one of the Sacred Harp Singings). Her name was Elizabeth Palmer before she married Cooper. The boys I know was Dr. Ellis Palmer, Preacher Bud Palmer, the one who married Clover and me, Joe Palmer (Russell's oldest son), Heze (Hezekiah) Palmer, Grant Palmer, Russ Palmer a writing teacher – the most beautiful writing I ever saw. He lived in Arkansas. His boy, Blue John they called him, is Clover's dad. Old Dr. Russell Palmer was father of all 12 boys and 1 girl. Dr. Russell's wife's name was Morning Dizenia (Mansell)." Morning Dizenia Mansell was the daughter of Morning Dove White, the Cherokee Indian who married William Mansell. So Cora Lee was able to remember much about her relatives and Clover's and was able to write letters to Roger giving a treasure trove of information. Another treasure trove was Clover's photography of many of these same relatives.

Cora Lee sent letters to Roger of great importance about her youth and early years with Clover as well, which gives insight into what their lives were like around the 1920's. Of great interest also, was more information on Mammy's relatives in one of her letters:"I'm thinking of some things you might like to know. Mammy's mother was an Armstrong and also Uncle Bud Palmer's wife was an Armstrong and they were sisters. Also Mammy's Dad and Uncle Bud Palmer were brothers, so Mammy's parents had double first cousins. So was Aunt Linda Kennedy who was a sister to Mammy's mother. She was an Armstrong before marriage. The three were sisters, Margaret, Linda, and Nellie, I think, was the name of Mammy's mother. Aunt Linda lived close to the White House Church of Christ, not but about 20 miles from Hamilton, Alabama. We would go up there (this is another church where the Sacred Harp Singings took place) when we were young in Clover's car back then 50 years ago before Harrison was born. Sometimes we would have a flat tire and he had to get out and patch it himself. Everybody took their patching material with them then. But you can imagine Clover's white shirt on that day. But we were young and gay and forgot about the tire. So we sang, and had dinner on the grounds tables. We had lots of fun meeting everyone. I loved Aunt Linda. I say Aunt, because Clover and Mammy said Aunt. Her children married Howels and Burlisons. So my children are related to the Armstrongs, Kennedys, and Burlisons that's up close to Haleyville, Alabama, 40 miles from Hamilton, Alabama. So my grandmother was a Hurt. Mary Homer Hurt visited me and Clover when Iva was a baby. We are related to the Wagners and Stephens. I'll write Rhoda and see who Uncle Bob Goodson's wife was before marriage – they called her Aunt Coon. Also, I'll find out who Aunt Laura Goodson married. I believe he is a German (Wasaman we found out later). I'll try to get the name of Aunt Coon before marriage. You see, this is my father's sister's (Laura) husband and my father's brother's wife, so I know you will want these, Roger. Uncle Tobe Driver's wife was Texanne Galbreath. Doc Galbreath is her brother and his children married Palmers, 3 of them. Talking about names, Harrison was named after a president, Herbert Hoover was named after a president, and Horrice Edward was named after a doctor, Doctor Horrice Edward + Palmer." So in this one letter we have a wealth of information about Cora Lee's and Clover's ancestors.

My Aunt Iva Louise Palmer was the third child of Clover and Cora Lee born February 25, 1924. My mother, Mary Elizabeth Palmer was the second child born March 24, 1922. Harrison Roe Palmer, the first child, was born January 23, 1920. The three other boys were Joseph Arthur born May 10, 1926, Herbert Hoover born April 2, 1928, and Horrice Edward born April 17, 1930. My mother and Aunt Iva were very close throughout their childhood and remained very close throughout their adult years until my mother passed away at age 84 in 2006. As stated before, they wrote each other at least twice a week all of their lives and we visited Aunt Iva and her family in Illinois every three years or so in summer and they visited us as often in Alabama. Our families were very close and remain so. I was especially close to Aunt Iva's children, my cousins Trudy and Bennett Gamel. In fact, Trudy and I had crushes on each other all throughout childhood, which I think is a common trait with cousins in the Palmer family.

To better understand Aunt Iva I think it is important for one to know of her childhood and how the tragic events that occurred within it affected her then and afterwards as an adult. Of course the tragic events that surrounded the death of her father Clover deeply affected all of his and Cora Lee's children. My mother was eight when Clover died on September 11, 1930 and Aunt Iva was six, so one can well imagine the traumatic affect that his death had on such impressionable young children.

Clover died as a result of a horrific auto accident that caused a fatal brain injury. He was only 31 years old and had just begun his promising and brilliant life as father, husband, and talented photographer, songwriter, and artist. He was a very handsome and dashing young man with dark wavy black hair and with the very prominent and distinguished features that most males in the Palmer family were known for. His father, grandfather, great grandfather, uncles and cousins were all known to be "lady killers" and Clover was the most dashing of all with the good looks of a "Valentino" silent movie star. Clover's endearing personality and winning ways matched his good looks and all his family and his friends loved and respected him deeply. So one can well imagine how his children must have idolized him, especially young Mary Elizabeth and Iva Louise.

When a neighbor came and knocked on Cora Lee's door that night of September 8, 1930 and told her that Clover had been in a bad car accident, she and her children had no idea how their lives were about to tragically change. Clover survived in a coma for three days in a Jasper, Alabama, hospital, before finally passing away. Cora Lee and his mother, Mary Dizenia (Mammy), sat by his side for three days and three nights hoping that he would regain consciousness but he never did. He groaned in pain and it seemed that he tried to speak but he could not.

The children visited the hospital while Clover was there and my mother remembered walking down the dimly lit corridor of the hospital that led to his room. She was with her mother, Cora Lee, and the other children on the way to Clover's room, all the while listening in fear and trepidation to her father's groans of pain as she hesitantly approached his room. My mother knew nothing of the future movies of Federico Fellini but this cold dark corridor must have had the same chilling surreal affect as her mother pulled her slowly toward what she sensed was the doom and darkness of her father's room. Iva was with her older sister and tried to match the courage that her sister managed to muster. Harrison the oldest boy was leading the way with Joseph Arthur timidly holding onto his hand. Harrison would now have to be the man of the family at 10 years old and Joseph Arthur at 4 years old would, doubtless, not remember much of what had befallen his family and him. Little Herbert at 2 years old and Horrice at 5 months old had been left with neighbors while the rest of the family visited their dying father.

The children that came had to endure the horror of what awaited them in their father's room. The person who lay there underneath the tightly made sheets of the hospital bed groaning with guttural cries of anguish that they had not yet witnessed on this earth could not have been their handsome, loving and nurturing father but instead must've been a gruesome stranger whose head was wounded and covered with white bandages. His eyes were black and blue around the sockets and his mouth grimaced with each struggling breath that he took. All of their father's beautiful, wavy black hair was covered with all the thick white bandages that were necessary to cover his awful head wound. His injury was caused when a long metal lever from his car's windshield had pierced his skull and passed through his brain. It was said when the accident occurred that a woman who lived in a white house next to the road had heard the loud crash of metal when the vehicles collided and went to see what had happened. She could see the awful head wound and the blood pouring from Clover's head as Clover's friends were removing him from the car. The woman asked how she could help and Willie Calvin, Clover's best friend, asked if she had some sheets at her house that could be used to bandage Clover's head. She returned quickly to her house and she brought back the sheets and a small silver platter to the crash site so that it could be placed over the open wound on his head where his brain was exposed. With the woman's help Willie managed to place the small platter over the wound and the woman tore the sheets into strips that they wrapped around Clover's head. It wasn't long before a limousine approached and they were able to flag it down and lift Clover up into the back seat and transport him to the hospital in Jasper, Alabama. Someone, we assume Willie, had to arrange that silver platter in place with the makeshift bandages around Clover's head and hold them in place with pressure applied until they made the thirty minute or so trip to the hospital. How Clover survived the long trip to Jasper hospital and remained alive for three days after was amazing and a testament to his strong will to live. He tried desperately to survive but sadly lost his battle on the third and final day.

Of course my mother and my Aunt Iva did not know at that time the extent of their father's injury or how it was caused or about the horrific details of it all. They just saw their father replaced by a monstrous presence that lay groaning in pain before them and that is what they remembered all the rest of their lives. Gone were the joyous, sunny day memories of sharing an outing getting an ice cream cone or having a hot dog in their father's café, or shopping for toys, costume jewelry, clothes, or dolls at the five and dime store with their beloved and handsome father. Gone were the sounds of his inspirational Sacred Harp music played on the organ in their house or sung with his resounding baritone voice at church. Gone were the stories about the "Old Set" of Palmers that he would tell them about around the fireplace before kissing them and sending them to bed at night. Never again would they see him cut hair in his barber shop or cook hot dogs in his café or develop photographs in his darkroom. He would never draw pictures for them or practice his "Palmer Style" handwriting for them ever again. They would never see him build a house or a barn with his own hands again and they would never go for a ride in the country on Sundays in his car again, for that car had fatally injured him and left in his place the monster that lay dying before them.

When Clover died he "lay in state" at their house overnight and was buried at the Palmer Cemetery after his service at the Palmer Church outside of Hamilton, Alabama, the next day. People old enough to remember said that there were cars lining both sides of the dirt road leading to the church and cemetery and many people had to park far away and walk a good distance to attend Clover's funeral. At the visitation at their house the night before all the Palmer and Goodson relatives and all Clover's friends and cousins attended and paid their respects including the families of the Burlisons, Boyettes, Kennedys, Armstrongs, Howells, Hurts, Wagners, Stephens, and Galbreaths, just to mention a few. They all tried to remember the good times they had with Clover and praise his contributions and good deeds that had benefitted everyone throughout the community over the years. They talked about what a good life he had led and how he would live on in people's memories long after his death.

All of the condolences and best wishes and praise didn't help my mother, Aunt Iva, or the other children much though because they had lost their father and so much of their young lives had been lost along with his that could never be regained or replaced. Mother remarked many times later that the casket should not have remained open and the children should not have been allowed to see their father covered with those awful bandages. The last memory that they had of their loving, beautiful father should not have been one of such abject horror that would deeply affect all of them the rest of their lives.

The next day after Clover's service at the Palmer Church they buried him at the adjoining Palmer Cemetery between the Indian rock graves of Russell Porter Palmer and Morning Dizenia Palmer, his great grandparents and the grave of his grandfather, Mammy's father, Zachariah Gaines Palmer. As if having to see their father "laying in state" in the open casket were not enough, the children now had to sit by their father's freshly dug grave and watch his casket being lowered into the ground. It was too much for Iva and she fainted. She was very deeply affected by it and she had trouble adjusting to being around people for a long time after that. She was just entering school at the little one room schoolhouse out in the country where they first moved to live with their grandpa, John Thomas Goodson, after Clover's death. They later lived in one of John Thomas Goodson's sharecropper houses for a while before moving back to the town of Hamilton and living in the house on Third Avenue that Clover had built for them. During her first weeks of school Iva had a hard time acclimating to the new social situation and schoolroom environment that was now thrust upon her. She was six years old and felt isolated in her world with no father to love her and protect her anymore. She did not trust the other school children and sometimes they teased her for being "a little orphan girl". She wasn't used to this kind of treatment as her father had always been proud of her and shielded her from all abuse. So Iva had a lot of adjusting to do and at first she did not want to participate and learn anything at school. She just wanted to have her loving father back again. Good for Iva there was an excellent teacher at the school that helped her regain her self confidence and instilled in her a new sense of pride and independence. Her teacher, Mrs. Dona Coffield, gained Iva's respect and admiration and Iva began to rise above the agonizing weight of grief that had held her down since her father's death.

Mrs. Dona Coffield was most adept at teaching Iva her ABC's, but more importantly, she brought Iva out of her shell and took what was a very shy, introverted and tragically sad child and produced a happy, outgoing, self assured and extroverted one. There was an incident at Iva's school, among many incidents, that made her feel unwanted, rejected and that reinforced her tendencies toward being a loner and a social misfit. After school one day some of Iva's older female cousins gathered together to gossip as they always did and when Iva and her young friends approached them to join in the conversation they were immediately scolded and told to go away. As Aunt Iva told the story, these were the older cousins' words: "You young uns go away cuz we old uns want to talk about our beaus!" This was just another slight and rejection that Iva had to endure and she and her young friends were downcast and walked away dejected and with tears rolling down their cheeks. Mrs. Dona Coffield was leaving the school house with one of her teacher friends and looked over and saw what had transpired with Iva and the other children. Dona was on her way to the new car that she had parked next to the school and was about to give her friend a ride home. Dona's car was a brand new bright blue Model "A" Ford sedan and was the envy of all the students and teachers alike. The students all wished that Mrs. Dona would give them a ride in her new car sometime. In fact, Dona used this to her advantage by offering to give rides to the students who excelled at their lessons and who achieved the most positive results with their schoolwork. So far none of the students had earned this honor and privilege of being the first to ride in Mrs. Dona Coffield's brand new shiny blue car.

When Dona saw Iva crying and dejected by her cousins, she got into her car, with her teacher friend sitting in the passenger seat, and she drove over next to Iva and her friends and announced to her: "Iva, how would you and your friends like to ride with us in the back seat of my brand new car? I can drive all of you home as it is on my way!" One must remember that this was at the beginning of the Great Depression in rural Alabama and people barely had enough money to buy food for their families much less buy a fancy new car. So when one had the chance to ride in one, one snapped it up like grabbing a shiny new silver dollar lying on the sidewalk in front of them. Aunt Iva's eyes brightened, her tears dried up and went away and she ran as fast as she could up to Dona's new car. Iva's friends were right behind in quick pursuit and they all jumped in the car as Dona's teacher friend swung the back door open. The children were like hungry bunnies hopping around in a carrot patch as they piled into Dona's back seat. Iva claimed the passenger side back seat next to the rear window so that all of her snobbish cousins could see her as the car approached them. Iva sat proudly upright with her head held high, beaming and smiling ear to ear as Dona drove right past her callous cousins that had humiliated her earlier. All the cousins were green with envy as Iva and her friends rode happily past them and the clouds of dirt stirred up from Dona's car wheels enveloped them in a fog of discontent.

With this event, a bright new day had opened for Iva. From that day forward Iva was a prize student in school and someday she would become a school teacher in a little one room schoolhouse in rural Illinois herself. From that day forward there was nothing that Iva could not accomplish because Dona Coffield told her so and, besides, she was a Palmer and Palmers can do anything once they set their minds to it. When Dona Coffield offered to give Iva and her friends a ride home in her brand new car it was like her father Clover was alive there with her again and driving her home from school just like he used to do when he took her for rides in his Model "A" Ford on Sunday afternoons. Iva understood from that day forward that her father would always be with her and that he would always love her and protect her – she felt this in her heart and a shining brightness took hold of her soul that cast away the darkness of Clover's death away forever. She knew that her father was in the hereafter watching over her and that someday she would see him again and that he would take her hand in his and show her the way as he had always done on earth.

Aunt Iva's letters to my brother reveal our past history in ways that we would've never known without her. I include this first one dated 4 – 3 – 1989: "I decided to get my old notes out of the Bank Box and put my awful scribbles into a form someone could read – the only people who can read my writing are Gerald, Elizabeth, Roger, Trudy and Bennett (and me). I wrote all this down in January, 1950 when Mammy came up to Rock Falls (Illinois) and stayed several weeks before and after Trudy was born. We had a lot of time to sit and talk and she gave me the full names of the "old set" and other info. Its lain in my box all these years except for when I gave a lot of it to you when you asked. I borrowed the info on Michael Goodson and Allen Berryman Driver from you. All else came from Mammy except for the legend of Russell Porter Palmer and his mom and brothers leaving Carolina because of his father's death and 2nd family being cut out, etc.- this is what I heard years ago from some other Palmers. Mammy did often speak of the little black boy and his chant to grandpa about breakfast – that always led me to believe they had at least house slaves or servants. Mammy also said North Carolina and I wrote that down in 1950 as she told me – bear in mind she was 68 at that time (that is my age now as I copy). You and Arthur say South Carolina and you are probably right. I wish we knew which county so we could go back there and research as you did on Goodson and Driver (my brother did do this in South Carolina in 1991). If there is any part of what I'm sending you don't agree with or wish to correct, just mark it out. Mammy's legend of why Grandpap (Russell Porter Palmer) stopped in Hamilton or Bexar was that, and here are Mammy's words "Grandpap said, when he saw Dizenia Mansell, I thought that was the prettiest girl I ever had seen!" I believe him! In her picture she is old but those features of face are still evident."

Aunt Iva includes in her letter "Conversations with Dizenia" her typed copies of all her notes with Mammy and everyone else's information. It is copied and included here:

"Conversations with Dizenia"

Palmer/Goodson families – as recorded by Iva Louise Gamel from conversations with Dizenia Palmer, her grandmother, during various visits to Alabama Also, there is included research by her nephew, Roger Brown. (notes are typed by Gerald Gamel – Apr., 1989)

Ancestors of Iva Palmer Gamel & My Brothers and Sister:

Russell Porter Palmer & Dizenia Mansell Palmer _ (parents of 11 sons & 1 daughter.) Russell Porter Palmer came to Alabama with his mother and two brothers, Joe and Ben, from the Carolinas, which one is not confirmed … possibly on the borders of the two states.(This was however later confirmed to be Union, South Carolina by my brother's research). They had come through Georgia and most of Alabama…and stopped at Bexar (in the SW part of Marion County, about 5 miles from the County Seat of Hamilton) where "Grandpap" (Russell Porter Palmer) met a local girl. Her name was Dizenia Mansell. She also was called "Morning Dizenia" but no one knows why (we now know that she was named after her Cherokee Indian mother, Morning Dove White Mansell). According to Mammy, Grandpap said "I saw the most beautiful girl I ever saw in my life!" So - he had no reason to continue their trip to Arkansas. His brother Ben went "north" (how far is not known!). Mammy wasn't sure if the other brother, Joe, went on or whether the mother stayed or went on with either Ben or Joe (we know now that she stayed and when she died was buried in Marion County, Alabama). Russell and Dizenia homesteaded near Hamilton….about 3 or 4 miles west. The area became known as "Palmer" (not incorporated) but still called that today!! All early and some recent Palmers are buried in the cemetery, and most recently, others than Palmers in the "Palmer" community.

Russell and Dizenia's children were: **1.** Joseph Howard Palmer – "Joe" **2.** Benjamin Franklin Palmer – "Ben" **3.** Hezekiah White Palmer - "Hez" **4.** William Russell Palmer – "Russ" lived in Arkansas (the father of John Russell "Blue John" Palmer) **5.** George Flowers Palmer – "George" **6.**

Thompson LaFayette Palmer – "Fayette" was father of Martha Ballard, 1st cousin & good friend of Mammy. **7.** Doctor John Howard Palmer – "Doc" not a title – a nickname probably! (This was Joel Palmer's great grandfather) **8.** Zachariah Gaines Palmer – "Gaines" our Great Grandfather! **9.** Estern Augusta Palmer – "Bud" father of Triforcia Palmer Nichols and Estern Palmer and Trivinia Palmer-------------- and Russ Palmer who's only child was Preacher Joel Reedus Palmer, whom Gerald & I met in Rock Falls in the early 50's when he conducted a revival at the Assembly of God Church there over a two week period! Trivinia was mother of Aussie Lee----------- --- Harrison was graduated with Dayton Nichols from HHS – Hamilton High School. Estern Palmer's son "Estern Palmer" was much admired by Gerald, who called him "A true noble Patrician! **10.** Alexander Sherman Palmer – "Alex" – A Physician & Surgeon who was graduated from medical college in Nashville, I understand. He practiced in Winston County, Alabama. I grew up hearing Mammy say that "Uncle Alex married a 'Nice Northern Woman' " After I met Gerald and developed a "Northern Awareness" I asked Mammy where in the north was Uncle Alex's wife from? She replied, "Paducah, Kentucky!" (I think to Mammy anything north of Alabama was "north"). **11.** General Grant Palmer – "Grant" – This General Grant name along with "Alexander" & "LaFayette" and "Sherman" indicates Grandpap's feeling for the Union (the North) – for strong leadership & loyalty also, for education, (Benjamin Franklin & William Russell), and knowledge of the Bible, (Hezekiah & Zachariah & Joseph). He must have been well schooled on that Carolina plantation/ farm from which he, his brothers, and his mother were forced to leave! Legend). **12.** Dizenia Elizabeth Palmer – "Sis" – Now we know from whom our Liz (my mother and Aunt Iva's sister) got her name and nickname! "Aunt Sis" married Jim Cooper, who lived near Sulligent, Alabama (this is the Jim Cooper whose mother carried him as a baby from Tennessee to Marion County, Alabama). These were known as the "Old Set"!

Now, I want to refer to our Palmer Antiques. The big spinning wheel Mammy gave Trudy, when she was 3 years old, was made for Grandpap's wife, Dizenia Mansell Palmer (Morning Dizenia), by her father in his woodworking shop. Grandfather Mansell gave it to her when she was married. Her first son, Joseph Howard Palmer, according to Mammy, was "almost" old enough to fight in the Civil War (we know now that he did fight and actually recruited others to fight with the Union)....so we estimate the wheel to be about 142 to 143 years old (in 1980) –and was probably made between 1846 – 1848. At her death, Grandpa's only daughter, Aunt Sis (Dizenia Elizabeth Palmer Cooper) kept the wheel for years after her mother's death. Then, Aunt Lucrecia, who was Uncle George Flowers Palmer's wife, had it for 3 or 4 years after Aunt Sis's death, then sold it to Mammy! Trudy's grandparents, William and Gertrude Gamel, gave Mammy the money to buy it from Aunt Lucrecia. After keeping it in her home for about two years, Mammy asked us to take it to our home to keep for Trudy until she was ready for it. This occurred about 6/7 years ago, when they bought their present home in Rochester, Illinois, just a few miles southeast of Springfield, state capitol of Illinois.

The other antiques include: A Civil War belt buckle with C. S. A. letters on it had been given to Mammy from someone in her family, which was divided…some Union…some Confederate. She said Russell Porter— (Grandpap) was on the Union side, but didn't fight as he was too old. And I'll add, had too many children to leave for war. We have Russell Porter Palmer's wall-mounted coffee grinder – more than 130 years old. She told me we could have it…and told Gerald to climb up into the attic of her little house in Hamilton and get it for me. He did. He also removed the rust…painted it with a black paint…mounted it on a special wood mounting he made…and we've had it on our kitchen wall in 3 different homes. Also Mammy gave me an iron wash pot on legs…so it could sit on hot coals in the fireplace. It's been in the family for years. We call them Palmer treasures…not antiques!

Mammy's other grandfather was named Armstrong. He was Irish. Her Grandmother Armstrong was Dutch. The Armstrongs came to Winston County, Alabama from Blount County, Georgia. Grandpap's name was James Stewart Armstrong. His wife was Mary Polly Armstrong. Their children were Mary Elizabeth (Nellie), who married Zachariah Gaines Palmer, one of the 11 set…Margaret married Zachariah Gaines' brother, Estern (Bud). Mammy was a "double" first cousin to Uncle Bud's children. Another Armstrong daughter, Linda (called Linde), married________ Kennedy. Also, the Armstrong girls had a brother, William (Billie), who made a little slate for Mammy's mother, Nellie, to use in school. This was passed down to Mammy who gave it to me. I, in turn, gave it to Trudy who became a school teacher. Grandpap Armstrong, prior to being in Blount County, Georgia, had been in the state of Ohio, according to Mammy.

As you know, people in Winston County declared themselves as "THE FREE STATE OF WINSTON" and many fought in the Northern Army. Zachariah Gaines Palmer and his wife, Nellie Armstrong Palmer's children were Elizabeth (who married Mr. Barnes). These were Destie Parrish's parents. Also, another daughter was Mary Dizenia Palmer (Mammy), and a son was named Zachariah Gaines Palmer. He and his wife Ellie had two sons...Taft Palmer and Ralph Palmer. Mary Dizenia (Mammy) also had a half-sister, called "Sister Lindy" Poore, and a half-brother, Gaither Weaver. Mammy became very close to Sister Lindy late in life, after Sister Lindy was able to get "out of the hills" and come to town more often. Sister Lindy had the soul of a saint and brought much companionship to Mammy in her later years. Mammy's full sister, Elizabeth, died at an early age. I'm not sure if Elizabeth had other children besides Destie.

Earlier I spoke about Grandpap Russell Porter Palmer, his two brothers and mother being "forced to leave their home in the Carolinas". According to the legend, my 3rd great grandfather came to North Carolina from England...some say Wales. He had many children by his first marriage. His first wife died. He married again (<u>she</u> was my 3rd great grandmother). They had at least three sons...Grandpap Russell Porter Palmer, Joe and Ben. Apparently, when their father died, the laws of the state gave his property to the <u>first</u> <u>family's</u> <u>sons</u>. (The laws of the first colonies were based on English law, and it is theorized that inheritances in early U.S. states followed the principle of oldest son as beneficiary.) I believe that Russell Porter Palmer's family in the Carolinas was fairly well off. Mammy, who spent several years, off and on, in her childhood at Grandpaps...told me that Grandpap often told her about a little black boy who served him as a child back in the Carolinas. He repeated what the little boy chanted to him each morning as he awakened..."some eggs...some sausage...some cakes...for mastah thisss mmoannnen...!?!?..."

In spite of my own early appreciation for my Palmer background, and my love and admiration for Mammy, I rebelled against the Palmers ONCE. It was during the deep depression of the 30's. Mammy would not allow me to spend a dime which was "burning my fingers"!! I rushed for paper and pen...and became an instant poet! I wrote—"SAVE SAVE SAVE, THAT'S THE PALMER WAY, SAVE SAVE SAVE FOR A RAINEY DAY! BUT, THAT RAINEY DAY HAS NEVER COME YET, AND THAT'S JUST A GOOD EXAMPLE OF

THE OLD PALMER SET!"

Now, let's turn to the Goodsons….Dizenia's son, Clover McKinley Palmer married Cora Lee Goodson in March 1919. Their six children… in order of appearance…were: Harrison Roe Palmer – born January 23, 1920 (Harry) Mary Elizabeth Palmer Brown (Sis) – born March 24, 1922 Iva Louise Palmer Gamel (Ivie) – born February 25, 1924 Joseph Arthur Palmer (Joe) – born May 10, 1926   Herbert Hoover Palmer (Herbert) – born April 2, 1928   Horrice Edward Palmer (Tubby – only used as a baby!) – born April 17, 1930 (Cora Lee was the daughter of John Thomas Goodson and Molly Driver Goodson).

Grandpa John Goodson, of English descent, came to Hamilton from Villa Rica, Georgia (midway between Atlanta and the Alabama state line) via Anniston, Alabama. His first marriage was to Mary Reagan. This union produced five children…Thomas Goodson…Rhoda Goodson Boyett…Rowena Goodson McKay Porterfield…Warner Goodson…and Mary Louis (Chip) Goodson Fikes. After Mary died, Grandpa Goodson married Molly Driver of Carrollton, Georgia, whom, I believe, had moved to Anniston, Alabama. To this union were born four children, two of which survived babyhood. They are Oscar Goodson and Cora Lee Goodson. John Thomas Goodson's father was Michael Goodson, 1st Lt. 37th Military District of Carroll County, Georgia. He served the Confederacy in the militia under Lt. Col. Ely Benson. Michael Goodson was an original settler of Villa Rica, Georgia according to Roger Brown's research.

Cora Lee's mother, Molly, was the daughter of Allen Berryman Driver and Martha Smith Driver. Allen's parents both came from North Carolina (Roger Brown research). Molly Driver had two brothers, Uncles Bill and Tobe (Tobias?) Driver. They went out to Texas where they became a part of the "oil rush" according to Momma and Aunt Rowena. They were big, powerfully built men. I remember seeing them on a rare visit to Hamilton. Arthur gave me a picture of one of Uncle Bill's granddaughters who visited Hamilton after World War Two. (I especially thank Roger Brown for his research on Molly Driver Goodson, because she died when Cora Lee was less than two years old, and because Momma could tell us nothing about her mother, except what she heard from Aunt Rowena and Aunt Rhoda. I always felt a real sadness that Momma could tell us nothing about our real grandmother on the Goodson side. Roger brought her "Alive" for us with pictures, with certificates, and information that he obtained on a trip to a

Georgia county seat. Momma was born January 2, 1902 in Bexar, Alabama (Barnesville Community). She died January 29, 1988 in Birmingham, Alabama, age 86. She was buried January 31st, 1988 at Hamilton City Cemetery on a spot where our home once stood. Clover was born January 8, 1899 at Hamilton (Palmer Community—in Grandpap's house). He died September 11, 1930 in Jasper, Alabama Hospital. He is buried in Palmer Cemetery. Mary Dizenia Palmer (Mammy) was born January 4, 1882 in Winston County (upon later research probably Marion, County). She died March 23, 1963 in Hamilton at age 81. She is buried in Palmer Cemetery.

Aunt Iva ends her "Conversations with Dizenia" with this note: "My best memory of Dizenia and Cora Lee was that, in spite of any differences between them, they had a singleness of purpose: To get Clover's little brood raised in a way that he would have been proud."

I think that Aunt Iva's letters and her "Conversations with Dizenia" add a richness to our family history that could not have been gained in any other way and that is why have included so many of them in my book. I have selected a few more insightful contributions from her and from other outstanding relatives' samples which will follow:

My Aunt Iva wrote many more letters to Roger and I found one in which she discusses "Blue John", Clover's father, to be of particular interest:"I'm sure that it was Uncle Russ who went to Arkansas who was the father of John "Blue John", father of Clover. Russ went to Arkansas and I understand he was in the jewelry, watch repair, etc., business and fairly well off. The son John was the only one I ever heard about, (Naturally it couldn't be discussed too much!) though, I'm sure there were other children. John just happened to be the one who spent summers at his grandfather's home in Alabama. Uncle Russ was also the talented one at decorative writing, the old fashioned type you see in the Bible, etc. The old set insisted that the Palmer method of writing which was used in schools by everyone my age and older was started by our ancestors. I have no way of proving this. My father (Clover) also did a decorative writing – beautiful hand."

In the same letter, Aunt Iva also discusses Destie Parrish who was Mammy's niece with whom I associate bad memories. I remember her at the visitation of Mammy's funeral in which Mammy lay in state overnight at her home. Destie had come from Arkansas where she lived supposedly to pay her respects but she was much more interested in scurrying about Mammy's house looking under things and behind pictures and beds, etc. We all figured out later that she must have known that Mammy hid her money in the house and didn't trust banks. Destie was looking for Mammy's money that she would tuck away in a safe place to pay bills or in case of emergency. Turns out that Mammy did tuck away about $600.00 in an envelope that my Uncle Horrice had found before Destie could get to it. Mammy had told Uncle Horrice where her hiding place was and that she had some money there to help pay for her funeral as she did not want to be a burden to her grandchildren. Destie certainly had other plans for Mammy's money and I have never had anything good to say about her since. Aunt Iva writes:"You see, Destie would be Daddy's age or slightly older, so would have been a child if she was born at all, when John (Blue John) came through Alabama. Mammy was Destie's aunt. Destie's mother was Mammy's sister Elizabeth. She (Elizabeth) married a Barnes. So there were Elizabeth, Dizenia, and Gaines, children of Gaines Palmer and Mary (Nellie) Armstrong. Then Gaines died and Mammy's mother later married a George Weaver. He was the bad stepfather that Mammy talked about."

This letter of Aunt Iva's is important as it establishes the beginning of a storyline about Blue John and where he came from and how he came to be in Alabama. He obviously visited Alabama each summer as Aunt Iva wrote, but he would have to have been there in spring of 1898 to have gotten Mary Dizenia pregnant with her child Clover that was born on January 8, 1899. Blue John Palmer stayed at his grandfather, Russell Porter Palmer's homestead, where Mary Dizenia Palmer (Mammy) would have been a frequent visitor. The two first cousins most likely were together often and most certainly developed a close bond early on which soon led to that fateful encounter in the "fields of clover". Of interest here too is the mention of Mammy's stepfather, George Weaver, who Mammy's mother Nellie married after the death of Gaines, Mammy's father and Blue John's uncle. Mammy told of him being the bad stepfather and one's imagination could run rampant with trying to ascertain why he was so bad. So we can begin to see a story unfolding here, albeit more legend than a story. Two young people who just happen to be first cousins are both rebellious due to their enduring of personal and/or family conflicts and are drawn even closer together as they commiserate about it quietly to themselves. Blue John may have been sent to Alabama to have his grandfather teach him lessons from the old set of Palmer discipline and work ethic to be gained from working in the cotton fields of Alabama. Old Doctor Russell Porter Palmer had most surely straightened out many a youth in his large family of twelve children with his numerous grandchildren and John Russell," Blue John" Palmer, would've been no exception. Mary Dizenia Palmer visited her grandfather often because she loved him dearly but also, most likely, because she needed time away from the bad stepfather, George Weaver, and she hoped that she would have courage enough to tell someone her plight. In her first cousin, Blue John, who was six years her senior, she may have found the older more mature person who she hoped would be a true friend, confidant, and father figure that she so urgently needed. Perhaps, over time, things plummeted out of control and the primal urges of overly passionate youth reaped havoc on what might otherwise have been a strictly Platonic relationship. One must read closely, ever so closely, between the lines, but the story is there to be found.

Many of the letters that Aunt Iva sent were very informative about Mammy's and our other ancestor's history and I will include the most relevant parts of those letters on the following pages.

From a letter dated 1-27-1990 Aunt Iva writes:"I keep remembering things Mammy told me as a child as I study these pages - things long forgotten. I made a mistake in my sheets I sent you from Mammy's sister of 1950 – at the bottom where I listed her birth and death, I said born in Winston County, January 4, 1882. I had been talking about the Armstrongs and Mammy's sister, brother, ½ sister and brother and all and because she talked so much to me over the years of her life and grandpa's and grandma Armstrong that she loved so much in Winston County and of playing on Natural Bridge as a small child and the White House (church) and all the relatives there, I got temporarily confused when I dictated that to Gerald as he typed from my "rough" notes. I think she (Mammy) was actually born in Marion County (maybe even in grandpa's Russell Porter Palmer's house. Clover, Harrison and Elizabeth were). You see, Nellie (Nellie Armstrong, Mammy's mother) had her first child Elizabeth "Sister Lizziebetts", then Mammy was born on January 4, 1882 and her dad Gaines died October 14, 1882 when Mammy was only 9 months old and Nellie was expecting Gaines Jr. – they always said Gaines was born after his dad died. So Nellie would probably go back to Winston County where her Mom and Dad were – hence all the talk about her (Mammy's) childhood in Winston

County and Natural Bridge, White House Church and all. Gaines was buried in Palmer Cemetery in 1882 which sounds like he and Nellie were in Marion County then. Anyway, after some time, Nellie married Mr. Weaver, "Ol Man Weaver" as Mammy called him, tho he was probably 35 or 40! Mammy said it was a terrible thing for he was mean to Nellie and to the kids too – he was not a kind and loving step dad to them. I think he already had kids older. I believe Mammy said she was 12 when her mother (Nellie) died and she had to look after Gaines Jr. her brother. I guess Elizabeth stayed back for she married young to a Barnes, had Destie and Chess (girl). She had a hard, hard life and died young. Mammy didn't think well of Barnes (maybe that's where Destie got her ways!) but poor Elizabeth could have been sort of forced into marriage when her mom died and no place to go. I'm not sure but Mammy <u>hated</u> her marrying Barnes (I can't remember his first name). Mammy and Gaines Jr. came back to Hamilton, Palmer area (a community close to Hamilton named for our ancestors) and sort of lived around "pillar to post" as Mammy described it. They stayed some at grandpa's (Russell Porter Palmer's) some at Uncle Bud Palmer's (Aunt Tryforcia told me this) and whoever would take them in for a time, I guess. It was hard to be an orphan in those days and tho I feel the "old set" was nice to them and grandpap (Russell Porter) and grandma (Morning Dizenia) too, it was still a life without real roots or a home. I'll always feel this "unsettled life" was why Mammy succumbed to the "Arkansas Glamour" (Blue John)! I saw his picture once, he was a cross between Clover and Herbert (the fifth child of Clover and Cora Lee) – real cute. I remember seeing this picture in Mammy's old family pictures when I was a child 12 or 13 or so and I said "Who is this?" and she sort of pretended not to hear or changed the subject. I just sort of knew, tho I couldn't be sure. I'm mad at myself for not managing to somehow get a hold of that picture."

This letter of Aunt Iva's is especially noteworthy because it provides a viable explanation of why Mammy may have been attracted to Blue John. She was in dire need of having someone to lean on and in dire need of having a loving family so she would've been highly susceptible to the "Arkansas Glamour" as Aunt Iva so well put it. It is a very insightful letter and I just had to include it. Aunt Iva closes this letter but then adds a P.S. that I think is of special interest as well:

"I saw on TV that American kids can't write and they are going back to the "Palmer Method of Writing" – the "old set", especially Uncle Bud, insisted that our ancestors started that method but you can see why I can't dare brag about that! Thanks for suffering thru my scribbling over the years! Love Aunt Iva "

Thank you Aunt Iva for all those letters you've scribbled to us over the years. We have a greater knowledge of our ancestors because of it and besides we scribble just as bad as you did and we have no trouble reading your letters at all. Clover took a Palmer Handwriting correspondence course and I have an example of his beautiful handwriting from a sheet of notebook paper that he practiced on framed and hanging on my wall today. There will be more of Aunt Iva's letters to come and so I continue. The following letter from Aunt Iva was dated 2 – 2 – 1990 and is rich in information about Palmers who fought in the Civil War and included stories about the war that Mammy told to Aunt Iva when she was a child. They are similar to the stories that Joel Palmer's dad and grandparents told him. I include it here:

"We were so pleased to get the mail - and the Palmer stuff too – its fun and I read it and then remember more of Mammy's stories I'd forgotten. She often talked of William Plummer Williams – as a child I thought that was a funny name! The Purser name was surely ancestors of Mama's (Cora Lee's) boyfriend, Walter Purser who was broken up because she met Clover and quit him! That was the Barnesville area where he was. Jim Cooper, the baby in the "Tennessee Walk", married Aunt Sis (Elizabeth) Palmer Cooper, only girl Russell and Morning Dizenia had. I remember Uncle Jim well. I've seen that picture of Uncle Joe (Joseph Palmer, oldest son of Russell Porter) you sent in Mammy's things. Daddy (Clover) took pictures like that – I don't say took that one. I can't remember when Uncle Joe died – it's probably in those papers you sent – but I know that picture well – I saw it as a child. Those stories about the Tories, Home Guard, and Rebels, Yankees, etc. sound like Mammy's many stories. I don't doubt that it's fairly accurate. She told me many times about some friend or neighbor of Armstrongs in Winston County who was taken away by the Rebel supporters and tied to a tree to die. She also told of her uncles, I'm not sure if it was Palmer or Armstrong tho, who was hiding out or lost from their camp and was starving and saw a snake and built a fire and cooked and ate it. As a child, that story "freaked me out"! She told another <u>sad</u> story of two brothers. I'm not sure if it was Joe and Ben Palmer, brothers of grand pap Russell, or if it was grand pap Armstrong's brothers, but I heard it many times. She said one brother rode many, many miles up to Tennessee by horseback. He loved his brother and missed him so much and wanted to see him. So he rode hungry, wet, cold, etc. and so tired but finally was thrilled to see the site and know he'd see his brother. But as he got near and almost got off his horse, he noticed an insignia or uniform or something which let him know his brother was on the wrong side. So he turned his horse around and started the long trek back without ever speaking to his brother! As a child I'd choke up on that one. Of course, I'd beg her to tell the story again later, just as I'd beg her to sing Barbara Allen and when she got to "Sweet William" dying for love and Barbara so mean I sat by the fireplace and hid my sobs, but later on, of course, we'd beg her to sing it again! She also told us (about war) that they came and got grand pap (Russell Porter Palmer) but I guess they thought he was too old or somehow they let him go. Joel's (Joel Palmer's) story says he was needed as a doctor, which makes sense. So the stories jive pretty well, I think. Mammy often told me about Aunt Nancy "Nannie"(Nancy Ozbirn, Newton Ozbirn's youngest daughter), Doctor John Howard Palmer's (Russell's youngest son) wife who were Joel Palmer's grandparents. She told me Uncle "Doc", as she called him, had a baby boy (Johnny) by a young girl long before he was married to Nancy – for some reason he <u>took</u> the baby to raise (perhaps the girl wasn't fit or couldn't raise it or even died or some reason), but Mammy would tell that Aunt "Nannie" "had her cap set" for Uncle "Doc", a dashing young man who had a young son (how well Mammy may have identified with this story as she remembered her own experience with Blue John). Aunt Nannie had an "accent" or speech impediment or something. I could repeat it as Mammy quoted her, but I can't write an "accent" (neither can I). They'd look in the coffee pot at grounds left in the bottom and tell their "fortunes"- see the boyfriends, etc., etc. Aunt Nannie would say when she saw grounds in the cup "I see Doc and Doc's little Johnny". The other girls and women would roll their eyes (when she couldn't see) and smile for they knew Nannie intended for Doc to marry her and she'd raise his little Johnny! You look at Doc's family and you'll see a John much older than his other children at the top of the list! I remembered Mammy's story, long forgotten, and ran and pulled out Joel's stuff and there was Johnny!"

It just doesn't get any better than this. Aunt Iva's letter about Mammy's stories puts me right there back with them and I feel as if I am right beside them listening to Mammy talk by the fireside. I hope that you do too! Aunt Iva, as you have no doubt now learned, was an avid writer and especially loved to write my mother, her sister. As I've related before, they would write letters to each other at least twice a week for over 65 years and I have tons of their letters saved for perhaps another book I will write later. I just hope that there is enough time left for me to write all the books that I want to write. Bear with me though, and I promise that I will finish this one first. Within the same envelope of the letter about Mammy's stories that I've just related to you, there was an additional letter written the next day on a greeting card with two note pages added inside. It has information about a book written about the "Free State of Winston" written about the pro Union county of Winston during the Civil War. Enjoy this story as well:

"I forgot to write about the book on the card that was in the letter I wrote yesterday. Gerald wanted to leave to get to Rio (Illinois) to the tax lady to leave something. Anyway, as I said, Joel's stuff on the Civil War sounded a lot like Mammy's stories, tho she didn't have later details, etc. and I never wrote her "war stories" down (but Aunt Iva had a pretty good recall of them).I wanted to mention a book we bought in Double Springs, Winston County, several years ago. We'd heard about it and asked at the courthouse and they sent us way out in the country. We went down a sandy, rocky lane, hardly a road and came to a gate. But beyond that was a nice brick house sitting out in "nowhere" and the lady we were to see to get the book was well dressed, had good grammar, etc. and was the librarian I think. I can't remember what I did with the book (and I'm afraid, Aunt Iva, we never will). If I gave it to you when you did your research, I did it because I wanted to, but we've moved twice and I can't remember. I can't even remember the little "Free State of Winston" but I'm not sure that is the title and I think a Mr. Wheeler, we'd met years earlier and talked to about the war, wrote it – but I'm not clear on it. But I know they would have used his info. He was smart and a good citizen of the town and older than Mammy was. The names of all Winston County families at that time (Civil War) were listed and children. James Stewart Armstrong (Mammy's Grandfather) and his family were listed, his son William (Billie) and all. If you ever get back, check at the library to see if the book is there. I believe some of Joel's stuff came from that book and some from stories of Palmer and other families. I'll check for the book too, if we ever get to Double Springs or Gaylesville. If ever you talk to Joel ask about Russell Porter's mother. She came with her 3 sons to Bexar, Alabama in the early 1840's as Mammy said and his stuff agrees but did she die there? Is she buried at Palmer, Alabama? I don't remember Mammy showing me her grave but maybe I forgot. Did she go north with Ben (her youngest son)?"

Joel Palmer did research this and found the cemetery and gravestone which answers all of Aunt Iva's questions. He took a photograph and it reads as follows:

"Grandma Elizabeth Roberts Palmer 1780-1851 Wife of Hezekiah Palmer, a Preacher and Farmer from Union Co. S.C. in 1816 moved to Georgia, then to Benton Co. Alabama (present day Calhoun Co.) in 1831. Hezekiah died there in 1839. She came with sons Joseph M, Russell P and Benjamin F."

The stone is located at Mt. Zion Cemetery, Marion Co. Alabama.

Aunt Iva had other questions though as I relate her words from her letter: "I'd always been told she was a 2nd wife. His stuff says they had 12 sons and Russell Porter was born 18 years after their 1st son who was born in 1800. Joe and Ben were much younger than Russell, so if she had 12 sons, and was the only wife of Benjamin Hezekiah and he died and she crossed the country at age 55 or 60 or so, married in 1800, got to Bexar, Alabama in 1844 or 1842? She would be a pretty strong "Mammy type" to weather 12 births and covered wagon trip and all." Aunt Iva makes some very good points here and possibly Hezekiah did have a first wife that died early in childbirth or some other cause and he remarried. But, as in many other missing pieces of ancestral research, there is no record of it.

Aunt Iva adds this to her closing: "Mostly, I'd like to know if she stayed there with Russell and died there at "Palmer". I never asked Mammy what happened to grandpa's mother. She just said grandpa came as a young man with his mother (widowed) and 2 brothers, Uncle Joe and Uncle Ben and stopped at Bexar, etc. etc." That is the main content of these rather long letters relating to information that Mammy told to Aunt Iva as a child and when compared to the information gathered by Joel Palmer all is fairly close. The wealth of information gained from Aunt Iva's letters helps to fill many gaps in our family's history and can be added to that of Joel Palmer's.

In a letter written by Aunt Iva to my brother on 1 – 13 – 1990 she discusses Joel Palmer and their relationship within the Palmer family and she also provides valuable insights and additional information about the "old set" of Palmers. I include it here:

"Thanks so much for the wealth of information! We've had plenty of time to read all the papers you sent. I'm so glad to have the names, dates, etc., of the wives and children of the "old set". The information I got from Mammy was pretty accurate but sketchy for I never asked for wife's and children's names when I talked to her. I got mostly her parents and grandparents info. I'm glad to know who Joel Palmer is. The only Joel I knew was Joel (Reedus) Palmer, only child of Russ Palmer, son of Uncle Bud (Estern). Of course Bud (Estern) had a son, Estern too, who lived in the (cabin) as we all grew up. I'm glad to know this Joel is son of Jim and Una "Unie" Palmer, Uncle "Doc's" son Jim. I used to "tag" along with Mammy to visit Uncle Doc's family. Most of them lived about 5 miles north of Hamilton and farmed and did truck farming, taking their produce to town. They were all smart people and had a pretty good life for themselves. I remember Jim and "Unie" very well. I had forgotten that their son was named Joel. His dad, Jim Palmer, was very smart. He was a country farmer but was an inventor. He could rig things up and had running water in his house and electricity when nobody out there had it. He had lots of interesting things before others had it. I was out there a lot for Mammy took us out in the summer to can "on the halves". Jim and "Unie" had lots of peaches, string beans, corn, etc. We provided the labor and took our own glass cans and we got half. "Unie" and Mammy supervised and we children just peeled huge zinc tubs of peaches, beans, etc. I can still remember it! But it was depression years and we needed the extra food for winter."

"I was surprised at Mammy's Daddy Gaines being in medical school. She never told me that. She always said he died of diabetes. After seeing Harry (Harrison, who was Clover's oldest son) in diabetic comas over the years, he looked like he was drunk or "on something". I wonder if Gaines (Zachariah Gaines) died in a coma instead of because of drugs. Mammy was a baby when he died so we could not have known. They say diabetes hits one in last generation. Harry got it but, so far, I don't know of any other of the children of the 6 "stair steps" (Clover's children) having it. As far back as I can remember I've always felt the old Palmers came from <u>quality people</u> back in Georgia, South Carolina or Virginia. The "old set" had a regal bearing one couldn't help but notice plus an inclination to do well, to school their children, etc. in an area where it was considered unnecessary. Their ability at decorative writing, drawing, etc. and music – it had to come from someplace. I knew little about the Drivers till you did your research. I'm so happy to have this on the Drivers. Poor little Arthur (her brother and mine and Roger's uncle who died young) wanted to get all this info together so bad. I'm glad we have a lot of the blanks filled now."

" Back to Joel Palmer. I remember Mammy talking about his Aunt Adline, Uncle Doc's daughter. She died young of cancer. Mammy said she endured Hell when she was dying of terrible pain. In those days people "sat up" with the sick at night all night and of course Mammy would be there. She said Adline begged and begged them to kill her and get her out of her misery. I'm not sure if morphine was hard to get in those days for patients or whether there was a religious reason for her not being relieved of her pain, but to this day, chills go thru me when I remember Mammy telling me how Adline died. Mammy had nothing strong to give and just had to treat with what they had. You would think they could have gotten morphine or something in 1921. Mammy never told me the reason and I was too young to really ask. The cancer was on top of her head. Mammy thought it was further irritated because she was young and didn't want anyone to see it and kept it covered when it should have been open when it started."

The letters from Aunt Iva are true gems of family history. Another letter that I found interesting was from my Aunt Iva (yes, one more from Aunt Iva) to my brother and includes a newspaper clipping with an article about Granny Ballard or Mrs. Martha Ballard of Detroit, Alabama, that is a few miles southwest of Hamilton, Alabama. Granny Ballard was the oldest surviving relative of Doctor Russell Porter Palmer at the time of this article. Aunt Iva relates this from her letter:"Martha Ballard in this story is granddaughter of Russell Porter Palmer. One of the 11 sons (I'm not sure which) was her father. He had 11 sons and 1 daughter, Elizabeth (Aunt Sis) Cooper who lived at Sulligent, Alabama. One of the sons Alec (Alexander) was a surgeon and family doctor in Winston County. He graduated from medical school in Tennessee or Kentucky – I can't remember which. He rode on a horse to treat people and was the only doctor in the rural and small town area of Haleyville, Alabama at that time". The newspaper article that she sent was written by staff writer Erna Oleson Xan. I include it here as I find it very informative about the medical practices of doctors like Russell Porter Palmer and the times that they lived in. The article reads as follows: "In her 92 years, Granny Ballard of Detroit, Alabama (Mrs. Martha Ballard) has gathered up a heap of memories which she passes along to Party Line through our friend, Joe Acee, SULLIGENT correspondent. My grandfather, Russ Palmer, she told him the other day, was a doctor. He would come riding up on his horse, and the first thing he would ask, is stick out your tongue. Then he would give you some bitter terrible tasting medicine that would make you vomit. His theory was that you had to clean out your stomach first, if you were sick. He would always say before he left: You send for the doctor, and he makes you sicker than you were before he came."

The "Granny Ballard" article continues with her words:"Because one could not always get a doctor, pioneers used old home remedies. Polk root was the remedy for itch, which was common then. They gave one butterfly root to raise a sweat. And this was supposed to get the poison from one's body. Ginger root was given for a cold. When the baby had colic, catnip tea was the medicine. For a bad case of La Grippe (flu), one made a tea of rabbit tobacco. Fat meat was placed on a rising or a boil, and when a person was bitten by a snake or rabid dog, the neighborhood mad stone was sent for. It was a stone taken from a deer. Put directly on the wound, it would draw the poison out. One had to be really sick before one sent for the doctor. When Dr. (Grandpa) Russ Palmer got there, his talk and psychology was always better than his pills." The home remedies mentioned by Granny Ballard remind me of ones that Mammy used and that were no doubt passed down to her from Morning Dove, her Cherokee great grandmother. Her description of her grandfather Russell Porter Palmer's approach to medicine gives an added richness to his story and to the story of his times. An actual accounting taken from the memories of his oldest living relative offer one as valuable a source of information as is possible. Granny Ballard offered some additional observations of her own as well about doctors:"All I have to do is call up the good old doctor I've had for 30 years. He knows by the sound of my voice how far to go with the prescription on the telephone, or if I should come to the office. Sometimes when I come to him he knows that nothing is wrong but a problem is worrying the life out of me. We talk it over, he gives me sound advice (and I'm sure some soda pills) and I get well right away. I often tell him, when the time comes and there's nothing else to do, I want you to be the one to tell me."

There are letters from other recently discovered relatives that I found interesting as well and I include them here as I close the chapter "Letters from Home". Cora Lee received a letter from Dorrie and Willie Driver from Overton, Texas which seemed to confirm what her father, John Thomas Goodson, had always told her. Dorrie Driver received a letter from my brother Roger asking about their Driver ancestors and this was her response to Cora Lee about how she had answered it:"We had a letter from your grandson (Roger) and he was wanting some information about his cousin Willie. Willie said all he knew about his Daddy's people was his Daddy and brother came to Alabama from England and he said his grandpa married an Indian woman. All he knew was one of his grandma's was a Smith. You write to Fannie and Jesker and I think Jesker has the old Bible and maybe she can tell you a lot more than I can. Jesker lives in Tyler, Texas. Fannie will give you her address when you hear from Fannie." From this letter and others, my brother was able to further research our Driver ancestral record back to Virginia and before that to England. Eventually my brother was able to trace the Drivers all the way back to 1623 in England. We know from Rhoda Boyett that she believed our Goodson ancestors came from Ireland, although there is no documentation to prove it. Also we know that our Palmer ancestors came from England and my brother was able to trace that back to around 1649. Rhoda Boyett, as I've stated, was Cora Lee's half sister and she had another half sister, Rowena Porterfield. Rowena also wrote letters to Cora Lee and my brother Roger about the Goodson and Driver ancestries which proved invaluable.

I found an interesting connection that Rowena Porterfield made with information received by Cora Lee from Dorrie and Willie Driver of Overton, Texas. Willie Driver remembered that he had a grandmother whose maiden name was Smith. Sure enough, Rowena remembered and wrote about the same grandmother. I include her words here:"I believe I told you that Elva, Uncle Bill Driver's baby daughter, had two daughters and one died on her sixteenth birthday after she just got in from church and fell with a heart attack and died immediately. That left Anna and she was oldest of the two and now lives in Anniston, Alabama. I got this information from James' widow. Uncle Bill Driver's son was James W.

Driver, now deceased. His sister, Lula, is also deceased but Aunt Nancy lived with Elva and Anna. Of course, when Aunt Nancy and Elva died, that left the Bible and a big picture album for Anna. I called Anna and she said it might not be much help but she knew positively that grandma's maiden name was Smith. Rhoda, my sister in Hamilton, is pretty sure and believed she was a Smith. Anna said they lived in Carrollton, Georgia and Carrollton is in Carroll County, I'm pretty sure. Papa's (John Thomas Goodson's) cousins lived in Carrollton when we visited them when I was nearly four, but I remember it all, place by place at the cousins' houses. Another Driver was nicknamed "Mouse" and his wife was named Emma. Anna said some of them came down there from Villa Rica, Georgia." So between information gathered from Drivers, Cora Lee and her half sisters, Rhoda and Rowena, we begin to get a pretty clear picture of Goodson and Driver ancestry.

There was a letter written by Cora Lee to our Aunt Iva that had a newspaper clipping about the 1920 tornado that killed her best friend that I have referred to earlier. This letter expands significantly on that horrific event and the accompanying newspaper clipping gives chilling details of what actually occurred on April 20, 1920. I begin with quoting the account from *The Birmingham News,* Sunday Edition, February 6, 1966, by Rose McCarley, entitled *Hamilton Remembers Day of Big Tornado:*"April 20, 1920 was the day a monster tornado almost leveled the town. Described by people who remember it, the tornado was a great roaring mountain of black rolling clouds and fire." Thomas Taylor and his wife Mamie, who was Cora Lee's best friend, died in this tornado along with their grandmother Taylor, a brother Jim Taylor, and his 8 year old son. A surviving nephew, Dewey Taylor, who was eleven at the time, speaks of the harrowing event recalling that it was a dark, dreary day when he left to help his father, Albert, with the plowing in the field below the house. Dewey tells the story for the article:"We hadn't been plowing long when the clouds began to get darker and lightning began popping off the wire fence. Papa said we'd better go to the house and wait until the rain was over so we took the mules to the barn and went up to the house. Mama wouldn't let us go to the storm house because she was afraid the wind might blow the chimney from our house down on us, so we got on the bed. We had been there just a short time when our clock struck 10 and about that time Mama called from the door that a cyclone was coming. We all ran to see it and there it came – a big, black cloud shaped like a funnel and it was coming right toward us. All we could do was huddle together in the house. We were all scared to death. ALL OF A SUDDEN, the house was lifted high off the ground and when it came down, everything was all gone and we were scratched up but alive. My baby sister was blown down into the field but was all right when we found her (our mother, Mary Elizabeth Palmer Brown, remembers her mother, Cora Lee, telling her about how the baby was found hanging by her hair from a tree limb but still survived unhurt). We looked around all around us and in the direction of Uncle Matt Taylor's house we could see some timber standing so we went over there. He and Papa went to see about Grandma Taylor who lived a half mile away and when they came back, they said Grandma Taylor, Uncle Jim Taylor, his eight year old son, and Uncle Tom and Aunt Mamie Taylor had been killed. Papa and Uncle Matt took the wagon and brought the bodies back to Uncle Matt's and laid them on the porch. It was such a sad time for everyone, and then the day they were buried in the Taylor Cemetery was another day I'll never forget."

That was the accounting of the horrific events of the storm given in *The Birmingham News*. Cora Lee wrote a letter to our Aunt Iva about the storm as she remembered it:"Iva, I'll send this clipping (the one just quoted from) I cut out of Sunday's paper. It's the storm we was in. Harrison was 3 months old. Hattie's baby was a little older. Burnice wasn't borned. That's Mammie and Tom Taylor's name on the tombstone (from the article photograph). She was my best girl friend. Tom lived through World War I and they got married and both got killed in the storm. Jim Taylor and his little boy and the old mother all got killed, 5 of them. Clover went to see about Hattie's folks as there wasn't any timber standing around that way. They drug through the timber and got to Matt Taylor's house for shelter. Then Clover and my father went and stayed with these 5 Taylors till help could saw timber out so they could get these people to shelter. There was not one thing to cover them with till help got them to a house." From these accounts, one can easily understand why Cora Lee was forever after paranoid about tornados. That letter and newspaper clipping gave an account of just how perilous it was to live in those days, especially if one had the misfortune to be caught in one of those horrific Alabama tornados that we still have in abundance today.

An interesting closing note to this chapter is an observation from another of Great Aunt Rowena's letters about Uncle Bill Driver and Aunt Nancy:"Uncle Bill and Aunt Nancy were divorced when they were 84 years of age. I think that is why Aunt Nancy was with Elva, I suppose. She (Nancy) was a fine person and she lost her voice when one of the children was born. She could hear but she couldn't speak. She was smart though and taught Uncle Bill to write his name and the alphabet and she was pretty and sweet. She was a Waggoner. Some of the Waggoner family is in Anniston I think." We know from Rowena that Uncle Bill Driver lived to be 107 years old. After his divorce he lived another 23 years. What an interesting story he could've told us about why he and Aunt Nancy divorced and what happened with their lives afterwards. They each had new beginnings in their lives at a very late point. The next chapter will be about new beginnings and will relate some of the special memories that have been passed down by our ancestors. Many of these memories have been passed down by word of mouth and many, as well, come from letters written to my brother or to other relatives of ours.

Chapter Ten

New Beginnings

The main thrust of Clover's existence as well as that of his family, was comprised of making daily existence as rewarding as the times they lived in would permit. Clover strived to make his family's life as spiritually, emotionally, and physically complete as he could. All generations are faced with their own unique set of challenges and the degree to which they are successful in responding to these challenges will lay the groundwork for the successes of the following generations. My great grandmother would quote Ben Franklin a lot and one of her favorite sayings was "Experience keeps a dear school, but fools will learn in no other and scarce in that". That was from Ben Franklin's *Poor Richard's Almanac* and I think the quote would work as well if the word "History" were substituted for "Experience". Learning from the school of history will better prepare us to negotiate our present and future lives.

From researching our ancestral history so well, my brother learned much about our ancestors and how they faced the challenges of their times. He wanted to know about his ancestral past and was curious about where he came from and what made him the person he was. I think he gained a better understanding of himself by learning about his ancestors and their personality traits. I too have learned from the research that he did and I am better able to understand my strengths and frailties as a result. By the same token, I am better able to understand Mammy, Clover and Cora Lee now that I have learned about the personality traits of the ancestors that came before them. I can envision how Clover and Cora Lee may have begun their new lives together. I have learned about their ancestors and the tough pioneer stock that they came from and I can reasonably conjecture that Clover and Cora Lee faced the challenges of their mostly agrarian lifestyle in much the same way as their ancestors did.

Clover lived with his mother, Mary Dizenia, in his grandfather Doctor Russell Porter Palmer's old log house. Russell Porter Palmer was 89 years old when he passed away in 1908 when Clover was nine years old but he had taught his grandson many valuable lessons before leaving this world.

His wife, Morning Dizenia, passed away about three years later in 1911 and had also instilled many lasting values into the lives of her children and grandchildren. Clover learned from his grandparents and shared in their pioneer spirit by learning the survival skills that they taught him. Clover was a prodigy and was a brilliant and talented lad that learned the skills his grandfather taught him in farming, carpentry, mechanics, medicine, writing songs and poetry and he learned as well from Morning Dizenia's knowledge of Indian medicinal plants and herbs, Indian hunting and fishing methods and Indian methods of making clothing and tools for farming and building. Clover was ready to begin his promising adult life and venture out on his own to begin a family that he would provide a rich future for. When he met the love of his life, Cora Lee, they married and lived at the Russell Porter Palmer homestead the first two years or so and they farmed the land as Russell and Morning Dizenia Palmer had done before them. Except for some of the modern inventions, their lives had remained pretty much unchanged from that of their parents and grandparents. Modern conveniences were slow in coming to rural areas like Hamilton and people still had wood burning stoves, kerosene lamps, mule drawn plows, horse drawn wagons or ox carts and used the same technologies that their parents had used. Although they had few conveniences, Clover did have a Model "T" Ford automobile that he drove around Hamilton and he did have a camera and homemade darkroom that he used after training himself by taking a photographic correspondence course. Mammy and Cora Lee made clothes for the family using foot treadle sewing machines and thread spun from spinning wheels like the old spinning wheel that had been passed down from William Mansell. Mammy still used the Indian herbs and medicinal remedies that had been passed down from Morning Dove White Mansell. They grew their own food, milked their own cows, slaughtered their own livestock or deer, hunted in the forests and fished in the creeks and streams just the way their ancestors always had done.

Clover and Cora Lee's first two children, Harrison Roe Palmer, and Mary Elizabeth Palmer (our mother), were born in the old Russell Porter Palmer home just as Clover had been over twenty years before. Harrison was born January 23, 1920 and Mary Elizabeth was born March 24, 1922. With the new camera that he had purchased Clover took pictures of his new family at the old Russell Porter Palmer place. There are photographs of Clover and Cora Lee that Mary Dizenia or Mammy took and there are also pictures of Mary Dizenia with her brother Gaines and her nephew Taft standing in front of the old house. There is a photograph as well of the oldest child of Clover, Harrison, standing amongst the chickens and feeding them corn. My mother Mary Elizabeth, who was just a baby, had her picture taken while cradled in an old horse collar that Cora Lee put her in while working in the fields. These old photographs show that life for them had remained much the same and their photographs illustrate well a lifestyle that continued to be like those of their parents and grandparents. Clover was always anxious to try the new conveniences though and he replaced his horse and wagon with an automobile and was very excited about learning photography and building his own darkroom. He would very early on start a clock repair business and eventually start businesses of his own such as a barber shop and a hamburger and hotdog cafe in town.

Clover was always trying to improve things for himself and his family so he built a new house for them just up the road from the old Russell Porter Palmer house. He started his first barber shop in the country and he began doing photographs for people's picnics, church and school outings and family portraits. He was also a talented song writer and wrote several hymns that were sung at the Sacred Harp Singings that were held in the area. Things were beginning to change for him and his family even though they were still farming the fields, plowing with mules, and picking cotton, corn, beans, sweet potatoes and other crops. Iva Louise Palmer was born at the new house February 25, 1924 and the family remained there for a year until Clover built two other houses, one for his new family and one for his mother, inside the town of Hamilton. The other three children, Joseph Arthur born May 10, 1926, Herbert Hoover born April 2, 1928, and Horrice Edward born April 17, 1930 were born in the new house Clover built for them in town. Mary Dizenia, Clover's mother, lived in her own little house that Clover built for her next to their house until about the 1950's when the kids had all grown up and moved out. Cora Lee also moved out and remarried and at that point Mammy rented out her little house and moved into the bigger one, remaining there until she passed away March 26, 1963.

When Clover moved the family to town he moved his barber shop business there as well and he had a shop next to the five and dime store. Sometimes the kids would come there with Cora Lee and sometimes the older ones like my mother would walk to town alone and her father would see her there and they'd take a break to go next door to the five and dime store where Clover would buy her some candy or an inexpensive toy. When she was a little older my mother would take Iva Louise, her sister, with her. Mother would've been about five or six and Iva about three or four. Jake Smitherfield, who owned the five and dime store, who thought a lot of himself, acted like a big shot in front of his friends and neighbors most of the time. This must've rubbed off on his eight year old son Sammy Smitherfield, because he had become obnoxious, disrespectful and bullied many of the younger kids who would visit his father's store. My mother, Mary Elizabeth, would go to see her father Clover at the barber shop, and if Sammy was around, he would make fun of her dresses because they were handmade and were not "store bought" in his father's store. He would sometimes block her way and not let her pass, forcing her to go out in the street in order to get to her father's barber shop. Sammy did this one time too many and my mother went and told Clover immediately what Sammy had said and done. Clover was not a person to be disrespected or made light of, especially when it came to his family and to his young daughter and so he was determined to straighten things out with Sammy and his father Jake.

Clover had been taught to respect his fellow man and to treat all women and men with dignity and he always tried to treat people fairly and forgive their shortcomings as a good Christian should do, but "turning the other cheek" was something that he never accepted to do. He could give people a good piece of his mind if they deserved it. So Clover stormed into that dime store and gave Jake Smitherman a piece of his mind telling him eyeball to eyeball:"My kids are just as good as yours and the sidewalks in front of your store are for all of us to walk on! Your son blocked my daughter from walking on the sidewalk in front of your store and made fun of her clothes that were handmade by my mother! My daughter's dress was sewn together from threads spun by my mother on a spinning wheel like my great grandfather made in his workshop over 100 years ago. Your store and the dresses that you sell in it do not hold a candle to the fine workmanship of my mother and great grandmother before her, so I think you best explain some practical knowledge, history, respect, etiquette and make yourself a better example to that young boy of yours, lest I have to take a rod to the both of you!" Jake was real flustered and red in the face, but like most blowhards, he fell deafly silent when overpowered by

Clover's loud baritone voice, feeling Clover's vehement wrath and seeing the fire in Clover's eyes. In fact, my mother says that she never had any trouble with Sammy from that day forward.

Those were the days that a half dollar took a long time to earn but could buy a lot of goods and Mammy would take a half dollar and turn it carefully around in her hand with her fingers and rub it as if she were making a wish as she carefully pondered what she would purchase with it. She could buy a big sack of self rising flour for 25 cents, and maybe some corn mill and some sugar that would help feed Clover's kids for a week or so. If she chose to buy the flour, the big bags always came with a floral print dish cloth sewn onto the bottom that she could use around the house or just cut and add to her scrap fabrics for making quilts or dresses. Mammy made extra money by washing people's clothes and ironing them and also by sewing and making clothes to order. She was an excellent seamstress and made all the kids' clothing on an old foot treadle sewing machine. They weren't "store bought" but they were high quality and lasted through the wear and tear that kids could put them through better than "store bought". Unlike Jake Smitherfield and his spoiled son, people from those days put great stock in having high quality, handmade clothing, so Mammy was able to provide extra income for her family by taking orders for handmade dresses, shirts, quilts and the like.

There was an old friend of Mammy's named Ana Bell Lovejoy that was always asking her to sew her up something nice that would make her look young, trim and "light on her feet" and Mammy would always joke back with her saying that she was "rode too hard and put away wet too long ago" for a pretty dress to do her much good any more. Ana Bell kept on about it though and finally Mammy gave in and said she would look around for some nice fabric with some spring floral print patterns on it that might just do the trick for Ana Bell. Actually Mammy already knew what material she was going to use for Ana Bell's dress and she had devised a plan that she thought would keep Ana Bell from worrying her anymore about trying to revive her long lost youth. Mammy had saved all those fabric samples from the flour sacks and they were mostly nice floral prints that would make a nice spring seasonal outfit for going to the Sacred Harp Singings or to the picnics on the grounds people would have after church. So Mammy worked steadfastly on a nice outfit for Miss Ana Bell (she was a "miss" or an "old maid" as people called them then). Mammy probably should've gone more gently with Ana Bell but Ana was really starting to get under her skin about making that dress and making her look young and spry again. This dress was going to be just the ticket and Ana Bell was never going to pester Mammy about making her a dress again.

By the time of the Sacred Harp Singing, which was the second Sunday in May, Mammy had finished the dress and she presented it to Ana Bell inside a nicely wrapped pink colored paper bundle with a red ribbon on top. "Now Ana", she said," don't you go and open this before the Singing. You just try it on quick like and come on down to church and you can show off to everyone then! I made it a special present for you, and I don't want a dime as pay!" Needless to say, Ana Bell was thrilled to have the dress all wrapped up and ready and even more thrilled that she didn't have to pay for it. The next day was Sunday and Ana couldn't wait to open the bundle up and try on her dress. It had a beautiful floral print pattern that was vaguely familiar to her (unbeknownst to her at the time, Ana had several of the same flour pattern cloths hanging in her kitchen that she used as dish towels and cloths). Without really examining the dress closely Ana, in her haste to get to the singing, quickly put on the dress and brushed her hair, whipping it up into a nice bun that she clipped onto the back of her head with one of her best pearl clasps. She powdered her nose, rouged her cheeks, and put on some shiny red lipstick as she sat looking at herself in the vanity mirror. Ana Bell thought: "Oh, I do think I look so lovely and I do think Mary Dizenia's dress has put some spring in my step!"

Ana Bell couldn't wait to get to the church and sit on the front row so that everyone could see her in her new dress. In fact, she was the first one there and was sitting there waiting as all the church goers came through the doors and sat there behind her. Everyone greeted Ana Bell and remarked about her dress and what a pretty pattern it was and how young and cheery it made her look. Ana Bell beamed with joy and responded: "It just makes me feel light on my feet and I want to jump right up and dance!" It wasn't long before the church filled and it was time for the Sacred Harp singers to stand up and begin their "do, re, mi, fa, so, la, ti, do". Being there on the first row, Ana Bell stood up with all the other singers who thought that she had come up front to sing with them and all at once there rose up a chorus of chuckles, giggles and downright side splitting laughter from the crowd behind. While Ana had examined the front of her dress pretty well as she admired it in her vanity mirror, she had not looked that close at the back of it where the words "Self Rising" had been sewn by Mammy directly onto the seat. Ana Bell did not speak to Mammy for a long while after that but they did both come to terms eventually. They, as well as all the other churchgoers, laughed about and told the story of the "Self Rising" dress that Mary Dizenia had made for Ana Bell at every Sacred Harp Singing and Picnic from that day forward.

There were special memories that my mother recalled from her growing up, and being the second child of Clover, she could remember some experiences that she shared with her father. She learned what hotdogs were for the first time when she visited Clover's hotdog and hamburger café in Hamilton. She did not like the mustard on them though and it was a while before she developed a taste for them with or without mustard. Still it was special to go there and spend some time with her father who would always take time to be with her and walk around town to meet some of the shop owners and see some of their friends and relatives that were in town shopping. There was a public well there in front of the courthouse square where everyone would bring a big metal bucket to draw their water and take it back to their homes. When she would walk there with Clover they would go to the courthouse which was an imposing, somewhat gothic building made of large gray blocks which gave it a great sense of character. It was located at the center of town as most courthouses were and there was a concrete wall that surrounded it. When they would go there on Saturday country folks would gather there and sit on the wall to share news, chew tobacco, dip snuff, and spit. Mother remembered that the women's bottom lips always bulged with a pocket of snuff between their lip and gums and the men's cheeks bulged with a lump of tobacco wedged in. Usually they would meet one or two of the old set of Palmers, like Uncle Grant Palmer or Uncle Bud Palmer (the one who married Clover and Cora Lee), sitting there on the wall chewing their tobacco and they would catch up on all the local gossip with them, being careful to keep a safe distance away from them when they spit. On the way back to his barber shop, Clover would always stop by the five and dime store with mother and let her pick out a small trinket such as an inexpensive toy, doll, necklace, bracelet or ring. There weren't an abundance of times that Clover was able to afford to buy things for his kids, but the times that he did so were very special to them.

Mother remembers the house that Clover built for them in town and the little house that he built for Mammy next door. She remembers the smell of the pungent fumes of kerosene lamps that they used inside for light before the days they were able to afford electricity. There was a storm house built into the side of the hill behind the house that they would take the kerosene lamps to in time of storms as well. There was no running water in those days and the kids had to go and fetch the water in big buckets from the well in front of the courthouse for Cora Lee and Mammy so that they could wash clothes, cook and prepare baths for everyone. The kids would take a shortcut through the cemetery on a trail that led into town that began on a steep hill behind their house. Mother remembers it as being very scary as they walked through the cemetery with great caution as old rusting iron gates, sinking slab tombs, and moss covered monuments abounded and towered over them. There were huge hickory nut and persimmon trees scattered throughout the area and the kids delighted in eating the nuts and fruits as much as the squirrels did. Green apples filled trees to the right side of Cora Lee's house and six little crabapple trees, one planted for each of the six children, spanned the distance on the left side along a path to Mammy's shotgun house next door. Cora Lee and Mammy would have the kids pick the green apples from the trees on the side of Cora Lee's house and place them on the tin roof of the garage next to Cora Lee's house in summer time. The hot sun would cook and dry out the apples so that Cora Lee and Mammy could make fried apple turnovers out of them and I remember Mammy making them for me when I was a small child as well (they were the best apple turnovers that I have ever had). The larger house of Cora Lee's was a double shotgun structure with an added kitchen in the rear. The kitchen had a dirt floor covered with linoleum and mother remembers many meals cooked there with fresh biscuits, cornbread, clabbered milk, fried okra and potatoes, and fried apple pies. I can remember Mammy cooking chicken and dumplings in that same kitchen for me when we would visit her and they were so delicious that I would gorge myself on them. Cora Lee and Mammy used to make hominy and soap using lye and ashes in a big black cast iron pot in the back yard. Of course there was no indoor plumbing in the houses either and there were two outhouses out back, one for each house with old Sears & Roebuck catalogs kept inside them for toilet paper (toilet paper at this point was a luxury item).

Mother and my Aunt Iva saved some special items that Clover had given them as kids and I still have some of my mother's things today. These were no doubt toys that Clover bought for them when he would take them to the five and dime store. They include miniature porcelain "Dutch Girl" tea sets, miniature pocket book mirrors with cases, miniature powder puffs with cases, small "Kewpie" dolls made from celluloid with cute white dresses with red polka dots, porcelain dollhouse bathroom tub, toilet, and sink and a variety of doll clothes accessories. One of the small "Kewpie" style dolls has a "Betty Boop" look to it and dolls like it may have influenced the later 1930 cartoon character that the "Betty Boop" dolls were made after. It is displayed in a cute box designed to look like a travel luggage chest with illustrated straps, hinges, lock, and destination stickers placed over the surfaces. This one was especially prized by my mother and my Aunt Iva had one exactly like it that she prized as well. They both put them away in special drawers and saved them as they would have prized possessions – and they were prized because they were childhood gifts from their father. Other items that my mother saved included dolls and other items that may have been Christmas presents or things purchased by Clover at state fairs or clothing stores. Again my mother stored these possessions with great care and almost never revealed them or indicated where they were kept. There was a larger doll of about 12" height with celluloid head, arms and legs dressed with white and small red dotted petticoat and white bloomers. The feet were painted to look as if they had red slippers on them and it had a white and red checked bonnet on its head. Another smaller doll, now deteriorating, had two sets of additional clothing included but with no shoes (presumed lost over the years). Of particular interest to me were two handmade dolls made from papier mache, one man and one woman, with painted on faces and very simply stitched handmade clothing. I can only assume that these were made by Clover or one of the old set of Palmers and given to mother as gifts. As I related, mother kept these treasures hidden away and I only rediscovered them after she passed away.

Clover did his best for his kids and bought them things that he could afford. Times were tough and money hard to come by so the gifts were rare but much appreciated when they were offered. Mother remembered one exciting trip on the 4th of July in the summer of 1930 that they all went on to the state fair in Tupelo, Mississippi, which was only about 30 miles west of Hamilton across the state line. Clover treated them all to hotdogs (mother still did not like the mustard) and he purchased nice coats for each of them to wear which were purchased from the vendors that made handmade clothing. Mother remembers the green wool coat with red plaid checks and a nice fur collar on it that she got and how proud that she was to receive a brand new coat. Clover bought all his children nice coats that day and they all had fun winning prizes at the game booths as well. Another thing that stood out in mother's memory was the fair's 4th of July fireworks celebration that Clover took them all to. She was absolutely petrified by the loud explosions and flashing lights spraying projectiles into the night sky. Unknown to Clover and the rest of the family, she went and hid in the back of the bleachers and ducked her body down between the seats so that she could hide from the death curdling shock of it all. She felt as if it were "the end of the world", and prophetically speaking, it may well have been because this most special part of her life was indeed about to end. This would be one of the last family outings they would take together with their father and at the time no one realized just how special an outing that it was. Summer was fleeting ever so quickly away and September was just around the corner, where our next chapter begins.

Part III
Spiritual Fields

Chapter 11

Road's End

My mother had memories of her father speaking about moving north to pursue a career that would improve his and his family's lot in life. Although my mother had no specific memory of where in the "north" he wanted to move or what career he intended to pursue, it is of special note here, that both my brother and I skipped a generation and moved "north" to Chicago, Illinois, where we attended and received MFA degrees in Fine Art from The School of the Art Institute of Chicago. Our Aunt Iva had also moved to Illinois many years before when she married our Uncle Gerald Gamel, whose family was from Rio, Illinois and he and my aunt lived in Dixon, Illinois a few years later. The symbolism of this appealed to my storytelling soul, so I decided, by artistic license, to designate Chicago as Clover's choice to move had he lived. Not knowing exactly what Clover had in mind, I created a storyline for him and his family that mostly consists of what ifs and unanswered dreams. Keeping this in mind we journey further into the realms of my imagination into what may have been and venture away from the actual paths of truth which with passage of time have become lost to us. The following pages from Chapters 11 and 12 are theoretical and have little basis in fact but live mostly in my imagination and within the imaginations of those who read and want to believe in magic.

Clover's dreams of a bright future for himself and his family, he anticipated, were about to come true. He had a plan in the making and was all set to initiate the first phases of it. He would travel to Chicago and stay at the YMCA for a week or so while investigating the possibilities for employment and also allow time for applying to schools where he could receive training or further education toward earning a college degree. There were several fields that interested him and he had experience and specific talents that made for a fine resume that would be a plus when making applications. He knew that his talents were being wasted in Hamilton, Alabama and that there were limitations on just how far he could progress and expect to accomplish for himself and his family. He was by now an expert photographer, songwriter, musician, and had talents as an artist and handwriting expert as well. He had read the classics of literature and the poetry books of his grandfather, Doctor Russell Porter Palmer, and had done extensive reading and research in the school library as well. He was mechanically inclined, and thanks to his grandfather who taught him, he had become a skilled mechanic and he had learned how to repair watches and clocks. There were many fields that he could explore and many roles that he could play. He was 31 years old and still young and just needed to get to the big city where opportunities were ripe and he could start fresh with taking advantage of the God given talents that he possessed.

Clover's idea was not devoid of concerns about the positive results that it might produce though. After all, the country was in a depression and jobs were scarce. There were food lines in Chicago with food provided by the gangster Al Capone who had the disposable gangland income to accommodate those in need in return for positive public support. Prohibition had made Chicago the capitol of gangland violence and the streets were not safe to walk on as gangland murders occurred nearly every day. Still, Clover was the eternal optimist and he felt as if this was his time to act. This was his time to rendezvous with destiny and he was right but destiny had far different plans for him than he would ever have anticipated.

Mammy, of course, wanted no part of his leaving and moving his family up north where she would seldom see him or her grandchildren again. She had grave concerns about plans to move north where it wasn't safe to raise a family. Mammy had raised him on Doctor Russell Porter Palmer's land and she wanted him to stay and farm it as her ancestors had always done. She knew her child was gifted though and that he wanted much more from life than just farming the fields every day. He had already started a barber shop business, a watch and clock repair service, and was becoming an exceptional photographer with his own camera and darkroom. He had taken correspondence courses in photography and the Palmer system of handwriting that was taught in most schools of that time. He was struggling to find a more viable livelihood that would enable him to move to the city and provide better lives for them all. He had moved his family a short ways up the road from Russell Porter Palmer's old homestead to a new home that he had built himself. He still farmed the land there but eventually the desire for a more challenging life would draw him to the town of Hamilton where he would build a house for his family and a separate one for his mother. They would move away from the country and from a life of farming. In town he opened a barber shop and later a hotdog and hamburger café which temporarily satisfied his hunger for change, but he longed for something more. Clover had read the newspapers and studied books in libraries as well as heard commentaries on the radio about the exciting life and golden opportunities offered in big cities like Chicago and he was ready to take the plunge. He had read the news stories about the food lines, unemployment and gangland violence as well but he was convinced that he had the talents, willpower and perseverance to overcome all obstacles. After all he was a Palmer and Palmers could do anything that they put their minds to. He was ready to leave his ancestral home of Hamilton and venture out into the world where endless hope and golden opportunities would be opened up to him and would enable him to provide a better life for himself and his family. He had read countless articles about success stories of young men just like himself who had gone to the big cities and found success. After all, this was America and if you worked hard, were blessed with skills and talents, and had a good education you could achieve anything and make your dreams come true. If he had to fight against all odds to accomplish his dreams then he would do so with his Palmer head held high.

Clover had discussed his plans with Cora Lee, and although the thought of leaving her home and family frightened her, she knew how much Clover wanted and needed to pursue his dreams. The way Clover put it was, moving their families in order to find a better life was not a new thing for the Palmers or for the Goodsons. Their ancestors had done it before them, in pioneer America, so it was really just a family tradition that they would be continuing. Cora Lee was willing to let Clover leave Hamilton on his own for a time just to see if he could find success in the city. He could get a job and earn much more than he could ever make from his barber shop or café. He could send money by Western Union money orders to his family and he could find a place for them to live after he established himself. She would miss him but she knew that she and Mammy could care for the kids until Clover found the answer to his dreams or until he realized that maybe Hamilton wasn't so bad after all and came on back home. She just hoped that he would not become another casualty within the unending flow of gangland violence statistics. Cora

Lee loved Clover that much and, even though she feared for his safety, she would still support him no matter which direction he decided to go.

Mammy was not so quick to go along with the idea though and it took some real persuasive power by Clover to get her to budge. Mammy was deeply rooted in Hamilton and all her kin folks were there. Farming was the only life she had ever known, and although she had never been rich, she had always had plenty of food, clothing, and a good roof over her head that she didn't want to jeopardize just to satisfy her son's whims. Mammy didn't fancy dodging bullets like her ancestors had done in the Civil War either and she made that fact very clear to her son. Clover approached Mammy with a few "what ifs" though in an effort to get her to understand just how badly he needed to pursue his dreams. Clover implored to her:"What if all goes well and I make it. What if I make a name for myself and earn a respectable living for all of us? You know that I will care for you and support you. What if I move you up to be with us so that we can all live together and have better lives? What if I find a safe neighborhood up north where we can all be secure? Besides our Palmer ancestors were loyal to the north and fought with them in the war, so we'd be right at home up there." Finally Clover promised Mammy if after a few weeks He had not found a job or had any successes in the big city, he would agree to come on back home again. Mammy had to admit that her son made some real good points and his promise to come home pushed her over the edge, so she finally grudgingly agreed to go along with his plans.

So it was all set. Clover would take the train up to Chicago after setting up a place for himself to stay at the YMCA. He would write the YMCA a letter and make all the arrangements and then he would drive to Muscle Shoals, Alabama which was just about 50 miles north of Hamilton to schedule his departure date and purchase his train ticket. He planned to have everything arranged and ready to go in about two weeks. That would allow him time to take care of important details around his business and his home. He would ask his good friend Willie Calvin to look after his barber shop and café for a while until he got things settled up north. Willie could cut hair as well as Clover and had helped out many times anyway, so he would be glad to help for the short term. As for the hotdog and hamburger café, Clover had been meaning to close it anyway, as it was just barely making ends meet. Having worked all the details out, Clover decided that he and a few friends would have a little celebration the night before he was scheduled to leave for Muscle Shoals to take his train to Chicago.

That night, before he was scheduled to depart for Chicago, Clover drove his 1930 Model "A" Ford taking the curving road over the steep and hilly landscape through Guin, Alabama and then proceeded toward Jasper, Alabama, which would be their final destination. Willie Calvin, his cousin Ollie, and a friend who worked in the café named Jeff, came along for the ride and for the celebration they would share in Jasper, Alabama at a popular "speakeasy" that they had all visited many times before. These were the days of Prohibition and if you wanted to have a few drinks together you either had to drink your own wildcat at home or go to a "speakeasy", if you could find one that the Revenuers hadn't crashed. So far the one in Jasper was still open and it would be the perfect place for them to have a few drinks, talk over Clover's plans to move north and just talk over old times together.

This night seemed odd to Clover because his recollection of events on that road through Guin and on the way to Jasper were not at all clear. It could've been that the wildcat they were all sharing along the way had fogged his memory but at some point things got all blurry and things began to happen that didn't make any sense. Everything was happening at a haphazard pace that seemed disorienting, dreamlike, and confusing. On a sharp curve in Guin, Alabama there had been a blinding flash as if another car's headlights had struck his eyes, and afterwards, things went blank. It was alright though because just a few seconds passed and Clover and the boys were speeding on down the road toward Jasper. It was scary to Willie, Ollie, and Jeff, because the road had a lot of sharp curves and steep hills and Clover was really driving too fast. Just as Ollie was about to say something about it to Clover, they all saw an old gentleman with gray hair and mustache dressed in a black suit and white shirt with tie standing alongside the road waving his hands like he was trying to get them to stop. These were the days when people still trusted strangers and tried to help people in need, so Clover slowed down and pulled his car over close to the old man to see what it was that he needed. Clover was shocked because the old man strongly resembled Doctor Russell Porter Palmer, his grandfather, and he looked just the way he last remembered him at his funeral over 20 years ago. The old man looked at Clover and smiled in such a way as to nurture trust in the most suspicious of souls. Somehow Clover felt that what was taking place was natural and he became enamored and totally accepting of what was taking place in front of him. It was strange and inexplicable but Clover was now alone in the car as he reached over and opened the passenger side door and invited the old man to enter and sit beside him. Clover spoke to the old man:"I know you will think me mad but you look just like my grandfather did just before he died over 20 years ago. You look just like him and you are dressed just like him. You are also carrying an old doctor's bag just like the one he used to carry."

The old man reached over and brushed his left hand, which seemed wet and cold, across Clover's cheek. Without speaking the old man communicated to Clover's consciousness that all was well and that he had come to accompany him to his destination. It did seem unusual that he communicated in this manner and that Clover was able to understand without his speaking the words. Clover continued driving his car along the steep winding road navigating the dips, curves and slopes as he had done many times before. It was exciting to drive his car on this road and it always got his adrenaline up when he would speed along the curves at breakneck speeds. Cora Lee would always tell him to slow down on those curves or it would be the death of them, so it was fun when he took the boys for a spin and he didn't have to be so cautious. Clover did think it was strange that his companions had abandoned him though. He wondered where they had gone and when they had left as he did not notice when they had gotten out of the car. He decided that next time that they did this they would have to watch out how much wildcat they were drinking and try to exercise more caution with the curves.

Clover had driven this road to Jasper many times before and it had never taken this long to get there. The road seemed familiar but the surrounding landscape was eerie with scraggly dead trees and long, spindly moss menacingly swaying from their limbs as the wind howled outside his car. There was no storm out before, there had never been trees like that before, and that kind of moss did not grow in this part of Alabama. Clover began to get a feeling of uneasiness about these unusual surroundings and his mysterious passenger that resembled his grandfather so. As he looked over at the old man he was again silently but effectively communicated with and he understood these words:"Have no fear for this road will take you where you want to go. All that is good will find you there and all that is empty within you will be filled. Trust me and I will take you there.

When we arrive you will travel new roads and this one will be no more. I have travelled this land 20 years or more and I know the way. Follow me and you will find all that you seek."

Clover knew that he must be dreaming and that he would soon awaken in his bed as he had always done. He would tell Cora Lee of his strange dream with all of the zeal that his lively imagination could muster and it would be a treat to repeat it to everyone, especially the kids, who would sit around the fireplace and listen with amazement. It would be like all those tales that Grandpa Russell Porter Palmer used to tell him when he was a kid and even better because Russell Porter Palmer was a major character in this one. But he wasn't dreaming and he wasn't in his bed. He had been driving in his car with his pals on his way to Jasper to have fun and celebrate the beginning of his new life up north in Chicago. Truly that is how it started but the kaleidoscope of life twisted fate and forced a detour upon Clover from which he would never return. The old man was truly Doctor Russell Porter Palmer and it was possible now for Clover to see him and communicate with him because they were both denizens of the same land – the land of the dead. Clover had crashed his car head on into a chicken truck coming in the opposite direction around one of those dangerous curves on the highway going to Jasper and the force of the impact had thrown Clover's head into the windshield of his car. A long metal lever that adjusted the windshield was thrust all the way through Clover's head and the blinding flash that Clover had experienced from it was the last conscious reality that he experienced of this world. Although he was not killed instantly and survived in a coma for 3 days, Clover had left his world instantly never to experience it in the flesh again. All of his dreams ended on that dark, dangerous road that night. He died 3 days later in a Jasper hospital on September 11, 1930.

There would be other chapters to follow for Cora Lee, Mammy, and the six children, but the chapters of Clover's brilliant and promising physical life had ended with a horrific automobile collision. He was the only one killed and all three of his pals escaped with only minor cuts or no injuries at all. The lives of Cora Lee, Mammy, and the six children were forever changed on that fateful night. Clover would continue to travel roads within a new and unfamiliar realm with his grandfather and others leading the way. They would stop at venues along the way that would offer entrances to new levels of existence with opportunities given to look backward or forward in time as its participants wished. The choices made would be crucial to their spiritual standing and to their attainment of the levels that they must complete to achieve total knowledge and spiritual wholeness.

Chapter 12

What Ifs Don't Count

Clover really had not totally accepted much less understood what had been happening to him. It seemed that he was in a strange limbo land and the world that he had previously known had been turned inside out. Nothing was as it was before. The roads were different and the landscape was an unfamiliar mix of foreign trees, hedges, convoluting hills and steep bluffs with jagged and threatening rock that jutted out precariously toward him like rusted stilettos. He and the old man, who he more and more believed was a reincarnation of his grandfather, had finally arrived at their destination. Clover did not recognize it though and it certainly was not Jasper, Alabama. Ever since that blinding flash it seemed that the whole world had changed and that he couldn't re-orient himself to the bizarre new one that he now found himself trapped within. They had arrived at a train station but it was not the familiar Muscle Shoals station where he had purchased his ticket to Chicago. It was all confusing because he wasn't supposed to take his train until tomorrow. Even time had fallen out of sequence and the minutes, hours, and days seemed melded together into one incoherent whole. He no longer had a grasp of where he was or what time it was or why he was in this strange new environment. Nevertheless he still had choices to make and he still must keep moving forward with his grandpa who was patiently guiding him toward the train station's ticket office. This train station was not like any he had seen before. It was a bright, silvery, gleaming, metallic artifice with an inner effervescence that brilliantly lit the surrounding twilight sky. As they walked toward the ticket booth which projected outward from the left side and had a shining, corbelled dome on its upper façade, Clover could see through the glass window that there was a woman inside. She was seated upon a golden throne with red velvet back and a velvety red cushion seat that was soft to the touch – he knew that it was soft because all his senses were acutely alive and he could "consciously" feel the softness of the fabric and the fill beneath it. There was an overwhelming yet exhilarating rush of sensory stimuli that came over him and he felt as if he had become immersed

170

within the essence of his everlasting soul.

The woman at the ticket booth looked lovingly into his eyes and he knew instinctively to reach inside his pocket, pull out his wallet, and retrieve the train ticket that he had purchased a few days ago. As he handed the ticket through the round opening in the glass, he at once recognized who she was or who he thought she was. She was beautifully dressed in a white buckskin dress with fringes on the sleeves and cuffs and colorful red, orange, and yellow beads had been decoratively sewn into a sunburst design that was located at the center over her breasts. Clover had never seen Morning Dove but he had heard plenty about her from his grandmother, Morning Dizenia. It was her. Clover's grandpa looked him in the eyes and smiled his acknowledgement and Clover knew that he was right. Clover had been led by his grandpa, who he had stopped and picked up alongside the road to Jasper, to a mystical new realm with a shining monumental train station at its entrance, where he presented his ticket to Morning Dizenia's mother and his grandmother, Morning Dove. Now the round arched, thick and heavy steel doors of the gleaming metal station opened as if by magic and a voice from within kindly beckoned him to come inside. Russell and Morning Dove accompanied Clover and all three stood before a conductor who was grandly dressed in an official blue cap with a golden sunburst medallion centered on its black band, blue coat with golden sunburst buttons, and blue trousers with thin golden flame like stripes running along the sides. Clover immediately observed that for such a large train station there was no waiting room or benches inside but just a large open space with tall metallic walls without a ceiling, and a floor of what appeared to be solid gold tiles. The conductor suddenly looked sharply upward, clicked his golden shoes together at the heels in military fashion, and raised both arms toward a midnight blue sky with brilliantly sparkling stars that shined through the opening where the ceiling should have been. When Clover looked up the sky slowly brightened and he could see billowing reddish clouds forming over a now brilliant daytime sky that seemed to filter the light of the sun which was shining behind them. Clover was reminded of a passage from the Bible that described Heaven as being paved with streets of gold as he glanced dreamily downward around the room at the golden tiles and tried to discern just exactly where he was and what was happening.

Finally a new ultra reality came rushing down from the open ceiling above with the hydraulic force of an all immersing waterfall and Clover understood that he was dead and had passed over to the other side. In fact, as he consciously made this analogy, an immense, sparkling crystalline waterfall cascaded down from the open ceiling above and swept him away into a vast river below with rushing currents that flowed like the spectrum of a rainbow. All of this had happened so quickly that Clover had no time to assess the all encompassing breadth and scope of it all. The multicolored currents were moving so fast around him that he had not noticed that he, his grandpa, and Morning Dove were all now inside a long boat with a large square windblown sail printed with a large golden sunburst over a band of red and white vertical stripes. The boat seemed to be coated in gold and it had a large mast on front with a large golden lion as a masthead. Clover thought that it looked like a Viking ship and he had no sooner thought that until the ship was populated with a crew of Viking oarsmen who began rowing the boat toward what he instinctively knew was a northerly direction. Clover was surprised by what had happened but not afraid – in fact it seemed that all fear had left him and serenity had prevailed over his entire being. He thought of Russell his grandfather and Morning Dove his great grandmother as he looked behind and saw them and wondered if Morning Dizenia would appear in this new realm as well. Within an instant Morning Dizenia appeared there at his side along with Russell her husband and Morning Dove her mother.

As they all stood at the front of the boat together, Morning Dizenia placed her hands on Clover's shoulders and smiled as she communicated to Clover's consciousness this message of warning:"Be careful, my son, what you think of here because it will come alive and become part of your reality. All is real here and all thought universally manifests itself. All that exists is here at once and forever. A mere suggestion or thought will bring it to the surface where it will share your plane of existence. This may seem a blessing but it may also be a curse because once a thought is manifested it can never be lost or made to disappear." Russell went on to explain to Clover that he must control his thoughts and follow his grandpa to the first level where Clover would learn how to control his power of thought and how to be selective in what he chooses to manifest. Having had this advice, the only thing Clover was able to do was think only of the boat with the Vikings rowing in a northerly direction with him and his grandparents and he concentrated on that only as they were rowed within the rainbow currents of the river. The four of them stood together at the front of the boat and emptied their consciousness of anything other than themselves and what surrounded them until they reached the first level.

"What we imagine to be is, and what is may be imagined. It is all there and is the same. There is no reality but the one we imagine and all that we imagine is real." Clover heard or consciously understood these words as they passed into the first level and the boat that had transported them there ceased to be. In fact all that Clover once knew to be physical truth ceased to be and there was only pure thought now. He saw everything at once, knew everything at once and understood infinity for the first time. Words were useless as knowledge replaced them. Physical reality ceased to exist as it was replaced and nullified by a spiritual wholeness that encompassed all. It became unnecessary to label or name or classify or even to comprehend. There were no differences, there was no good or evil. There was no controlling force or energy for there was God and that was all. God is all and all is God. At the end of physical time all goes to God and becomes one with God as that is where all things originate from. Clover had arrived at the first level and he at once understood these truths as if they had always been a part of him because now he was once again part of them. He was communicated another message which welcomed him and comforted his being which stated:"Welcome young soul who enters the first level. As you reexamine the old, fear not as you are not lost yet are found and comfort may be taken as you look within to ultimately understand what seems unknown from without."

Clover now possessed that which all had received who reach the first level. He had the gift of partial knowledge which would grow upon completion of each additional level that he attained. Clover's life and all those lives in God's infinite universe had been, are, and will continue until the end to be a constant pursuit of knowledge. He knew now why complete knowledge had not been made a gift to us by the creator. If we had been given it then we would never have pursued it. We as humans accomplish all through our pursuit of knowledge and we find knowledge only a bit at a time. We never realize that we will be given the opportunity to possess all knowledge at the end. Having complete knowledge would be a beautiful thing but pursuing it is what makes life worthwhile. God created us to pursue knowledge but only God provides complete knowledge as we become one with him. We must be willing to take the journey and follow the guides assigned to us that will show the way toward attaining the levels necessary to complete our quest.

These were the truths that Clover understood upon entering the first level. Now he was able to think freely and explore the fresh opportunities that were presented to him upon entrance to this level. He was free to look backward and analyze his past and also free to look forward and view what other directions his life might have taken. First Clover wanted to see what would have happened if he had not died September 11, 1930 and he had been able to take his trip to Chicago. It would mean nothing as all things physical were past, but at least his curiosity would be satisfied upon discovering what his life would've been like and what he would've accomplished. It was simple now and Clover could just open his consciousness and view what might have been. It was much like watching a cinema and it flashed before his consciousness like this: After their night out to celebrate Clover's upcoming trip to Chicago, Clover drove back to Hamilton, dropped off Willie, Ollie, and Jeff, and he went back to his house to get some sleep. It was after midnight and Cora Lee and the kids were all in bed asleep. Mammy, who would have been in her own little house next door, was now there at Cora Lee's house. It seemed she had woken up and come next door to see about Clover and inquire why he had been out so late, knowing that he had to get up early to catch the train. Clover greeted her there and explained how he and the boys just needed some time to talk over old times and say their goodbyes because it might be a while before they all got together again. Clover could see these scenes playing out before him but it was muted as if being projected through a rainbow colored mist that he was suspended inside of. He had seen impressionistic paintings in books that had the same feeling to them. It all seemed real and as if he were living the whole experience out but it was an out of body experience and it was like he was all spirit and had no flesh, bones, or body and, of course, he didn't. Mammy seemed satisfied with his response and she gave him a big warm hug as she sent him off to bed."We'll get up around five and I'll fix you a good hearty breakfast of eggs, grits, bacon, biscuits and sawmill gravy", she said. That sounded great to Clover and he turned in for the night without waking up Cora Lee who was sound asleep beside him. He had gone into the kids' bedrooms to check on them and Harrison was awake and crying about a bad nightmare he'd had where his father had been killed in a car crash. Clover tried to assure Harrison that all was fine, but he could not hold back his own tears.

Clover got up early to discover that everyone was awake and making preparations for getting the kids off to school and the little ones, Arthur, Herbert, and Horrice would stay home with Mammy and Cora Lee. Arthur was four, Herbert was two, and Horrice was just a baby of five months old, so likely Arthur was the only one who would remember him, Clover thought. Clover hugged and kissed Harrison, Elizabeth, and Iva as they finished up their breakfast and hurried off for school. All of this seemed real enough but it was if everything was being acted out within the scenes of a cinema. Cora Lee and Mammy, who were now together in the same house, both hugged and kissed him and held him tight as if they wanted to keep him from leaving them; it was almost as if they sensed that once he left they would never see him again. Clover kissed and hugged them both tightly as he headed for the door and looked back with tears in his eyes for one last time. This would be the last time Clover would see his beloved family, cinema or no cinema, and he tried to slow it all down but to no avail. The cinema, like life itself, was fleeting and those special loving moments that we experience each day are gone all too quickly never to return, so we must be grateful for each day.

His best friend, Willie Calvin was at the door waiting for Clover so that he could drive them to the train station in Muscle Shoals, Alabama where Clover would catch his train. On the way to Muscle Shoals Clover had time to look over his ticket information and study a map of the route provided by L&N (Louisville & Nashville) Railroad. He looked at the map and it was if he could see the layout on a huge cinematic screen inside his head. He could see a national map indicating the separate states with the cities indicated by dots that the railroad passed through and made stops at along the way north to Chicago. There was a new importance to the viewing of this map with all the stops on it because Clover knew that once he passed through all these towns that he would never see them again. It was that way with all he experienced and he was overcome with an oppressive sadness as he viewed his life's essence literally slip through his fingers and out of his grasp forever. He thought that it would've been good to see how things could've been but he now realized that what could've been would never be because of the events of that fatal night of September 8, 1930. He was aware that the life flashing before him was more a dream than reality and that the ideas, events, and people within were mere phantoms of an alter existence that could never be. But, at least, he thought he would get to view his life as it could have been even if he could not live it through means of his physical being which was now lost forever.

He therefore closely perused the map and began by noting his starting point of Muscle Shoals, Alabama. He would depart from there and the next town would be Lawrenceburg, Tennessee where they would stop to take on passengers. The next stop would be Columbia, Tennessee where they would disembark and board another train that would take them to Nashville, Tennessee. The Muscle Shoals to Columbia line was a short route that connected Alabama to Tennessee and places north. After passing through Nashville they would stop in Amqui, Tennessee and then continue north to Guthrie, Hopkinsville, Atkinson, and Henderson, Kentucky. Clover could see the names of towns that they would pass through with such clarity that he could've been the engineer with the railroad looking out the train's window as it approached each one of them. When they crossed into Indiana he could see that they would pass through or stop in the towns of Evansville, Fort Branch, Vincennes, Terre Haute, and Clinton, Indiana. After entering into Illinois, they would make stops in Danville, Rossville Junction, Woodland, and Momence on the way north to Chicago. With all the stops at the numerous towns along the way to let off and take on passengers, it would take nearly a whole day for them to arrive in Chicago at around 7:30 am the following morning. Clover had never heard of most of these towns on the way but they were all as crystal clear to him now as if he had traveled this route every day.

Once they drove up to the station in Muscle Shoals, Alabama, Clover already had a precise picture of where he was heading from having viewed the cinematic map that seemed magically projected inside his head. His friend, Willie Calvin, helped him with his two bags, one packed with his clothes and the other packed with tools and supplies for work that he might find in Chicago. Everything at this train station was the same as it had been when he had purchased his ticket several days before and he and Willie went inside and Clover presented his ticket to the agent at the ticket window. The ticket agent said that the train would depart in about 10 minutes so he and Willie walked through the exit doors onto the train platform next to the track where the #907 steam engine train bound for Columbia, Tennessee was waiting. Willie helped Clover with his bags and they entered the train where the porter showed them to Clover's seat. As Willie put Clover's bags into the overhead bin over his seat, he told Clover not to worry about his barber shop or café and that he would keep both running smoothly until Clover returned. He would check in on Cora Lee and the kids as well and make sure that they had all that they needed. Clover thought to himself what a good friend he had with Willie and what good times they had shared together over the years. He gave Willie a big hug and thanked him for all the things he had done for him. Willie hugged him back but said not to worry and not to act like they were never going to see each other again. Willie got off the train and waved to Clover as the train slowly pulled away from the station. With tears in his eyes, Clover thought that this was another very special part of his life and another very special friend that was slipping away forever.

Suddenly it became obvious to Clover that all that had been precious to him was now lost. He had lost his family and his friends and with great sadness he realized that anything he might have accomplished in Chicago or anywhere else would not have taken the place of them. He thought what difference would it have made how successful he might have become if he could not be alive to share his successes or even his failures with the ones he loved. After Willie left, Clover was overcome with the oppressive weight of sadness that all that truly experience love must endure when losing a family member or friend and realizing that the loss of them can never be replaced and the place vacated by them can never be filled. He sat alone in the passenger compartment of the #907 steam engine train as there were no other passengers making the trip from Muscle Shoals to Columbia, Tennessee that day. He had time to think about all he had lost before he reached the stop at Lawrenceburg, Tennessee where they would pick up more passengers. Clover dozed off as the "clickity clack" rhythm of the steel wheels on the track lulled him past the tranquil pastoral scenery of the north Alabama hill country. As the train sleepily chugged along it was almost as if he were alive again and that all of this that had happened to him was just a strange dream that he would soon awaken from.

Clover was awakened but not from a dream. He was awakened to his ever present new reality by the metallic screeching of the wheels on the track as the train slowed and pulled up to a halt in front of the Lawrenceburg, Tennessee station. Almost immediately Clover saw a young woman dressed in a very elegant, long, white chiffon gown. The gown was bunched and pouched at each shoulder, ruffled at the cuffs, and it ballooned out in neatly arranged and puffed pleats which flowed gracefully down from her waist beneath a maroon colored velvet belt to the shining maroon slippers on her feet. The gown was being blown by the wind and the fabric was rippling fitfully with the motion of the approaching train. Some of the steam from the train's smokestack surrounded her like clouds wafting in a crisp, clean, and azure spring sky. She appeared like a vision, vixen like, outside Clover's window as he stared mesmerized by her deep blue green eyes. She had on a wide brimmed white chiffon hat with a smooth rounded top and a bright maroon ribbon tied around it as a band with a puffy maroon bow with two long ribbons trailing from it in the wind. The wind blew recklessly through the long freely flowing strands of her strawberry blond hair as she stared back at Clover with those deep pools of blue green eyes that seemed to beseech him to plunge into the very depths of her soul. Clover was instantly entranced and totally enraptured by this woman who had stolen his heart and would no doubt try to steal his very soul. Clover had never seen a woman more beautiful than this vision of femininity which was being presented to him by this" heavenly" muse. Clover thought to himself about the warning Mammy had always given him about people:"If someone appears too good to be true, then they probably are". Thanks to the cautious upbringing of his mother, Clover was at once on guard and mistrustful of this lovely creature. He knew that he must be dreaming as beauty such as hers simply could not exist and his male sensibilities could not possibly absorb and fathom the depths that had immersed him within those blue green pools that traveled to her very soul.

She was unaccompanied as she stood by a porter that had stacked her luggage upon a cart that was waiting to be unloaded onto the train. The porter, who seemed unaware and unaffected by the beauty beside him, brought her luggage into the passenger compartment where Clover was sitting and she came up and sat directly across from him in the seat next to the opposite window. Clover could not believe that she had chosen to sit right across from him as she could have chosen any seat in the entire compartment and this made him even more suspicious of her intentions toward him. After arranging her luggage and settling down in her seat she looked over at Clover, smiling as she parted her lips and revealed her perfect pearly white teeth. "Hello!" she said, "My name is Charlotte

Carlisle and I am travelling to Chicago on business. What brings such a handsome and dashing man as yourself to these parts and for where are you bound?" Clover responded in as authoritarian manner as he could muster:"I am Clover McKinley Palmer, a man of many talents who is on his way to Chicago to pursue the brighter paths that await me there".

Clover continued to explain to her that he was a photographer as well as a song writer and that he wanted to pursue the avenues available to him in the big city that would enable him to expand his horizons. Charlotte smiled broadly and seemed impressed with what Clover had told her. She told him that she was a fashion designer and model in Chicago and that the gown, hat and slippers that she was wearing had been designed by her. Clover commented on how beautiful the gown was and how it had totally captivated him as he had watched her from his window and observed her boarding the train. Just then the porter came by to take Charlotte's ticket and to give them a copy of *The Birmingham News* which Clover was glad to receive as he had missed out on all the news for the last few days. Charlotte did not seem interested in having a copy so she declined and began combing her beautiful strawberry blonde hair that had been tossed into disarray by the wind. The front page headline of the paper flashed out toward Clover like fire as he read with utter devastation these words:"Lawrenceburg Senator's Daughter Killed in Fatal Car Crash". Clover read on and found that Charlotte Carlisle was the daughter of Samuel Carlisle, Tennessee's state senator from the Lawrenceburg district. She had been on her way to catch the train after a visit with her parents and had a blowout on one of the tires of her vehicle. Her father had left for Nashville, the state capitol, the night before and had told her to just use his white Lincoln convertible to drive to the station the next morning. Her outfit was perfect for the trip back and it matched perfectly the elegant style of her father's fine white Lincoln convertible, so what could've been better? When the tire blew, Charlotte lost control of the car and went crashing through a guard rail over a steep cliff and into a rocky ravine below. The car exploded into flames and Charlotte was killed instantly. Again the kaleidoscope of life had turned its wicked lenses in unpredictable directions and one could never know when the lens would snuff out the lives within.

Clover went on to read the obituary page expecting to find out more about Charlotte's death when he noticed a few lines down on the same page another startling entry:"Clover McKinley Palmer, local Hamilton merchant, killed in violent head on automobile collision on Jasper Highway." The obit went on to describe the wreck which happened on September 8, 1930 and Clover's passing away from a serious head injury three days later on September 11, 1930. The funeral was held in the Palmer community at the Palmer Church and he was buried afterward at the adjoining Palmer family cemetery just outside of Hamilton, Alabama. He was survived by his wife, Cora Lee, his mother, Mary Dizenia, and six children: Harrison, Elizabeth, Iva, Arthur, Herbert, and a five month old infant, Horrice. If he had not realized by now the reality of what had happened to him, it certainly all came crashing down upon him now. Clover looked over at Charlotte who was still combing her beautiful strawberry blonde hair and handed her the newspaper. "You need to read this" he said.

A torrent of tears burst forth from Charlotte's blue green eyes that flowed down her still rosy cheeks after reading the articles and she sadly implored to Clover:"I knew that something was strange when I did not see any other people at the station or any other people inside the passenger compartment but you. I remember a blinding flash before I arrived at the station. It was odd because everything changed after that and the next thing I knew I was already at the station waiting with my bags. I thought it very strange but I never suspected that I had died and was now in the hereafter." Clover replied:"Yes, I experienced the same feelings and it took some time for me to finally accept the reality of what had happened to me". Clover and Charlotte were both overcome by the tragic loss of their earthly lives and between the two of them a mutual bond of allegiance was born. They knew now that they would be sharing eternity together and whatever roads that lay before them, they each must make their own choices about how next to proceed. What could have developed into an intimate and loving relationship between them had now become a joint reckoning, the flesh was left behind and a mutual pact was made between them to pursue only the loftiest of goals along the paths that they must each travel.

They had no sooner thought these thoughts than they saw a female figure approach them from the distance. Strangely they were no longer on the train but each of them was alone walking on paths individually meant for them. Clover found himself amongst a glowing field of yellow jonquils like the ones that grew in fields around Hamilton, Alabama. The rapid pace of the changing habitats around him no longer confused him and he was becoming accustomed to the juxtapositions of time and space that this realm's kaleidoscopic lens had forced upon him. He felt sad that Charlotte was now gone but he realized that she had her own paths to travel. When he saw that the woman now approaching him was Morning Dove in her white buckskin dress he was not surprised but welcomed her freely and openly from his heart of hearts and soul of souls. These are the words that he understood her to say:"You have now mastered the first level and have understood the true value and meaning of life. Nothing is as valuable as a single moment shared with those we love. Nothing can replace a love once lost and nothing attained in life can equal that love in value. Without love given and shared with others and love received from them in return, nothing else in life can complete you and make you whole. A person without love will never be complete and can never attain the levels of knowledge that lead to spiritual wholeness. One must leave earthly pleasures behind and be open to the truth that lies within this level and the ones that follow."

Upon learning about and accepting this universal truth about love, Clover had now successfully gained entrance to the first level and was ready to begin his journey toward the second level and to face the challenges that it held. Morning Dove prompted him to follow her and she led him through the glowing field of yellow jonquils toward a crystal clear lake that had a glowing effervescence within it that seemed to draw him closer with each step forward that he took. A resounding voice came forth from the pristine lake that seemed to propel itself forcibly upward within a purplish waterspout that spiraled swiftly toward a sunset sky of yellows, oranges, reds, pinks, and blues that was muted and misty as if seen through the lens of an unfocused camera. The voice communicated as if by sound waves and the pitch was higher or lower depending upon how far away or how close the waves rotated toward Clover. These are the words that Clover understood as the waves rotated there in front of him:"The journey from the physical to the spiritual requires relinquishing the ties that bind you to the physical world. With each new level attained you will remember less of what was important on a physical level and retain increasingly more of the love that truly gave value to your existence. That love in its purest form will be what will comprise your spiritual being and when that love becomes sublime within you the final level awaits you and will accept your entrance therein."

It was so obvious to Clover now and his being was infused with a sense of utter elation and serenity. Morning Dove who had been there with him all along now signaled to him with a motion of her raised arms to follow her onto the surface of the silvery shining lake. They both treaded across the gently flowing surface with the ease of weightlessness that things spiritual possess. A great funnel like vortex opened beneath them and their beings flowed into and through it until they approached a crystalline tetrahedron globe that had round arched doorways upon each of its faceted surfaces. Upon arrival to this vast globe like structure, Morning Dove announced to Clover that their journey together had ended and that he had arrived at the entrance of the second level and would have to make a choice about which of the arched doorways he would pass through. The vast crystalline globe began to spin around slowly on an unseen centrifugal axis and upon each facet an arched doorway revealed a glimpse of what lay within. Clover knew that he was being tested as most of the doorways revealed visions of earthly treasures such as monetary wealth, fame and fortune, sexual ecstasies, unlimited political power and influence, and a mind boggling assortment of the vain and glorious possessions that humans strive to attain all of their lives on earth. Clover was not fooled by all of this though because he had already learned from the previous level what was truly valuable and that to be complete and attain true knowledge only the love that one possessed for others could lead the way. Clover's instincts were correct and he was being tested to see if he could be lured back into the traps and pitfalls that life in its physical form would offer.

Clover was ready to take the journey forward and he chose the doorway into which he could see love manifested from the faces of and outreached hands of his ancestors who had come before him. He saw John Palmer and Friday each riding spotted stallions on the fields of their South Carolina farm. He saw William Mansell in his Tennessee workshop working on the spinning wheel that he would give to his daughter Morning Dizenia upon her marriage to Russell Porter Palmer. He saw Newton Ozbirn riding his chestnut colored stallion Rex alongside a cascading mountain stream with his faithful dog Captain running ahead of them protecting the way. He saw Cora Lee's best friend Mamie Taylor and her husband Thomas B. Taylor who had both been killed in the April 20, 1920 tornado that struck Hamilton. They were now embracing in a radiant field of four o'clocks, zinnias, cockscombs, verbena, sweet William, thrift and a variety of flowers the like of which Mammy would grow in her garden by their house in Hamilton. The flowers swayed in the warm loving winds that enveloped the couple, surrounding and eternally protecting them from all future harm.

It wasn't hard for Clover to choose and he willed his being through the arched doorway of his ancestors as a chorus of hymns arose from the ranks much like the songs of the Sacred Harp that Clover had loved so much on earth. What he heard now was similar to the hymns he had sung at the White House Church and at other Sacred Harp Singings but was sung in one collective voice that was richly melodic with a metallic and horn like rhythm to it. It was as if do, re, mi, fa, so, la, ti, do was being played by a horned instrument but at the same time was sounding out words that rhymed like iambic pentameter poetry. His being absorbed its meaning and he at once recognized that he was listening to John Donne's "Holy Sonnets, Sonnet 10" as all voices coalesced and sang these words:

> *Death, be not proud, though some have called thee*
> *Mighty and dreadful, for thou art not so:*
> *For these whom thou think'st thou dost overthrow*
> *Die not, Poor Death, nor yet canst thou kill me*
> *From rest and sleep, which but thy pictures be,*
> *Much pleasure; then from thee much more must flow,*
> *And soonest our best men with thee do go,*
> *Rest of their bones, and soul's delivery.*
> *Thou art slave to fate, chance, Kings and desperate men,*
> *And dost with poison, war, and sickness dwell,*
> *And poppy or charms can make us sleep as well*
> *And better than thy stroke: why swellest thou then?*
> *One short sleep past, we wake eternally*
> *And death shall be no more: Death thou shalt die,*

Clover remembered John Donne's "Death be not Proud" as he had read it many times from his grandfather's poetry books and Russell Porter Palmer had said many times that their Palmer ancestors had been fond of the poem and recited it many times by heart. The ancestors were proud that Clover remembered the poem so well and that his grandfather had passed it down to him from his ancestors. The poem was vital to Clover's success and his knowledge of it would allow him to pass the test he would soon be given upon his arrival at the second level.

No sooner had Clover recognized the poem than a tall gaunt bearded man in 17th century attire stood before him and recited the first lines again as the chorus sang behind him. The man asked Clover when he finished his recital:"Who am I ?" Clover immediately answered:"You are John Donne and you have recited Sonnet 10 from your poem 'Holy Sonnets' or as I like to call it, 'Death be not Proud' that you wrote in 1618."

Upon successfully completing this test from his ancestral second level, Clover was transformed from his individual entity into that of his ancestral whole that occupied the second level along with all the others who were now one entity and would await the opening of the third level where they would face other spiritual challenges. The song they now sang surrounded their entity and their combined voices brought forth the deepest and purest sensation of love with an all consuming force that forever cleansed their combined immortal souls. Clover was with his ancestors now and all temptations from his physical past ceased to exist. By choosing the arched doorway of his ancestors and accepting their unconditional love for him he had successfully passed into the second level. An amazing sensation overtook him as his ancestors all seemed to coalesce into a unified mass with him as an integral part of it. He was no longer just an individual being but was now capable of existing unilaterally alongside his ancestors or he could meld himself within their common entity depending on how his will wished to perceive and relate to the spiritual forces around him. So in this new second level there was a dualism that involved free choice of the party concerned and therefore one could manifest oneself in an individual form or become part of a massive collective entity of souls with the collective knowledge and power that it entailed. Usually there were no separate entities unless these individual entities wanted to manifest themselves separately or unless there was a new entrant to the second level that needed the reassurance of seeing them and recognizing their familiar traits. This is why Clover saw and felt the love of his ancestors as he looked through the arched doorway of the globe. His ancestors became individually known to him first and once Clover recognized and accepted them as his ancestors they then opened themselves up as a collective entity of which he could now become part. They explained to Clover that the third level that they would all eventually attain was a holding area where all souls will remain as one until the end of physical time on earth when all individual entities will be judged as worthy or unworthy to enter the fourth and final level. Those judged worthy would join the unified deity that is God and become one with him. Those judged unworthy would become phantasms that would wander uncharted realms of God's universe where there exists no time and no physical or spiritual constraints or barriers but just infinite, non navigable darkness without light, without communication, without sleep and without hope. In the fourth level the lost may become found and find hope if they are found worthy. To be found unworthy is to be lost forever.

The third level would be a final testing zone for all beings, including Clover. Having made it that far was an accomplishment that few attain because of the many temptations encountered along the way. For example, if Clover had chosen to accept Charlotte's advances and had not shown her the newspaper headline announcing her death, she may well have encouraged his desires for her. They both could have submitted to the carnal desires that they each had for each other and an intimate relationship could have developed between them. They both could have continued their journey together on the train and once they had both arrived in Chicago they could have entered into a love affair that could've offered infinite pleasure and infinite opportunities for the advancement of their social and cultural existence. Many would've chosen that path and never have made it to the third level and, of course, many would've not even made as far as the second level because of similar temptations. Clover and Charlotte made a pact that they would pursue the true path of enlightenment that was there for all to see if they open their souls and allow God's wisdom to enter. It is true that Charlotte's path was necessarily different than Clover's because the demands and challenges facing her were not the same as those that Clover would face. We must all take our own paths but if we travel them well we will reach the same source of knowledge that we strive for – which, in essence, is God.

The third level then will be inhabited by the sum total of all successful souls that have made the correct decisions that enable spiritual purity to grow within them. Each level is a growth process and the successful completion of one leads the traveler to the beginning of the next. Doom awaits all that fail to achieve entrance to any level, but that doom and the judgment awaiting them is relative to the degree of accomplishment or failure that each one of them attains. There are planes of existence ranging from the darkest depths of oblivion to the brightest omnipresence of God which accepts all that attain successfully the fourth level. The third level then is not a guarantee of God's acceptance but it makes for a much smaller crowd waiting at "Heaven's Gates". Clover would now wait there and continue to grow in knowledge with each test that he successfully negotiates. What is different about the third level is that it offers the inhabitants the chance to learn from their mistakes and then move forward. The tests offered in the third level are not of a physical nature as the inhabitants there have now moved far beyond the physical toward a truly spiritual existence. Now they must learn how to maneuver within the spiritual realm and how to exist as a universal entity before they seek acceptance at the end of physical life and time on earth with the fourth level. These levels of afterlife will either be attained or not as we all eventually arrive at them and we, like Clover, will have decisions about what choices to make at each level just as we had decisions to make about which roads we chose to take in life. As with Clover, the roads we choose determine where our future will take us. God gives us free will to choose whatever paths we want, but in the end our choices must be worthy ones if we expect to find God's love at our final destination.

Part IV
Triumphant Fields

Chapter 13

The Agony of Grief

In the physical world Clover had been seriously injured in a car crash and was taken to a hospital in Jasper, Alabama where he lived on for three days before passing away. This period of time from the instant of the blinding flash of his car collision to his final breath and last moment of life exactly corresponded to the period that he spent with his grandfather, Russell Porter Palmer, his grandmother, Morning Dizenia Palmer, and his great grandmother, Morning Dove Palmer as they journeyed together in pursuit of the three levels. Where we left Clover at the third level after his discovery of what the fourth and final level held for him was the exact moment that his life ended on earth. With death and what comes after, time has no meaning and a day can be a year or a year can be a century and the span of a human life on earth may equal a millennium and physical reality ceases to exist and is replaced by pure thought. Once Clover finished his journey to the third level and discovered what awaited him with the fourth and final level, his journey was complete and his physical being passed away to all on earth September 11, 1930. His spiritual entity now existed along with all others who have passed and will be collectively called to God at the end of physical time. Death returns to birth as birth and death are the same in the kaleidoscope within which all life must travel. Those individual entities within that are judged worthy will be joined with God in everlasting love and peace and those judged unworthy will not.

Clover's transition into the everlasting began as it may have begun, as I have projected, over 30 years before with his conception in that beautifully windswept field of clovers. Symbolically, the fields of clover his life began within may await him and one can imagine him gliding magically through their wafting purplish heads as he speeds forward to the entrance of the fourth level and so his essence can be seen returning to the source from which it came. The length of this hypothetical journey to that level cannot be measured in terms of real time but on September 11, 1930 Clover's life tragically ended on earth before he ever had the chance to fulfill his ambitions and dreams. He joined the countless millions of other victims,

188

young and old, whose lives had been taken because of wars, accidents, murders, or just from being in the wrong place at the wrong time. He like so many others was a victim of the twisting lens of life's kaleidoscope that propelled him into the precarious realms of no return. He was 31 years old and had just begun to live his young life when it was so violently taken from him on that dark curved road just three days before on September 8, 1930.

The journey for Clover's loved ones on earth was a grim one as the shock of what had happened began to slowly come into focus. The night of the accident Clover was driving himself and three others around a dangerous curve on the road to Jasper, Alabama. In the car with him were two friends and a distant cousin. As the car veered around the curve it crashed head on into a chicken truck that was coming from the opposite direction. Had Clover's head not been thrust onto a metal lever that was projected out toward him he might have survived the crash. Some cars during the 1920's and 30's had a metal lever on the side of the windshield that enabled one to adjust the angle of the glass so that it could be opened or shut. The force of the impact was so great that Clover's head was forced onto the lever and it pierced through his skull and passed all the way through his brain. He somehow survived for three days and nights after being taken to the hospital but never regained consciousness. Death was no doubt merciful because had he lived it would have been in a vegetative state at best. Except for just minor cuts or bruises none of the other passengers were hurt including the driver of the truck.

The passengers in Clover's car and the truck driver were able to flag down an approaching car which turned out to be a Packard limousine owned by a wealthy senator named Rankin Fite from Hamilton. A daughter, Carolyn Fite, was a passenger and was a school friend of Harrison Palmer, Clover's son. The chauffeur of her car and Clover's friends were able to remove Clover and place him inside the limousine so that he could be taken to the hospital in Jasper. It was lucky that the limousine came around because there were no ambulance services to be had in that part of Alabama in those days. Caroline Fite had to ride on the running board and hold on to the door as there was no room left inside the car for her as they sped toward Jasper. A neighbor that lived in a white house close to the accident managed to help bandage Clover's head with her torn sheets and place a silver platter over the gaping wound in an effort to prevent any further bleeding. Somehow Clover survived the trip and was placed in a room at the Jasper hospital. Because of the seriousness of the wound there was very little that could be done except to stop the bleeding and place bandages over the top of his head. There was no plastic surgery in those days and due to the severity of the wound, surgery wouldn't have helped in any case. It was just a matter of time until he would pass away. He would groan in pain and it appeared that he was trying to talk at times but he never regained consciousness.

Cora Lee found out about the accident when someone came to their door that night and told them that Clover had been in a bad wreck. Mammy and Cora Lee stayed with Clover in the hospital for 3 days and 3 nights where he tried to talk but only groaned. The kids stayed with the Henry family in Hamilton while Mammy and Cora Lee stayed with Clover. The kids did visit though and one time my mother remembers walking down the corridor of the hospital to her father's room. She remembers him loudly groaning from inside the room as they approached but she mostly shut out the memory of anything else. My mother remembers one day that the kids were all playing softball at the Henry's home when someone came up to say that Clover had died. Having this happen to her at such an early age and to have her handsome, beloved father taken away in such a horribly tragic way deeply affected my mother the rest of her life.

The next event that vividly stood out in my mother's memory was the funeral of Clover. As was the practice in those days he lay in state in an open casket in the living room of their home and all the relatives and friends came to view the body and pay their last respects. This was horrible for mother and all the kids old enough to remember and especially so for my Aunt Iva who was six years old at the time. What was so striking to my mother was that Clover's head was covered with white bandages and his face was also partially covered. Clover had a beautiful head of thick black hair and it was all covered with bandages that were necessary to cover the awful head wound. It was horrible to see her father that way and the memory of it always remained with her. She said that it would've been better not to have had the kids see their father in the open casket that way. After the visitation mother remembers that they all went to the cemetery where they all witnessed his casket being lowered into the ground. Iva fainted when she witnessed this and it was very traumatic for her then and later when she started school.

After Clover's death they all went to Cora Lee's father, Thomas Goodson's place, as he thought it would be better to raise the kids in the country. Mother remembers him saying:"You wouldn't be no good in town!" That was where they lived when Iva started to school in the little unpainted schoolhouse in the country and where my mother and Harrison, the oldest boy, also attended. Mother remembers that the kids all got up in Thomas Goodson's grape vines and picked "possum grapes" as they called them very shortly after Clover's death. Not many memories were good ones though and things didn't work out all that well living in the house with Thomas, so they all moved to Thomas Goodson's sharecropper house to live for a while. Mother and Iva had good memories of going to the little country school though and mother learned her multiplication tables there under instruction of Mrs. Dona Coffield. Mrs.Dona Coffield was the daughter of the Coffields that had moved to Alabama from Georgia along with Thomas Goodson many years ago. Mrs. Coffield taught Iva as well and she helped Iva adjust emotionally to the loss of her father. They all got a good education at the little school and it was really one of those schools that taught to "the tune of a hickory stick", as the discipline was strict and if you misbehaved you got a good "paddling".

There were some unpleasant things though that mother remembered happening to her while she was at the little school. She was in a children's play that she had to sing a silly little song and dance a silly little dance around in front of the parents and students. It was very embarrassing then and still so to even talk about it later. The song went like this:"Sing a little, sing a little, sing every day, and sing your cares away." This was a very paradoxical experience for my mother and I doubt that having to perform this cheery little song for everyone when she had suffered so much helped my mother deal with the death of her father. Another thing that mother talked about was an obnoxious little boy who always brought his lunch to school in a bucket. His name was Hamilton Green and as if bringing his lunch in a bucket wasn't odd enough, he would eat from it like a pig. He enjoyed showing off and would pick up the bucket and slurp his food out of it making noises like pigs when they eat slop. Of course the teacher, Dona Cofield, got on to him and chastised him for acting like a pig and eating like a pig from a slop bucket. Mother said he didn't really care though and was proud to show off that way but she and every one of the girls in the class stayed away from him and thought he was gross. The boys, of course, encouraged him and got a big laugh out of it.

Clover's kids were all young at the time and it was hard on them to lose their father so tragically. Socially it was hard also because they were treated like poor little orphans and sometimes people could be insensitive to their feelings. There were many occasions that arose that made life for them challenging to say the least. One time that they all remembered concerned a man that had hired them all to pick some velvet beans from his field. They all worked in the fields and helped Mammy and Cora Lee to earn extra money to pay for food and clothing so it wasn't uncommon that they would be offered work picking cotton or other crops. But being "orphans", sometimes people would try to take advantage of them and try to cheat them out of their proper wages. A farmer named Mr. Duke contacted Mammy and asked her if she would send the kids over to pick some velvet beans in his field. This was not a fun thing for anyone to do, especially kids, because picking velvet beans would rub your fingers red and raw and give you an awful itch. Besides, the day Mr. Duke wanted them to come was the day of the air plane show and there were going to be a lot of planes doing stunts that the kids were looking forward to seeing. They needed the money though, so Mammy told them they'd have to go and pick Mr. Duke's velvet beans. They wouldn't have had the money to purchase tickets for the air plane show anyway but they could've got close enough to watch if it weren't for having to go and pick Mr. Duke's old beans! So while all the other kids were either at the air plane show having fun or at least close enough to it to see some of the stunts, Clover's kids were all in Mr. Duke's field picking velvet beans getting itchy and rubbing their fingers raw. They could only glance up from time to time and see a plane or two in the distance and it was really heartbreaking to be the orphans that missed out on all the fun. They did their jobs though and picked a bunch of velvet beans for Mr. Duke. When they finished and brought their beans to be weighed like everybody else, Mr. Duke cheated them and didn't give them the same price per pound as he did everyone else. After all, he thought, they were just orphan kids and shouldn't be paid like the adult pickers. They only got paid a small portion of what was due according to the pound weight and they were all upset and went home and told Mammy that Mr. Duke had shorted them.

Mammy was furious and she decided to waylay Mr. Duke the first chance she got when they went to town. She watched out for him and followed him when she saw him in town one day. He went into a general store where there were a lot of local townspeople shopping and Mammy followed him inside and cornered him. She stuck her finger up in his face and shook it violently while all the people inside watched in amazement. She hollered out at him in a loud chilling voice:"I want you to know Clover's kids are just as good as yours. They deserve to be paid full price for the velvet beans they picked for you and not to be cheated and taken advantage of because you think they're just poor little orphan kids. So you better look all these nice people in the eyes and say you're sorry for the way you treated them and pay up the difference or, by the good Lord above, I will never let you hear the end of it!"Everyone in the store was surprised that Mr. Duke would do that to innocent little kids and that he was the kind of person that would take advantage of the less fortunate and they all gave Mammy a standing ovation. Needless to say, Mr. Duke settled up with Mammy and went on his way trying not to look his friends in the eyes as he went.

Another heartbreaking memory that my mother related to me concerned the second youngest son Herbert. He was only two years old when Clover was killed but he noticed his dad was gone almost immediately. The reason was is that Clover would often take Herbert for rides in his car and Herbert really looked forward to seeing him when he would come home, come inside and pick him up in his arms and say:"I'm home son. You want to go for a ride in the car with me and go get an ice cream cone?" Now suddenly there was no daddy to come home and Herbert just could not understand why. It was hard on him and he would often ask Cora Lee:"Where Daddy? Where Daddy?" Cora Lee had to put away the pictures of Clover to keep Herbert from asking where he was.

Life was hard for them all and at first they tried staying at houses of their relatives but eventually moved back to town to live in the houses that Clover had built for them. They all started going to school in town and spent much of their free time picking cotton and other crops to help with buying food and clothing. They were very poor and Mammy and Cora Lee did washing and sewing for people to help pay the bills. Sadly, Clover had taken out a life insurance policy a few months before his death but he wasn't able to keep up the payments on it and it had lapsed just before his fatal accident. This left Mammy, Cora Lee and the kids to fend for themselves during the midst of the depression in the best way that they could. There was no Social Security, Welfare, or Food Stamps to help them but just their own backbreaking hard work and their Palmer pride. Of course they all picked cotton until their fingers were red and raw and the girls did house work for people in town when they got older. These were the jobs that enabled them to buy a nice dress for church or school activities or just to buy a special gift for themselves or someone else. All their food was grown and canned, they made their own bread, made most of their own clothes, and all that was bought was lard, sugar, flour and meal. Coffee was bought also and Mammy would often criticize the way Cora Lee would make it. If it was weak it was like "stump water" and if it was too strong it was "double up a hill and kick up behind" which described the way you would force a stubborn mule to go up a hill.

What had happened to their father weighed heavily upon the kids and at times it was necessary to act out their grief in what may have seemed unusual ways to those surrounding them. The neighbors around Mammy's house remembered the funerals that the kids would give for baby chickens, birds, or other small animals domestic or wild. Understandably, death was a serious thing to them and so they would have funerals for the poor animals that they had for pets or to whom they had become attached to. They all would get together on the side of the house and have a ceremony where they would bury the animal and decorate its grave with honeysuckles. The oldest boy, Harrison, would preach a sermon with his deep voice and all the kids would sing songs like "Rock of Ages", "When the Roll is Called up Yonder", "The Old Rugged Cross", and sometimes, if it was a pet lamb, they'd sing "Mary Had a Little Lamb". They were always very somber and serious and in some ways maybe it helped to alleviate the grief they all suffered from the loss of their father. The neighbors were all very nosy anyway and were always looking for something to gossip about when they sat in their porch swings every evening after supper. For example there was an eccentric neighbor of Mammy's named Mrs. Fowler, they liked to gossip about, who liked to go out in the field next to her house and pray because the pasture out there reminded her of the stable and the manger that Jesus was born in. Mrs. Fowler would often go out there and raise a glorious ranting and raving as she looked up to the heavens and praised God in her own peculiar manner. Mammy always thought she was a hypocrite though and tried to be deceitful with people and she used to call her "Old Decateful". When Mammy compared her pious antics to the heartfelt and genuine songs and sermons of the children with their animal funerals, "Old Decateful" could never hold a candle.

Aunt Iva liked to tell the story of how she rode in an ox cart when she was a little girl. No one really believed that it was possible but it actually did happen. Mammy had relatives that lived way out in the country and in those days it was inaccessible with few roads and mostly just narrow dusty trails. In fact many people used to say you had to swing on a grapevine just to get out there. Harlon Boyette, Mammy's nephew, had an ox cart left over from pioneer days that he still used to travel on the trails to and from his farm. Mammy had let the kids go out to visit her sister, Rhoda Boyette earlier in the day by hack or horse and wagon and the driver, a neighbor, came on back to town. Harlon Boyette had offered earlier to drive them home in his ox cart and Mammy trusted Harland to take care of them and agreed. When it was time to take the kids back Harlon hitched up the ox cart and loaded up the kids. Iva remembers being afraid because the ox cart was shaky and very unsteady on just two wheels and the trail was full of rocks and holes and was bumpy all the way back to town. The days of ox carts had long passed but Iva and the other kids got a chance to feel what it must've been like for their ancestors when they traveled by them to Alabama over a hundred years ago. She remembers the steep hills and mountainous countryside as they were jostled along and recalls looking at the terraces that the farmers had built alongside the hills to grow their crops. We later discussed how similar they must've been to those still found in France and other places in Europe. It was getting dark on that scary old trail though and Iva couldn't wait to get back home to Mammy. Mammy was worried too and was real happy to see them all when Harland pulled up front with all the kids shook up but safely inside.

The sense of loss strikes hardest during the holidays when one has lost loved ones that will never be there to share the joy again. Aunt Iva recalled what that first Christmas was like without her father. After Clover died they all moved out to Grandpa Goodson's place. It didn't work out too well though and they later moved back to town to live in their houses that Clover had built. The kids were told not to expect too much for Christmas that year because Clover was gone. However, there was a very happy ending because Santa Claus brought a bunch of toys anyway. Santa Claus turned out to be Aunt Rowena Porterfield, Cora Lee's half sister, who brought the toys. She owned a beauty school in

Birmingham, Alabama and her husband was a railroad man with the L & N (Louisville & Nashville) Railroad. They drove 100 miles from Birmingham to Hamilton to bring toys to the kids late Christmas Eve night. Iva got a baby doll cradle and stroller that she treasured and saved and they both belong to her daughter now. My mother got dolls, doll clothes and a doll tea service, and the boys all got softballs, bats, toy guns, toy cars and trucks, cowboy suits, Indian headdresses, drums and just the really nice things that little boys love. So Santa Claus did come after all and didn't forget the orphans who'd just lost their father. My Aunt Iva believed to her dying day that there really was a Santa Claus. As long as there are good people like Aunt Rowena and her husband the railroad man there always will be a Santa for little girls and little boys who will keep Santa in their hearts just as my Aunt Iva did.

This chapter has been about the agony of grief and how the death of Clover affected the lives of those that loved him. Mammy had much grief and sadness to deal with in her life starting with the death of her father Zachariah Gaines Palmer when she was nine months old and later, when she was twelve, with the death of her mother Mary Elizabeth (Nellie) Armstrong Palmer. She was raised by stepparents which according to Mammy's own accounts was not a pleasant experience for her. At sixteen she became pregnant with the child of her first cousin, John Russell or Blue John Palmer, who I have reason to believe she truly loved. She and Blue John of course had to remain apart because of the stigma of what they had done but Mammy seemed to have made consistent efforts to see Blue John in Arkansas many times throughout her life. Add to this the horrific loss of her beloved son Clover in an automobile accident when he was only 31 years old and you have a shattered human being who has suffered loss almost beyond endurance and comprehension. Different people have different ways of dealing with grief such as this and Mammy dealt with it by concentrating all of her efforts on the raising of Clover's children and ensuring that they grew up to be fine upstanding human beings. Mammy and Cora Lee together accomplished that goal and much more but Mammy had another means of assuaging her grief which offered her great solace throughout all the years of her life. No one knew it at the time but the folk ballads that Mammy would always sing when she would work around the house or comb her hair at night in the porch swing were songs that she deeply indentified with and she shared truly with the content and feelings of the songs' lyrics. In Chapter 14, my last chapter, I will share with you these songs and the sadness that they conveyed and how they closely mirrored the agony that my great grandmother must have endured in her life.

Chapter 14

Ballads for Mammy

I found when doing my research from my brother's collection of family letters a hand written copy of a song that Mammy used to sing. The copy was faint and hard to discern but I did my best and copied it down as precisely as I could. The handwriting was not immediately recognizable but upon comparing it with all the letters that Roger had received and saved and with other notes and records I finally was able to assess that it was copied by Clover himself. I was able to compare it to some notes and music sheets with handwriting on them by Clover and they matched. This was a song that Mammy sang all her life and obviously Clover must have listened closely and copied it down at some time. I am very grateful that he did because it gives us a factual accounting of one of the songs that many in the family have heard Mammy sing. When Mammy would sing she would sing in the old Gaelic dialect in strophic form which was the common structure used for ballads such as these in days past. I can remember her singing them when I was a child and we would visit her. She would have me sit next to her on the porch swing of her house and she would sing to me as she brushed her hair before going to bed at night. She had committed these songs to memory just as her ancestors had done before her and carried on a tradition of folk ballads that originated in Ireland, England, and Scotland as far back as the 1600's or even further. As I understand it, the strophic form used by her is the simplest and most durable of musical forms which extends a piece of music by repetition of a single section and that is how I remember the songs that she sung being structured. This reminds me a little of the structure of the Sacred Harp music that Clover and all the Palmer relatives would sing and that Clover would use when writing hymns.

I could hardly contain my excitement when I researched the internet and found the song that Mammy sang all those years ago. I was able to copy it down almost exactly as Clover had written it almost 100 years ago. I typed in the first two lines from a stanza and searched the internet and to my great joy the exact same ballad that I had copied from Clover

198

came up. I read each line of each of the 17 stanzas and found them to be identical almost to the word to what Clover had copied and to what we in the family have heard Mammy sing countless times. After having read the ballad many times over I was struck with how profoundly sad it was and how truly it mirrored the sadness that must have filled my great grandmother's life. It was like an epiphany to me because I at once understood why Mammy sang these ballads when she would meditate and rest during the day or at night. She identified with the structure of the melody and the rhythm and with the lyrics that told of such sad lost loves or ruined lives of the characters within. I instantly knew that Mammy herself could have fit remarkably well into one of these ballads as a main character. Indeed these ballads speak to all who have loved and lost and have suffered tragically because of it. This was so true of what happened with Blue John and Mammy and especially true later when Mammy lost her son Clover, the love of her life. Mammy lost both of her parents when she was young and was raised by stepparents, who at the very least were unkind. Her stepparents disowned her and Mammy had to live with her grandfather and grandmother when she became pregnant with Clover. Her only safe haven and place of love and care was with her grandparents. So all of this sadness fits collectively well within the subjects of the ballads. What better way of lamenting could there be than to sing these ballads when one meditates alone and has time to grieve over the loss of one's loves.

Because I believe it is so special to the enrichment of the understanding of Mammy and of those like her I will include the words here of the ballads that Mammy used to sing. The first one is titled "McAfee's Confession" and this copy was submitted by a Mrs. J.S. Thurmond Alderson in March of 1927 and is almost exactly the same as the one Mammy sang. She learned it from her father, Jackson B. Huddleson, more than thirty years before and this puts it right into the time frame of when Mammy would've sung it.

"McAfee's Confession"

Draw near young men and learn from me
My sad and mournful history.
And may you ne'er forgetful be

Of all this day I tell to thee.
Before I reached my full fifth year,
My father and my mother dear
Were both laid in their silent grave
By Him who did their beings give.

No more was I a father's joy,
But a poor little orphan boy;
No more a father's voice I heard,
No more a mother's love I shared.

Then to my uncle's friendly roof
From want and danger far aloof;
For nine long years it sheltered me,
As safe and good as need to be.

But I was thoughtless, young and gay,
And often broke the Sabbath day.
In wickedness I took delight
And often did what was not right.

And when my uncle did me chide,
I turned from him dissatisfied,
And turned again to wickedness,
And Satan served me with eagerness.

At length arrived the fatal day
When from my home I ran away,
And to my sorrow since in life,
I took unto myself a wife.

And she was kind and good to me,
As any woman need to be,
And living yet would be no doubt,
Had I not seen Miss Hetty Stout.

Gregory Hugh Brown

Ah! Well I recollect the day
When Hetty stole my heart away;
T'was love for her controlled my will
And caused me my wife to kill.

T'was on a pleasant summer's night,
All things were still, the stars shone bright,
My wife was lying on the bed,
When I approached her and said:

"My dear, here's medicine I brought,
This very day for you I bought;
My dear, I know it will cure you,
Of those vile fits; pray, take it, do."

She gave me a tender look
And in her mouth the poison took,
And by her baby on the bed
Down to her last long sleep she laid.

My heart was then filled full of woe;
I cried, "Ah, whither shall I go?"
How can I quit this mournful place!
The world again how can I face?"

I'd freely give up all my store,
Had I ten thousand worlds or more,
If I could bring again to life
My dear, my darling murdered wife.

Young men, young men, be warned by me,
And shun all evil company,
And walk in ways of righteousness,
And God your souls will surely bless.

201

As recorded in the internet version there are two more stanzas that were not included in Clover's copy. I do not know if he overlooked them or if Mammy chose not to sing them or if she forgot them over the years. There could've been a reason that she just chose not to add them. I am curious as to why they were left out because the first 15 stanzas were in Clover's copy almost word for word. Here are the last two stanzas from Jackson B. Huddleson:

The moment now is drawing nigh
When from the world my soul must fly,
And meet Jehovah at the bar,
And hear my final sentence there.

To all my friends I bid adieu;
No more on earth shall I see you,
But upon heaven's flowery plain
I hope we all may meet again.

These last two stanzas are a final goodbye and it just could've been that Mammy didn't want to sing a final goodbye yet. She still had Clover's kids to love and cherish as she helped raise them and she still had many unfinished issues to face with his father Blue John. The last two stanzas are those sung by sad souls ready to meet their maker and at this point Mammy was not ready to meet him yet. I believe the last two stanzas to be as beautiful as the rest of the ballad and I believe that Mammy left them out on purpose rather than include words she was not yet prepared to sing.

My brother, like Clover before him, copied down another ballad that Mammy used to sing and I think it is just as revealing of the sadness Mammy suffered and may have offered some solace to her when she sang it. It is the famous ballad *"Barbara Allen"* and I include it here:

"Barbara Allen"

Was in the merry month of May
When flowers were a-bloomin'
Sweet William on his deathbed lay
For the love of Barbara Allen

Slowly, slowly she got up
And slowly she went nigh him
And all she said when she got there:
"Young man, I think you're dying."

"O yes I'm sick and very low
And death is on me dwellin'
No better shall I ever be
If I don't get Barbara Allen."

"Don't you remember the other day
When you were in the tavern
You toasted all the ladies there
And slighted Barbara Allen."

"O yes, I remember the other day
When we were in the tavern
I toasted all the ladies there
Gave my love to Barbara Allen."

He turned his pale face to the wall
And death was on him dwellin'
"Adieu, adieu, my kind friends all
Be kind to Barbara Allen."

As she was walkin' through the fields
She heard the death bells knelling
And every toll they seemed to say
"Hardhearted Barbara Allen."

"O mother, mother, make my bed
O make it long and narrow
Sweet William died for me today
I'll die for him tomorrow."

They buried Willie in the old churchyard
And Barbara there anigh him
And out of his grave grew a red, red rose
And out of hers a briar.

They grew and grew in the old churchyard
Till they couldn't grow no higher
That lapped and tied in a true love's knot
The rose ran around the briar.

"Barbara Allen" has the same tragic sadness that would have pervaded the life of my great grandmother and, although neither Blue John nor Mammy died from their love affair in the "fields of clover", much the same overtones must have been there. Two lives were lost in the hopeless shuffle that life's kaleidoscope sometimes casts upon us. Alfred Lord Tennyson wrote from the poem, 'The Way of the Soul", these lines:

I hold it true, whate'er befall;
I feel it when I sorrow most;
"Tis better to have loved and lost
Than never to have loved at all.

"It is better to have loved and lost than never to have loved at all". I am not sure that my great grandmother would agree with Tennyson but I am sure that his words would ring resoundingly within her being.

Both of the ballads I've shared may have originated from ancient Scotch ballads which were passed down from Mammy's ancestors from Ireland, England and Scotland. There were many versions made of them as time passed and generations of people moved from Europe to America. They were handed down mostly by word of mouth from grandparents to parents to their children and to us and their deeply moving and meaningful lyrics are just as profound today as when they were written long ago. I was fortunate to have relatives that thought enough of their great value to copy them down as Mammy sang them.

It is said that as long as someone loves you and remembers you that you will always remain alive in that person's heart. When you are loved and sung about or written about in songs, poetry, or novels then your memory will live on the hearts and minds of countless thousands of those that experience them. Clover left a wife, mother, and six children who loved and cherished his memory until their dying days. Their children, including myself and my cousins, continue that love and remembrance and I am sure those that come after us will love and remember as well, just as all our ancestors have done before us. The memory of Mammy singing those ballads will remain with me and I now have a much greater understanding of why she loved to sing them so.

As I close I say this is not "The End" but just another link that I have tried to establish with the past and, God willing, connect with the future. God Speed Clover, and may there be grand ballads sung for you and your mother in the glorious skies of the hereafter and to all that read may you find the peace in knowing from whence you came.

Recipes:

Mammy's Dumplings for rabbit or chicken

Ingredients for dough   Boil chicken or rabbit until tender,
tasty and slice

2 cups flour
3 tablespoons of shortening
1 teaspoon salt
¼ cup water

Directions for cooking chicken or rabbit:

Get a 3 or 4 pound chicken or rabbit, wash it well and let soak 1 1/2 to 2 hours. Drain well. Place in a boiler and bring to a rolling boil, then lower heat to medium high and cook 2 hours or until tender, checking to see if it is done. Let cool. Take off bone, slice and place on serving dish. Save the broth. Keep in the refrigerator (or icebox) overnight.

Directions for cooking dumplings:

Mix together flour and salt. Cut shortening into flour using a fork, two knives, or a blender. Stir in water to form soft dough. Keep cool overnight so that the dough will roll well.

On a lightly floured surface roll out the dough to about 1/8 of an inch thick with a rolling pin. Cut into 1 inch wide strips with a sharp knife. Cut strips into 1 inch or longer pieces of dough and drop into a simmering broth made from the boiling of the chicken or rabbit.

Cook 10 minutes with the pot lid off, then 10 minutes with the lid on. Add more broth and sliced chicken or rabbit to the dumplings as needed and serve.

Eat em' up and enjoy!

Jeanne Catherine Mallard's rabbit and noodles

I include my wife's grandmother's recipe for rabbit and noodles because it is somewhat similar to the recipe that my great grandmother used, except for the addition of such ingredients as shallots and white wine which generally were not available to people in rural Alabama in the early 20th century. Jeanne Catherine (Benedict) Mallard was my wife Benedicte

Retrou-Brown's grandmother. She was born the second child of a family of twelve (large families were common in France as well as here during those days). She was born in Brixey, France, a small town a couple of miles from Doremy, the village where Joan of Arc was born. She married Paul Mallard, a young man from Doremy, whose home was right behind the house of Joan of Arc.

My wife's grandparents, like my own, lived in the country and worked the land and their life styles in France in the early 20th century were much the same as ours here, where my ancestors farmed in rural Alabama. My grandmother and great grandmother loved to cook as did my wife's grandmother in France and the recipes that they used were to a great degree determined by the agrarian lifestyles they lived and, of course, upon the availability of products that could be obtained. That is why my great grandmother's rabbit and dumplings were, in many ways, similar to the rabbit and noodles of my wife's grandmother in France during almost the same time period. That is why I have included Jeanne Catherine Mallard's recipe for rabbit and noodles here as well, just so the reader would have the benefit of comparing one recipe to the other.

Lapin aux Nouilles/Rabbit and Noodles

Ingredients
1 rabbit (3 to 4 pounds)
¼ pound bacon, cut into small dices
4 or 5 shallots
2 tablespoons flour
2 cups dry white wine (vin d'Alsace or dry German wine)
1 cup chicken or beef stock
3 teaspoons salt
1 teaspoon black or white pepper
¼ cup sugar
3 tablespoons wine vinegar

Directions for cooking:

Cut the rabbit into pieces (split each hind leg in half, the 2 front legs, 2 pieces from the back and 3 pieces from the front ribs and neck). Save the liver and have it for breakfast with an egg.

Saute the bacon in a large pot until it turns crispy and brown. Pour all the liquid fat into a large pan. Add the shallots to the frying pan and brown on all sides. Add the bacon to it. Brown the rabbit on all sides in the same manner and add to the pot. Mix the flour with ½ cup of the wine and add to the pot. Pour in the remaining wine, stock, salt, pepper, and bring to a boil. Simmer for 1 hour and 10 minutes. Meanwhile, combine the vinegar and sugar in a sauce pan and cook on high heat until it turns into a caramel.

Pour the caramel directly into the rabbit stew and mix carefully. Simmer for 10 more minutes and serve with fresh made noodles.

Like my great grandmother from Alabama, my wife's grandmother from France would sometimes not use vinegar and sugar. Instead, she would add some cooked mushrooms (which my great grandmother did not) and crème fraiche (Half and Half) just a few minutes before serving. Then she would cut up some fresh parsley from her garden and sprinkle some over the noodles.

Ingredients for noodles:

My wife's grandmother, like my great grandmother, made her own noodles or dumplings as my great grandmother called them. These were the ingredients which are similar, except for adding the egg:

2 cups of plain flour
1 egg
3 tablespoons of oil
6 cups of cold water or stock
Salt and pepper to taste
Directions for cooking:

Combine egg, water, and oil. Add flour, a little at a time, until the dough is very stiff. Knead until all flour is used. Sprinkle some flour on a cloth and roll out the dough. Wait a couple of hours, and then cut the dough into long strips. Wait another couple of hours to let it dry. Turn the noodles on the other side, so they dry well. Bring water or broth into a boil and drop the noodles, one at a time. Cook about 8 to 10 minutes. When the noodles are cooked, drain them and add them to the rabbit sauce.

Bon Appetit!

Mammy's Fried Apple Turnovers

Ingredients for dough

  2 cups flour
  ½ cup shortening chilled
  1 teaspoon salt
  ½ cup cold water

ingredients for apple filling

  2 cups dried apples
  ¼ cup white sugar
  1/8 teaspoon ground cinnamon
  lard or shortening for frying

Directions for cooking/cooking time:

preparation 45 minutes, cook 15 minutes, ready in 1 hour

Sift flour and salt together. Mix in shortening with spoon or blender until it looks like rough crumbs. Add cold water one spoon at a time and mix with a fork. When flour is mixed and moist form it into a ball, wrap in wax paper, and chill for 30 minutes.

Dice the dried apples and put them in a saucepan. Combine the sugar and cinnamon and pour over the apples and toss to coat them. Cook in a covered saucepan on low heat until soft, then mash mixture with a fork until thick. Let the mixture cool.

Put the chilled dough ball on a lightly floured surface and roll it out to 1/8 inch thick and cut rounds with a large jar lid or cookie cutter 4 inches round. If larger pies are desired, simply cut larger rounds and add more apple mixture.

Place in each round 1 heaping tablespoon (or 2 if larger turnovers are desired) of apple mixture. Moisten the edges of the dough with cold water, fold in half, and press edges with the end of a fork to seal them. Repeat for all turnovers.

Heat in a larger frying pan to 375 degrees, frying the pies, a few at a time, 2 to 3 minutes on each side until the crust is golden brown. Remove and drain on dry towel.

Eat em' up and enjoy!

Ancestral Photographs

Clover McKinley Palmer and Cora Lee Goodson Palmer photo taken after their wedding in 1919

Clover McKinley Palmer in 1919   *Cora Lee Goodson Palmer in 1919*

Doctor Russell Porter Palmer and Morning Dizenia Mansell Palmer, "Mammy" Dizenia Palmer's grandparents and Clover McKinley Palmer's great grandparents., photo taken circa 1900

"Mammy"
Mary Dizenia Palmer in 1960

"Mammy"
Mary Dizenia Palmer in 1955

"Mammy", Mary Dizenia Palmer, Taft Palmer, her nephew, and his father, Zachariah Gaines Palmer, her brother, photo taken circa 1910

"The Stair Steps", Clover's first four children with Cora Lee, left to right Harrison Roe Palmer, Mary Elizabeth Palmer, Iva Louise Palmer, Joseph Arthur Palmer photo taken circa 1927

Mary Elizabeth "Mollie" Driver Goodson (Cora Lee's mother) photo taken with her family circa 1895

Left to right, Clover with oldest son, Harrison, in his lap, John Thomas Goodson, Cora lee's father, and Boyette neighbors, photo taken circa 1926

Cora Lee Goodson Palmer photo taken Christmas 1945

James Gordon Brown, our father, James Roger Brown, my brother age 3, Mary Elizabeth Palmer Brown, our mother, photo taken circa 1944

Mary Elizabeth Palmer Brown and her sister, Iva Louise Palmer Gamel, photo taken circa 1944